ART ATTACK

Second Edition

ART ATTACK

Second Edition

Mike Faricy

Library of Congress Control Number: 2023915517
paperback ISBN: 978-1-962080-31-6
e-Book ISBN: 978-1-962080-32-3

MJF Publishing books may be purchased for education, Business, or promotional use. For information on bulk purchases,
please contact the author directly at mikefaricyauthor@gmail.com

Published by

MJF Publishing
https://www.mikefaricybooks.com

Acknowledgments

I would like to thank the following people for their help and support:
Special thanks to my editors, Kitty, Donna and Rhonda for their hard work, cheerful patience and positive feedback.

I would like to thank Ann and Julie for their creative talent and not slitting their wrists or jumping off the high bridge when dealing with my Neanderthal computer capabilities.

Special thanks to Ann for her patience.

Last, I would like to thank family and friends for their encouragement and unqualified support. Special thanks to Maggie, Jed, Schatz, Pat, Av, Emily and Pat for not rolling their eyes, at least when I was there, and most of all, to my wife Teresa whose belief, support and inspiration has from day one, never waned.

Prologue

Myles Rossler struck the paint brush on the canvas, creating the exclamation point behind his signature in the lower right-hand corner. He set the brush in the jar of turpentine and stepped back from his easel. This had to be his best work to date, but then, he always thought that. "I think that should just about do it. Another work of genius, if I do say so myself." Come on over and take a look," he said to the naked beauty stretched out on the red velvet couch.

She sat up on the antique couch, smiled, and ran her tongue seductively over her lips. Her tanned skin, juxtaposed to the small patches of white a bikini had covered only served to highlight her attributes. She stood and stretched, diverting his attention from the canvas to her figure. Once she had his full attention, she strutted toward him.

"Oh, Myles," she said, leaning over and nibbling his ear lobe. "It's marvelous. Beautiful! How do you do it?"

"I can't help it. The good Lord blessed me with a marvelous talent."

"As he did me," she said and fluttered her eyes. "Ready for a down payment?"

"Sounds wonderful."

"Why don't you get undressed, and I'll meet you in the sauna. I'll mix up a pitcher of vodka martinis for us and join you for the first of a number of workouts."

She placed one bare foot in front of the other, and strutted into the kitchen as if she was walking down a fashion show runway, aware without looking that she had his undivided attention. She assumed a pose, bending down into the lower cabinet, arching her back, and slowly reaching in to grab the glass pitcher. Before she stood, she looked over her shoulder and said in a tempting tone, "Baby, hurry up and get in there. I want you all to myself."

As Myles hurried out of the kitchen, he tossed his t-shirt on the living room floor. He unbuckled his jeans as he picked up speed and hopped out of them halfway down the hall. His socks and boxers came off just outside the sauna before he stepped inside. It was wonderfully warm, bordering on hot, as he closed the door behind him and climbed up onto the top wooden bench. A pair of pink plastic handcuffs hung from a brass hook on the wall. He stretched out along the bench, centering himself, leaving just enough room for her to position a leg on either side.

She placed the pitcher on the counter, took the bottle of vodka out of the freezer, and arranged the stemmed glasses on the tray just in case he peeked out. She waited a couple of minutes before wrapping the towel around her. She hurried down the hall, quietly slipped the four solid brass deadbolt locks into place, and dialed the thermostat up to the number ten setting, two hundred and forty degrees Fahrenheit. It had been a relatively simple procedure to override the high-limit switch, so she turned the timer all the way to the maximum three-hour mark before she headed into the bathroom to shower.

She heard soft thumping on the six-inch insulated sauna door when she stepped out from her thirty-minute shower. She turned on the hair drier and spent the next half-hour drowning out any sound he might make. She took her time dressing in-between watching a Kardashian special on the cable channel then spent fifteen minutes looking for her car keys. Once she found them, she slung her purse over her shoulder and double-checked herself once more in the mirror before setting out on the forty-minute drive to work.

As she walked past the sauna door, she gave a quick glance at the four deadbolt locks. They appeared undisturbed, and when she placed her ear against the door, she was unable to detect any sound from inside. The timer showed slightly more than twenty minutes remaining. She turned it back to the three-hour mark, just to be sure.

One

I'd just been paid, in cash, and was thinking things couldn't get much better. True, at least for the moment.

"Congratulations again on your successful investigation," Louie said. He laughed and pushed his empty glass across the bar. "I should probably take off, Dev. I'm in court first thing in the morning."

It was our fourth round, not that it mattered. I was feeling no pain, in fact, I was buying. My Golden Retriever, Morton, was at the foot of the barstool, half-asleep after finishing his second bag of pork rinds. An inner voice said something along the lines of *'You idiot, get in the car and go home.'* But why listen? Instead, I said, "Hey, Louie, let me get one more round."

"Well, since you twisted my arm. How can I say no? So, tell me again how this went down."

"It's not all that complicated. My client, the insurance guy, called me and said they had a question on some woman's claim for benefits. Apparently, she went blind from working on her computer all day."

"Working on . . . that sounds like some weird preexisting condition that was either exacerbated by staring at a screen or the computer had absolutely nothing to do with it. Sounds like whatever caused her blindness might have happened anyway."

"Yeah, only not quite. It turns out, she was in a relationship with an eye surgeon, and he filed a series of false reports. Once the insurance checks started coming in, she dumped the guy. After groveling in front of her for a week or two, he contacted my client and came clean."

"But you only investigated for a couple of days."

"Just one day, actually. I parked in front of her place at eight in the morning, and forty-five minutes later, out she comes, hops in her car, and drives to the casino."

"She's driving?"

"Yeah, in her new car, a 2019 Nissan. I followed her inside the casino. People who work there are saying, 'Hello Betty. Nice to see you again, Betty. Have a nice day, Betty.' Come to find out, she's a regular. She played the slots for three hours, took a break for lunch, then played until almost four in the afternoon before she headed out to the grocery store. She did a little shopping and went home. I was still parked in front of her place at eight-thirty that night when out she comes, dressed to the nines. She went dancing and brought some guy home around twelve-thirty. Amazingly, the guy is a chiropractor, and she'd been talking to him about filing a back injury claim if only he would help her out."

"Sounds like a pattern," Louie said and took a healthy sip. "She's liable to end up doing some time."

"The eye surgeon has already agreed to testify. Said he couldn't live with himself after falsifying documents. I'd guess he was just pissed off about being taken for a ride. He's retired, so losing his license wasn't that much of a threat. The chiropractor has an attorney, and he's agreed to testify as well. You'd think, under the circumstances, she'd want to keep a low profile, but that thought didn't seem to enter her mind."

The front door to The Spot suddenly flew open, and eight women stepped inside. The noise level went up about a thousand percent, shrieking, laughing, and yelling back and forth, obviously not their first stop. There were only three other people in the place besides Louie and me. A blonde woman, definitely over-served, was wearing a white lace veil. She was surrounded by the others, all laughing and raising the beer cans they'd carried as a toast. She had a sign on her back that said something about it being *'Her last night to misbehave.'* One of the women had beautiful blonde hair and a well-endowed figure. She maybe looked familiar, but I couldn't place her.

"Appreciate the drinks, Dev, but I think this is the warning that tells me it's time to go home," Louie said.

"We're right behind you, Louie. Come on, Morton," I said. We gave Mike, the bartender, a wave and headed out the side door. He waved back and rolled his eyes at the hen party. Although it's not like any of us hadn't done the same thing in our day.

TWO

Morton and I slept in the following morning and headed to the office around 9:30. I pulled behind a black Toyota and parked. As I let Morton out of the backseat, a voice said, "Dev Haskell?"

I turned and gazed at a beautiful, blonde-haired woman wearing tight jeans, a short sleeve blouse, and pink lipstick. She looked somewhat familiar. Morton immediately approached and thrust his nose between her legs.

"Yes?" I said.

"Dev, it's me, Kristi McKenzie. Long time no see."

Her voice sounded as sexy as I remembered, and as she said her name, the slightest hint of a beautiful perfume drifted over me. For a brief second, I was seventeen again. Kristi Mckenzie. High school homecoming queen, princess for the prom, and my senior year sweetheart. Oh, the things we taught one another that summer. Kids. She dumped me for some college art school student the following September, and I went into the Army. I think her first beauty pageant had been when she was five, Miss Kindergarten or something. She won Sandbox Princess at age eight and went on to become a professional beauty pageant contestant; St. Paul Winter Carnival Princess, Miss Ramsey County, Queen of the Mississippi River Headwaters, Miss Upper Midwest, Princess of the Prairie, the list went on.

"Kristi? Wow. Sorry, I didn't recognize you. I guess I never expected to see you again. I'll say it's been a long time. What was it? September after high school graduation. You, well, you look great. You still competing?"

She shook her head. "Dev, that was another lifetime. I gave all that up. How many times do you have to win a pageant before it just gets boring?"

"I guess I never considered that."

"I thought it was you in The Spot last night," she said. "Long, crazy, night. I was going to talk to you for a minute, but when I turned around, you had already left. I asked the bartender—"

"Mike."

"He never told me his name. I asked him if it was you, and he said it was. Then he told me this is where your office is. I think he was trying to come on to me." She turned and glanced at the building. "He said you're a private investigator. No offense, but I thought you were dead. Otherwise, I would have—"

"Don't believe everything you hear. So, you were with the bride to be last night. The girl with the wedding veil. Isn't that wedding later today?"

"Not until late this afternoon. It's over at Lookout Park."

"Right, on Summit and Ramsey Hill, nice location."

She nodded and said, "I was wondering if we could maybe talk. I'm thinking of hiring someone to find a missing person."

"A missing person? Tell you what, if you have some time, come on up to my office. I'll put some coffee on, we can catch up, and you can tell me what you're thinking. I mean, if you have time."

"Oh, Dev, thanks, so much. I'd love to. Sorry to just show up, but I didn't know how else to get in touch with you."

We headed up to the office. Morton seemed more interested in Kristi than anything else. Louie Laufen, my office mate, had already been in, and the coffee was on. If I remembered correctly, he had a 9:00 court date.

"Grab a chair, Kristi. You take cream or sugar?" I said, hoping she didn't because we were out of both.

"No, black is just fine."

Fortunately, she seemed to be focused on Louie's picnic table desk, which gave me a chance to dump his half-empty mug into the sink and refill it for her.

"Here you go," I said, handing her Louie's refilled mug. It wasn't lost on me that the next two buttons on her blouse were suddenly undone. A large diamond pendant was wedged in her cleavage. "Grab a seat and tell me what you've been up to," I said as I stepped behind my desk and sat down. Kristi looked at the chair with the masking tape over the arms and took the other one. She couldn't have weighed more than a hundred and fifteen pounds, but the chair creaked as she settled in, compliments of ne'er do well crime lord, Tubby Gustafson's occasional visits. "So what are you doing now?" I asked.

"Oh, you know, a little bit of everything. Now, be quiet for a minute and listen Dev. Before we go any further, I just want to say that breaking up with you was probably one of the dumbest things I've ever done. No wait, it was the worst thing I've ever done. Since then, nothing seems to have gone right for me. I literally kick myself every day for being so stupid."

"Oh, I wouldn't be too hard on yourself. I think we were headed in very different directions. You were going off to college and all those beauty pageants, and I was going into the Army."

"When I heard you'd been killed, I was absolutely devastated. By that time, I was in Paris, at the Sorbonne. I was crowned 'Princesse de la Sorbonne'." She paused for a moment to let that sink in. "I couldn't get back home, it was the end of term, and I had papers due, not to mention all my French Princess duties. You know how it goes."

Actually, no, I didn't, but I shot her a smile and nodded all the same. "So, you mentioned you might need help finding someone?"

She set Louie's coffee mug on the edge of the desk and smiled. Another wave of beautiful perfume floated over, and I inhaled deeply. "Yes. It's my husband, actually. Well, former husband, to be more accurate."

"When did you get married?"

"A couple of years ago, common law to be honest. We've been together, more or less for seven or eight years."

"Oh, gee, I'm sorry to hear that."

"What? That I have a husband?"

"No, I meant—"

She laughed and slowly ran her tongue back and forth across her upper lip. "Thanks, but its okay. He was starting to go batty, and then one day, he just up and disappeared."

"You've checked with his family? Friends?"

She nodded and said, "Yep. I even went so far as to place an ad in the paper. He's a painter."

It wasn't lost on me that she used the present tense. "He's a painter? Houses? Offices?"

"An artist," she corrected. "A very good artist, as a matter of fact. The occasional portrait but mostly landscapes. He's a modern impressionist. I even talked with the galleries that handled his work. It's like he just up and vanished into thin air."

I was taking notes as she talked. "What was his name?"

"Chandler Hancock. He's originally from St. Michael, Minnesota. We met in college, went our separate ways for a bit, and then reconnected and suddenly I looked up and we'd been together for a number of years."

I stopped writing for a moment. Chandler Hancock. She met him before college. He was the reason she'd dumped me. I'd wanted to kill him, but instead, I went off to basic training with the idea I would hone my killing skills and pay him a visit down the road. By the time I came back home, I couldn't have cared less. Amazing.

"How long has Chandler been missing?"

"Five or six months?"

"So tell me about it. What happened?"

"Not much to tell, one day he's there, and the next day he's gone."

"Anything like a ransom note, an affair, or maybe mental instability?"

"No nothing," she said and didn't even blink at the suggestion of an affair.

"Did he pack a suitcase? Has there been any online interaction? Tweets he may have posted?"

"No, no, and no. Nothing, Dev. He simply disappeared, not so much as a word or a post."

"Did you contact the police?"

"I guess I never thought of that."

I had to fight to keep my eyes focused on the notes I was taking. Finally, I looked up. "You never contacted the police?"

Three

I watched out the window as Kristi left the building and walked across the street to her car. A couple was walking down the street, the guy was pushing a baby stroller. While he stared at Kristi he ran the stroller into the fire hydrant, and his wife slapped him hard on the arm. I took out my binoculars and waited until she pulled away from the curb so I could get her license plate number. I ran a quick check on her plate. She came up clean.

I phoned my friend in homicide, Aaron LaZelle, and left a message. I Googled Chandler Hancock and came up with as many women as men with the name. There was an image of a landscape entitled 'Season Opener.' A lake scene actually, painted by Chandler Hancock along with a picture of him. I remembered seeing him once or twice but only from a distance, and that was at least fifteen years ago.

His online picture made him look like a clueless young eccentric. He was sitting in a chair in front of a fireplace. He appeared to be wearing a smoking jacket. He had a pipe in his mouth and what looked to be a tweed cap on his head. There was a landscape painting hanging above the fireplace but no indication whether or not he was the artist. The article was almost two years old and said the lake scene painting was on display at the Find Art Gallery down on Fifth Street. I phoned the gallery, but no one answered.

I was about to head out when my phone rang. "Haskell Investigations."

"Dev, Aaron, returning your call."

"Hi, Aaron, thanks for calling back."

Aaron headed up the city's homicide unit. I'd known him since we were kids playing hockey.

"What can I do for you, Dev?"

"I've got a strange deal. A woman stopped by and asked me to help find her missing husband. Common-law marriage, not that it makes any difference. He's been gone for six months, according to her. Strange thing is, she said she never bothered to contact you guys."

"Sounds like she might be happy that he's gone and just wants to play the part of the concerned wife. It's happened before. You suspect foul play?"

"No, I don't think so. At least she doesn't strike me as the type."

"And just what type would that be?"

"Point taken. Can I give you the guy's name and have you check to see if anything turns up on your records?"

"Give it to me. I'll run it right now."

"Chandler Hancock," I said then spelled out the last name. I heard the keyboard clicking in the background.

A moment later, Aaron said, "Nothing coming up on our records. Never reported missing and, according to our records, never involved in anything. Not so much as a parking ticket. No indication of a domestic situation if you were thinking in those terms."

"Okay. Sorry to take up your time."

"Not a problem. Nice to hear your voice. We're overdue for a get-together."

"You usually have more on your plate than I do. Give me a call when you have some time, and we can grab dinner."

"Thanks. Anything pops up with this Hancock thing let me know. Later," he said and hung up.

I phoned the Find Art Gallery again. This time, I got a recording that said they were open from 11:00 until 7:00. It was almost 11:30, so I hung up, filled Morton's water dish, left a note for Louie, and was about to head out the door when Louie stepped into the office.

"You coming or going?" Louie said.

"I'll be gone for maybe an hour. Ignore my note on your desk. Everything go okay in court this morning?" Louie had built quite the reputation in town for the guy to go to if you were charged with a DUI.

"Well enough. I've got another hearing scheduled for three o'clock downtown."

"I should be back long before that. Just on my way to an art gallery."

"Is there a display of coloring books?"

Four

I parked a block away from the Find Art Gallery on Fifth Street. It was located in a red-brick building built in 1885 and just across the street from the Top Hat bar. The front window looked in on an impressive gallery with polished maple floors that were probably original to the structure. I stood on the sidewalk and peered in for a minute or two. There were a number of large paintings hanging on the walls. Abstract Expressionism things, drips and drizzles on canvas, like the stuff Jackson Pollock created. I never got the attraction, and the paintings I could see through the window wasn't going to change my mind.

The door had an image of a clock face hanging on the inside with a sign that said 'OPEN.' The hands on the clock were set for 11:00, almost an hour ago. As I opened the door, I heard a tone sound in the rear. A moment later, an attractive woman stepped out from the back room.

"Good morning," she said. "Can I help you with anything or just looking?"

I glanced at one of the drip and drizzle paintings on the wall. It was entitled 'D'; the painting next to it was entitled 'E.' I didn't want to ask about the titles, so I said, "A while back, you had a painting by Chandler Hancock. I'm interested in his work."

"Oh, really? I believe we've three of his works in the back that I could show you."

"Would you have time?"

"Certainly, if you'll wait just a moment," she said and walked to the front door. She locked the door and adjusted the hands on the hanging clock sign. "Come on back. I'm Diane Turner, by the way," she said, holding out her hand. She had dark hair, brown eyes, and sparkling white teeth that looked even brighter next to her suntan.

"Dev Haskell," I said as we shook hands. "Do you handle a lot of his work?"

"Chandler Hancock, yes, from time to time, we've sold a piece. He's got a bit of a following. We have an exclusive with him, so we're the only local gallery. Now, I know he deals with a gallery in New York. I think Tampa and San Francisco as well. I'm not sure about New Orleans," she said as we made our way toward the door she'd stepped out of only a moment ago.

"Do you sell any of this?" I said, indicating the abstract work on the walls.

"Oh, there's a market," she said but didn't elaborate as she opened the door to the backroom. A cubicle with a countertop, two chairs, a laptop, and a sandwich next to the laptop was positioned in the corner. The ten-foot ceiling in the room was open, exposing solid wooden floor joists that were at least a hundred and thirty years old. Row upon row of eight-foot high shelving filled with cloth covered paintings extended toward a distant back wall. She stepped into the cubicle and flicked three light switches, illuminating all the shelving.

"Let me just check the location. You said, Chandler Hancock?"

"Yes, that's right. The piece I saw on the internet was listed as 'Season Opener,' I think."

"Mmm, a Plein Air. I remember it, a lovely work." She placed a napkin over what was left of the sandwich and slid it behind the laptop then said, "Yes, here we are, beta seven-four," she said and headed for one of the shelving aisles. She stopped maybe halfway down, reached up to a shelf, and pulled out a canvas. There was a small extension attached to the front of the shelf, and she set the canvas on it and carefully removed the bubblewrap covering it. The painting was the same one I'd seen online, although it was a hundred times more attractive.

"Yeah, that's the one. 'Season Opener'."

"He completed it in one day. Most of his work has been done in that manner, following Van Gogh's convention. It is very lovely. Let's view it in the light booth. Shall we?" she asked and, without waiting for my response, slipped the bubblewrap over the canvas and headed back down the aisle.

The light booth was just that, a metal cabinet on legs. The cabinet was maybe six feet wide and four feet high. The interior was white. She uncovered the painting, leaned it against the back wall of the booth, and turned on a switch. The lights in the booth came on immediately.

"The light temperature is five thousand Kelvin."

"Perfect," I said, not knowing what she was talking about.

She shot a quick glance in my direction but didn't comment.

It really was a lovely painting. A narrow beach, small waves, a clear sky. I felt like I could put a worm on a hook and catch a sunfish. I figured the thing probably had a price of close to five hundred dollars. "Just for the sake of discussion, what price do you have on this piece?"

"It's a real steal at fifty-one, five."

"Five thousand, one hundred and fifty dollars?" I couldn't believe it.

She looked at me, shook her head, and then smiled. "No, the price is fifty-one thousand, five hundred dollars."

"What?"

"You're not a collector, are you, Mr. Hassle?"

Five

I was sitting in the cubicle with Diane. She was working her way through the second half of her sandwich while I finished up her bag of potato chips. "So these guys actually get that kind of money for their paintings?" I said.

"Some do. You have to understand it's a tough business and an ever-changing market. To be honest, our showings, like the one out there right now, don't create a lot of sales. There might be one or two sales, possibly a few more for an artist with a large following. What the showing does create or enhance is just that, the following. For many people, when they come to one of our showings, more often than not, it's their initial introduction to a specific artist."

"So the stuff you have hanging out there now, does anyone really like that? It just doesn't appeal to me."

"Sure, I get that. But in this business, the person who likes the contemporary work out there now may not enjoy the more classic or traditional work of someone like Chandler Hancock. Which one is wrong or right?"

"Definitely I'm right, and they're wrong."

"Okay, but if you're running a business, do you want to eliminate them from your list of potential customers?"

"So how often do you get new work from an artist, say, for example, Chandler Hancock?"

"It's all across the board. Some try to get us to take a new work on a monthly basis. Others, it might be one per year. Chandler Hancock, I think we were averaging maybe two annually. For his last show, we had four new works along with sixteen of his from other galleries. It was a year-long traveling event, ninety days at four different galleries around the country. We were fortunate enough to be first on the list."

"But you said he was dealing with three or maybe four galleries around the country."

"Yes, and to be honest, none of us have heard a peep from him over the last half year or so."

"Is that unusual?"

"For Chandler, yes. If nothing else we'd get a newsy email or a card. But of late, nothing."

"If I bought that painting today, where would you send his portion of the payment?"

"We require every one of the artists we represent to provide us with bank details so we can make a direct electronic deposit into their account. We send them a 1099 at the end of the calendar year. The days of writing a check or, God forbid, paying in cash are long gone."

"And could he show up here unannounced and demand to leave with his works?"

"He could. That's happened once, no wait, twice, in the seventeen years we've been open. As you might expect, there can sometimes be a darker side to the artistic personality."

"If I wanted to find Chandler Hancock, where would I go?"

"In today's world? I think your best bet might be to attempt to contact him online and see if he would agree to meet you. I'd be happy to give you a mailing address, but it's a P.O. Box."

"Would you mind?"

"Not at all, but what's all this about? Is he in some trouble?"

"I hope not," I said and pulled out my wallet. I handed my business card and P.I. license to Diane. "I'm a private investigator. I've been asked to try and locate him."

"Has he done something wrong?" She asked and stuffed the final bit of sandwich into her mouth.

"No, but some family members haven't heard from him for a while, and they're understandably concerned."

"His wife?" she said, sounding a little disappointed as she clicked on her laptop.

"No, why? Do you think there's a problem?"

"A problem? No, not exactly. I've only met her twice, but she struck me, I don't know, odd. Maybe not as supportive as she could be, certainly a bit self-absorbed if I recall." I nodded and decided not to elaborate on my knowing Kristi in high school.

"Didn't she win a beauty pageant or something once? Although, God only knows ninety-nine percent of our clients would require someone with a great deal of patience in order to put up with them."

"You're back to the artistic personality," I said as she began tapping the keyboard. "And you're right; from the laundry list of beauty pageants Hancock's wife recited to me, she sounded more like a professional." The printer suddenly fired up and, a moment later, spit out a sheet of paper with Chandler's Post Office Box address.

"Here you go. His address, such as it is. Listen, if you learn anything, let me know. Not wishing him any ill will, but if you discover the worst, I can double the price on the three works we have and run a memorial service."

"A memorial service? Where you would offer the paintings for sale?"

"Yeah. Of course, we'd wait the appropriate length of time, you know, six months or so."

"I'll keep it in mind, Diane. Thanks for your time."

"Come on. I'll let you out. You sure you don't want to put a deposit on 'Season Opener'?"

"Fifty-one grand and change, that's a little out of my league."

When I climbed into the car, I checked the zip code on Chandler's P.O. box. 55107. I knew the post office. It was just across the river over on the west side. I drove across the Robert Street Bridge, took a left onto Plato Boulevard and a right on Eva. The post office boxes were all lined up on the far wall as you walked in the door of the post office. Box 457 was about a third of the way down the line and sat chest height. The small door to the box had a keyhole, the box number, and a glass panel, so you could look in and see if there was any mail. There was an envelope waiting in the box. The envelope, a number ten business size, was leaning against the side of the box. There was a return address sticker on the back of the envelope, but I couldn't read it.

I made a mental note and headed back to the office. I typed out an anonymous letter addressed to Chandler Hancock's Post Office box. In it, I said I had a thousand dollar cash payment 'per our agreement.' I said I would be in town on the 19th and would meet Chandler at the Depot Bar at 5:00 that evening. I placed the letter in an envelope. Drew a line with a yellow magic marker along the front and back of the envelope and attached a stamp. I put the leash on Morton, and we went for a quick walk to the mailbox two blocks away. I mailed the letter, and we headed back to the office. A note from Louie taped to my computer screen said he was over at The Spot if we cared to join him.

Six

ouie drained his glass and pushed it across the bar. We were sitting at the end of the bar. "Are you kidding me?" Morton was at my feet happily chewing on a bone Mike had picked up at the butcher shop.

"No, Louie, she was serious. Fifty-one grand and change for that painting of the lake."

"How big was the thing?" He held up his empty glass and signaled Mike at the end of the bar for another round.

"How big? I don't know, maybe twenty-four by twenty-four."

"Feet?"

"No, inches, Louie. You know, it's a painting you'd just hang on the wall."

"For fifty grand? I'm out of that demographic," Louie said and shook his head.

"Well, and the other thing she said was that, often-times, the price doubles if the artist dies. All of a sudden, I'm wondering if that could be an incentive to kill some guy or make him simply disappear. I mean, think about it. Some guy hides somewhere, so it looks like he's dead. He sells a bunch of his stuff at the inflated price and then suddenly reappears, say after twenty-four or thirty-six months."

Louie studied me for a long moment before he shook his head. "You're nuts, Dev."

"Think about it, Louie. I mean you got folks dropping thousands on this abstract drizzle stuff any four-year-old could do. So what's so crazy about disappearing for a couple of years, maybe live in a lake cabin, on the beach out in California, or down in Florida? Makes me want to get a bunch of color crayons, melt the things, pour it on a piece of sheetrock, and call it art."

Louie shook his head as Mike delivered the next round and said, "Hey, Dev, did a hot looking woman with blonde hair and a major league rack get in touch with you?"

"Kristi? From the hen party that was in here last night?"

"God, my ears are still ringing. Talk about loud. Every one of them screeching and talking over one another, no one listening. It was crazy. They stayed for one and went on to the next place. Not that any of them needed another. But she called you?"

"No. As a matter of fact, she was outside the office this morning when I pulled up. We chatted for a while. I'm gonna help her find someone."

"She wasn't hard on the eyes," Mike said, just as a guy at the opposite end of the bar called his name.

"Where are you going to look for this Hancock fella?" Louie said.

"That's the big question. I'll give Kristi a call tomorrow. I need to get a sense of where they were living, what he did in his spare time. All that stuff."

"You don't mind me saying, it's sounding stranger and stranger, the more you tell me."

"Yeah, maybe. We only chatted for about fifteen minutes, and then she had to take off."

"Okay, Dev, that doesn't strike you more than a little strange? Her husband has been missing for half a year. She hasn't bothered to contact the police. Now she's talking to an old high school sweetheart, asking for help to find the guy, and she'd love to tell you more, but she has to go somewhere. Something ain't adding up here. In fact, none of it is."

"I'll get more information from her tomorrow."

"Yeah, if she'll even meet with you. Sounds to me like she's bringing you onboard just to cover herself in case someone asks what she's doing to find the guy. Watch yourself on this one. I don't care how good looking she is."

"Her looks aren't going to affect my judgment, Louie."

Louie looked at me and shook his head.

Seven

Morton and I hadn't been in the office long enough to pour a mug of coffee when my cellphone rang. "Haskell Investigations."

"Mr. Haskell, please," the woman said. Her voice sounded familiar, but I couldn't place it.

"Speaking."

"Oh, Dev, hi. It's Diane from Find Art. I hope I'm not interrupting."

"Hi, Diane. No problem, just going over some paperwork," I lied. "What can I do for you?"

"I was thinking about our conversation yesterday and you looking for Chandler Hancock."

"Yeah. I'm really just getting some general information at this point. I don't have anything specific to tell—"

"Yeah, I gathered that from our conversation yesterday. I have another name that you could add to your missing artist list if you're interested."

"Oh?"

"Have you ever heard of an artist by the name of Oscar Callum?"

"Can't say that I have."

"Somewhat famous, a bit of a recluse. Charming enough if you met him in person. It's just that, after our conversation yesterday, I got to thinking, and Oscar Callum would seem to fit the same profile. Up and coming, and suddenly he disappears, not so much as a peep from him. After you left yesterday, I phoned a gallery that handled his work out in L.A. It sounds like a similar circumstance in that he seems to have simply disappeared. No one has laid claim to his works they have on hand. There's really no indication anything has happened to him, other than no one has been able to contact him for almost two years."

"And he lived out in California?"

"Originally, but he moved here to Minnesota maybe twenty years ago. The L.A. Gallery remained his primary market."

"Hmm, interesting. What makes them think he's missing rather than retired or maybe just taking a break?"

"Well, for starters, there is an account sitting with a fairly substantial six-figure balance, and it hasn't been touched in two years. They've repeatedly attempted to contact him through the mail, registered post, online, telephone, but they've never received a response."

"And let me guess, his work has increased in value."

"Yes, but not because of what I think you might be suggesting. The value has increased only because there hasn't been anything new in the last twenty-four months.

But that increase might be a ten or fifteen percent increase. If it was reported that he had passed away, we'd see an immediate jump of fifty, maybe even a hundred percent. He's quite famous in certain circles."

"And you want me to try to find him?"

"No, and I apologize if that's the impression I gave you. It just strikes me as odd that this is the case and that Chandler Hancock's situation appears to be heading down the same path. Both artists have apparently disappeared. Wouldn't it seem logical that someone, somewhere, would miss these individuals? I mean are their property taxes current? Did they own a car? Where is it? Their home? However much of a recluse, they must have had a power bill or a water bill. I mean, my God, Chandler Hancock was living with this Kristi person for God's sake, his wife, or girlfriend, or whatever, and only now she's wondering where he's been for the last seven months?"

"Well, with other people's relationships, who really knows? Do you have an address for Oscar Callum?"

"I have a Post Office Box in a town called Warba. It's up on Highway 2 outside of Duluth."

"Why don't you give it to me. I can't promise I'm going to drive up there, but if I learn anything, I'll let you know. His name is Oscar Callum?" I said, spelling it out as I wrote it down.

"Yes, that's correct."

"Just for the record what kind of work did he do?"

"He is, or rather was, a sculptor."

"You ever meet him?"

"I did, oh, maybe four or five years ago. Nice enough guy, certainly on the shy side, but quite the talented sculptor. I've had a couple of showings of his work."

"Anything strike you as odd?"

"Odd? You mean mannerisms? No, nothing like that. Of course, in this business, you meet all kinds, and as I mentioned yesterday, there can certainly be a dark side to the artistic personality, but Oscar didn't seem to present that. At least not to me. He was just very quiet, umm, thoughtful. So often in this business, it's the artists who are content with simply producing their work and don't seem to be concerned with whether or not it will sell that end up the most successful both personally and financially. Oscar Callum certainly fit that description."

"Any idea how old he is?"

"If I had to guess, I'd say mid-fifties, maybe, but no older than sixty, and he could be substantially younger. No family that I'm aware of."

"Diane, thanks, I'll keep you posted if I come across anything."

We disconnected, and I decided to phone Kristi McKenzie. I dialed her number and listened to the phone ring a half-dozen times. I was just about to leave a voice mail when she answered.

"This is Kristi."

"Hi, Kristi, Dev Haskell. You have a minute to talk?"

"I do and thanks for calling. I was going to call you later this morning."

I waited a long moment to hear why she was going to call, but she didn't say anything.

"The reason I called is, I wondered if I could stop over sometime later today and just take a look around. I'd like to try to get a sense of Chandler. Maybe see his studio, check his records. You know phone calls, people he may have socialized with, besides you of course. Anything you might think of. Did he have a favorite bar, or a grocery store, or something? Was he involved in any local art or neighborhood groups? Did he attend a church? Basically, when he wasn't working, how did he spend his time?"

"Well, this will work out just great. I was planning to call and ask if you could come over for dinner tonight, you know, if you don't have anything going on."

"Tonight? Yeah, I suppose I could do that. What time did you have in mind?"

"Why don't you show up around seven? We can have a glass or two of wine before dinner. Nothing fancy, just plain food."

"Seven tonight, I'll see you then. All I'll need from you is an address."

"Oh, silly me, yeah sure." She gave me her address. I actually knew the building. It was one of a half-dozen or so along the Mississippi River just below downtown. Someone had tried to shoot me down there a few years ago. Fortunately, they had lousy aim. Now they've got another fourteen years left to serve, giving them plenty of time to contemplate the wisdom of their action.

"I'll see you tonight at seven, Kristi."

"I'm looking forward to catching up, Dev. It's been way too long. Rest up," she said and disconnected.

I was still sitting at my desk five minutes later with a surprised look on my face, reviewing images in my mind Kristi's 'rest up' comment had generated, when Louie walked in.

"Hey, good morning. You able to drop that missing artist case yet?" he asked and wandered over to the coffee pot. He stared at his coffee mug and said, "What the hell?" He picked up a paper towel next to the coffee maker, rubbed pink lipstick from the rim, and tossed the towel into a wastebasket. "So what's the latest?"

"I'm going over to her place tonight for dinner."

"Are you kidding me? Dev, she's going to be serving herself up for dessert, and in the process, eliminating you as a credible witness if she's ever nailed for murdering her husband. By the way, not if, but when you spend the night, play it safe and make sure you sleep with one eye open."

Eight

etween googling Chandler Hancock and Oscar Callum and talking to people in various art galleries around the country over the course of the day, I figured I knew more about the current state of the art world than most people graduating with a degree in art. Like every other small business, it was a tough racket. Morton and I headed home around five. I took him for a two-mile walk, showered, put on a clean pair of jeans and a newer rugby jersey, and headed for the wine store.

Solo Vino is just a block away from my place. I figured the odds were fairly good Kristi would be serving either steaks or some kind of roast, so I grabbed a bottle of red wine, a Pinot Noir. The more I thought about it, the more it seemed two bottles might be the better idea. I grabbed a second bottle and headed for the cash register. Chuck was working.

"How's it going, Dev?"

"Good, Chuck. How are things on your end? How's the daughter?"

"Just like her mother, she's giving me directions."

"She can talk now?"

He gave me a funny look. "Yeah, she's heading into first grade this fall. She can already write her name and read some words."

"First grade? I thought she was born last summer."

"You got the time of year right. You're just off by almost six years."

"No one's surprised," I said.

He rang up my purchases, then gave me a head to toe evaluation. "Date night?"

"Not exactly. Just having dinner with a client."

He looked at the two bottles of wine. "Let me guess. You're going to have just one glass or maybe take a pass altogether and only drink water. Meanwhile, you'll keep her glass constantly filled."

"Not that I haven't tried that in the past, but tonight I intend to be the perfect gentleman."

"Let me know how that works out," he said, shaking his head and handing me the bag with both bottles.

I drove down Ramsey Hill, across West Seventh Street and took a left on Exchange. I drove past the Alexander Ramsey House. He was the first governor of Minnesota, and his home is now a historical site with tours. I took a right on Eagle Parkway, drove over the railroad tracks and across Shepard Road to the Upper Landing Apartments along the Mississippi. Kristi's unit, number 312, was on Mill Street and overlooked the river. She buzzed me in, and I took the elevator up to her third-floor unit.

I knocked on her door, and she opened it immediately, suggesting she was probably watching me through the peephole as I came down the hallway. "Hi Dev. Any problem finding the place?"

"No, I knew right where to go," I said, deciding there was no point in mentioning the shooting incident down here five years ago. She was barefoot, and her toenails were bright red. She wore black shorts and a black V neck halter top that looked about two sizes too small for her enhanced attributes. Not that I was complaining. I handed her the bag with the wine bottles.

"Oh, thanks, this is very nice. You didn't have to do it but much appreciated. If it's okay, I've got some little snacks set up. Let's sit out on the balcony, have a glass of wine, and we can enjoy the view. It's such a lovely evening."

"Sounds great," I said, looking around. "Oh, look at this." I picked up a framed photo sitting on an end table. Kristi getting crowned as homecoming queen our senior year in high school. "Long time ago. You haven't aged one bit, still look great."

"Yeah, thanks, it's a constant battle."

I wasn't going to touch that line. "Lovely unit you have here."

"Thank you. I really like it. It's a three-bedroom. One of the bedrooms is Chandler's office, and another is his studio. Why don't I pour us a glass of wine, and I'll give you the two-minute tour."

"Sounds perfect," I said, remembering Chuck's joke about just drinking water and keeping her glass filled. I followed her into the kitchen. I stood on the visitors' side of the counter while she opened one of the bottles of wine and filled two glasses. It was a twist-off cap on the bottle, another thing I liked about the brand. We clinked glasses and took a sip before we headed out of the kitchen.

I noticed a framed picture on the kitchen wall just above the toaster. Kristi in a dark-blue, floor-length gown. She wore a string of pearls, and her blonde hair was piled on top of her head. A sparkly crown rested on her forehead just at the hairline. She appeared to be twelve or maybe thirteen.

We walked down a hallway, past an open bathroom door. The lights were off in the bathroom, but two lit candles sat on either end of the marble-topped double vanity. The candles gave off a pleasant scent I wasn't able to identify. A framed rectangular mirror was centered above each sink. Four drawers ran down the center of the vanity with matching cabinet doors beneath both sinks. The bathroom looked to be about the size of my guest room with a white tile floor. A giant, free-standing bathtub that looked like a large soup bowl was in one corner, and a walk-in shower with two shower heads took up the opposite corner. A toilet and a bidet were opposite the vanity.

"Dev, down here," Kristi said.

I came back to the here and now, not realizing I'd stopped to stare at the bathroom, and hurried down the hall. She waited until I caught up before she opened the door.

"This is Chandler's studio. Usually, I'm not allowed in, but since he's not here." She chuckled as she opened the door. The lights automatically flashed on as the door opened. The carpeted floor was covered with heavy plastic, and the ceiling had maybe twice as many lights as normal. The room held two easels, each with a partially painted landscape. At the top of both easels sat three photographs of the image that was being painted. A counter along a wall had a sink, tubes of paint, and about a hundred different sized brushes arranged in a row of mason jars. A viewing booth just like the one I'd seen at the Find Art Gallery sat against the far wall. There was just the slightest scent of turpentine, and if I didn't know better, I would have thought he had finished working just fifteen minutes earlier.

"How much time did he spend in here on any given day?"

"Hours. It wasn't unusual for me to wake up in the morning and he'd already been in here painting for a few hours. Some nights I'd go to bed, and I wouldn't know when or even if he ever came to bed. Life with an obsessed person. Come on. I'll show you his office."

The office was next to the studio and about half the size. There were three framed photos, maybe sixteen by twenty inches. Each photo was Kristi in different beauty pageants. In two of them, she was wearing floor-length formal gowns, and in the third, she was in a one-piece swimsuit that appeared to be wonderfully small. She wore a crown in all three photos and in the swimsuit photo, she had a banner across her chest that I think said Mississippi Headwaters Queen. Unfortunately, due to her pose with her hips cocked and her left hand resting on her hip, it read Miss Head Queen, which could lead to all sorts of mistaken assumptions.

Other than the framed photos, the office looked pretty normal. Two four-drawer file cabinets were against the wall behind the desk. A large computer screen sat on the desk with the keyboard resting on a pullout shelf below it. An adding machine with maybe twelve inches of tape hanging out the back was positioned on a corner of the desk. A comfortable-looking black desk chair was pushed up against the desk.

"Did he spend much time in here?"

Kristi took a long sip of wine and shook her head. "No more than an hour a day, except at the end of the month, then maybe the better part of the morning. Hey, my tummy's growling. Let's have some snacks out on the balcony."

"Sounds great. You lead the way."

She closed the office door behind us as I stepped into the hallway. She ignored a closed door I presumed was the bedroom. We walked past another half-dozen framed beauty pageant photos of Kristi hanging on the wall that I'd failed to notice earlier. She refilled our glasses, almost emptying the bottle, and slid my glass across the kitchen counter. We clinked glasses in another toast. "This way," she said as I stepped aside and she walked across the living room and out to the balcony.

Nine

It was a gorgeous summer evening. The sun was sinking lower in the sky, still an hour and a half away from setting. It reflected off the Mississippi flowing past three stories below us. Occasionally, a boat drove by, heading upriver. Kristi's balcony had four comfortable wicker chairs with cushions. The chairs were arranged on either side of a wicker coffee table with a glass top. Other than the occasional boat, there was no sound from the river, and since we were actually on the back of the building, we couldn't hear any of the traffic noise from Shepard Road.

Kristi had arranged three platters of hors d'oeuvres on the coffee table. One held grapes, another held apple slices arranged around a dish of honey, and a third held orange sections with coconut sprinkled on top. I took another sip of wine and looked forward to the anticipated activity later in the evening. I had a half-dozen grapes in my hand and ate them one at a time as we watched a cabin cruiser move slowly upriver.

As the cruiser disappeared around the bend Kristi took a large gulp of wine and said, "So, Dev, what have you found out so far?"

"Not much, other than Chandler had a pretty good reputation. A number of art galleries said they would love to see more of his work coming their way."

"Which ones did you talk to?"

"Here in town? Diane over at Find Art."

"What a bitch," Kristi said and took another sip.

"I found her pretty nice. In fact, she was the one who, more or less, connected me to the galleries in New York, San Francisco, and down in Tampa. She took the time to explain some of the ins and outs of the industry to me."

"Oh, really, and what did she say?" Kristi said and followed up with more wine.

Her tone suggested there was maybe an unpleasant history between the two of them. I promised myself I wouldn't react. "Basically, she explained how it's a very tough business, and people's tastes are all over the place, from abstract to Plein Air and everything in between."

"I was lucky if Chandler would sell three paintings at any of the shows at Find Art." She shook her head and followed up with more wine.

"Yeah, she mentioned that was fairly standard. How did he do in the other markets?"

"Well, about the same, but after all that was New York and San Francisco. It's really hard just to get in on either coast, let alone make a sale."

"So here, in Saint Paul, the world's biggest small town, he sold as many pieces as those much larger markets. Sounds to me like Find Art did a pretty good job."

"Well, whatever."

"You ever hear of a sculptor named Oscar Callum?"

"Rings a bell, but I don't know why," she said and took a couple hearty gulps of wine, draining her glass. "Back in a minute," she said and hurried into the apartment. When she returned, she carried the second bottle of wine. She filled both of our glasses and set the bottle on the coffee table.

"Figured I might as well grab the wine. Chili is ready whenever we are. You know, Dev, I wasn't kidding the other day when I said dumping you wasn't the best thing I've ever done."

Hmm-mmm, if I recalled, she'd said it was the worst thing she'd ever done, and now, two days later, she up'd the rating to 'it wasn't the best thing.' "Kristi, we were two kids heading down completely opposite paths. I wouldn't lose any sleep over it. Besides, if you'd stuck with me, you probably wouldn't have entered all those competitions you've won. Look at the lovely place you're living in. You've got a gorgeous view. I'd say you've done pretty well without me messing things up."

She seemed to beam at the mention of the competitions, then went on to describe in detail a half-dozen of them. By the time she finished, the second bottle of wine was empty. I'd heard more about beauty pageants in one evening than anyone else heard in a lifetime. It was dusk. The rare boat now on the river had all its lights on. Finally, Kristi said, "Well, what do you say? Shall we eat?"

"You bet." I jumped to my feet, picked up the empty wine bottle, and followed her inside.

Ten

I recognized the landscape hanging over the fireplace as the one I'd seen in the online image of Chandler, where he looked like a clueless idiot wearing a tweed cap and smoking a pipe. "Did Chandler do this painting over the fireplace?"

"Oh, that thing? No, a man named Malcolm Webster did it. He painted it especially for Chandler. I don't like the thing, but Chandler loves it. He can talk about it for hours, given half the chance. Malcolm Webster was a mentor to Chandler when he was first getting started. To my knowledge, they haven't corresponded in the last few years."

I stepped up to the painting and looked at the signature, Malcolm Webster, with a line beneath the signature. I made a mental note of his name and followed Kristi into the kitchen. "Can I help you with anything?"

"I think I've got everything covered. Tell you what," she said, handing me a pack of matches, "if you could light the candles on the dining room table, I'll dish up and bring the food out. Here, you can take this too." She handed me a wicker basket with what looked like four ciabatta rolls.

The dining room table was set with sterling silverware and linen napkins. There were six candles in a silver candelabra, and I hadn't quite finished lighting all of them when she came out carrying two steaming bowls of chili and set each one on a plate. "You know, I guess I forgot to mention I'm a vegan. Hope that's okay. I made a vegan chili."

"Sounds delicious, Kristi," I said and quietly swore to myself. Ever the gentleman, I pulled out the chair at the end of the table for her. As she sat down, she said, "Dev, grab that other wine bottle on the kitchen counter, will you?"

I brought the wine bottle in, set it next to her, and sat down just to her right. She raised her glass. "Bon Appétit," she said and proceeded to gulp down half the glass. "Hope you like it." She followed up with a spoonful of chili and smiled.

I took a spoonful, fully prepared to be thoroughly disappointed, and to my surprise, it was actually pretty good.

"What do you think?"

"I think it's really good, Kristi. How long have you been a vegan? I just remember, after we went to a dance, you always made me take you to McDonald's or a pizza place."

"I did that for you, Dev. It's not like you didn't eat anything while we were there."

"Yeah, true, I guess."

I'd like to say we chatted about everything and nothing over dinner, but actually, I sat there and listened to Kristi continue on and on about various beauty pageants she'd been in. She told me about the preparation, the exercises, the workouts. I listened to tricks regarding facial creams and various makeup techniques. Way too much information about shaving. She was about three glasses of wine ahead of me at this point. I'd say we, but actually, she finished the better part of the third bottle. It was approaching midnight, and we were more than halfway through the third bottle when she looked at me through glassy eyes and said, "Dev, I'm counting on you to spend the night."

"Oh, Kristi thanks, but—"

"No, Dev. I really mean it. I want this to be a night we'll both remember. Please? I really, really want you to."

"Okay, yeah, sure, I mean, I'd love to. Thank you."

"Good, I can't wait. This wine has made me, mmm, ready for bed. What do you think?"

"Sounds like a great idea."

"Oh, you're so sweet. Come on." She pushed her chair back and staggered to her feet. Before I could get out of my chair, she stepped behind me and began to give me a shoulder rub. It felt wonderful, and I was beginning to think there was no way I ever wanted to find Chandler Hancock. She kept the shoulder rub going for a good few minutes then pressed the back of my head between her large, surgically enhanced breasts, and kissed me a number of times on the top of the head.

"Okay, baby, come on. Let's go to bed." She took my hand. We left the dishes on the table, the candles burning, and we headed down the hall to the bedroom. Along the way she reached behind her neck and unhooked the strap on her halter top then pulled the top down, almost, but not quite exposing her breasts. I was afraid she was going to hear my heart thumping.

She stopped in front of the bedroom door and said, "Which do you prefer, Dev? Top or bottom?"

"Whatever you want is just fine with me," I said. If she couldn't hear my heart, I was positive she could hear my heavy breathing. I was already panting like I'd just run a mile. No doubt, this was going to be a night to remember.

She opened the bedroom door, and a very dim, blue-tinted light automatically came on. "Alexa," Kristi said, "turn off the light in two minutes." I stepped into the room, reached around her shoulders, and pulled her top down. "Oh thank you, Dev, but you better hurry. The lights go off in about ninety seconds." She staggered toward the bunk bed against the wall.

"What the hell?"

"Yeah, that ladder is no fun at all. Thank you for a wonderful evening. See you in the morning." With that, she pulled her halter top over her head and tossed it off to the side. She unbuttoned her shorts, pulled them down to her knees, and kicked them off into a corner, revealing a very small black thong just as the lights went out. I stood there in the dark, listening to her crawl into bed, waiting for the invitation to join her that never came. A minute later, I was treated to wine-induced snoring.

I debated just going home but thought maybe there was hope for a morning romp. I undressed in the pitch dark and moved forward an inch at a time until I ran into the bunk bed. I felt around to my right until I located the ladder. I cautiously climbed up the ladder one step at a time, reaching for the upper mattress. Once I found it, I started to hop in, only to slam my forehead into the ceiling. I saw stars, and dropped a rung or two on the bunk bed ladder before I was able to stop the fall.

"Serves you right, Chandler," Kristi mumbled and went back to snoring.

Eleven

I woke early the following morning feeling like I'd slept on a railroad track. I lay in bed and slowly turned my head and shoulders from side to side. I heard audible cracking sounds. I looked at the two windows on the back wall. A faint grey light was peeping around the edge of the wooden Venetian blinds. It was barely sunrise. I leaned over the edge of the bed and looked down on sleeping Kristi. She had a sheet more or less draped over her. One perfect, bare leg was completely exposed. I stared for a long time waiting for her eyes to open, wink, and beckon me forward, but it never came. At least the snoring had stopped, I thought, just as she started up again.

There were two thin pillows on the top bunk. I took one and cautiously dangled it over the edge then dropped it on Kristi's face, hoping she'd wake up. Instead, she slipped her exposed leg beneath the covers, pulled the pillow I'd just dropped over her face, and turned onto her side, facing the wall and completely eliminating any hint of the gorgeous figure lying down there.

I carefully climbed down the ladder and stood for another five minutes staring and wondering how I could wake her without being obvious. "Kristi, are you awake?" I said a couple of times, but with the pillow over her head, she remained oblivious. So much for my plans.

There was a statue on the dresser with a black thong hanging from it. Kristi must have tossed the thong just after the lights went out. The statue was maybe ten inches tall, a naked woman with her clothes piled around her ankles. I stepped over and examined the statue. Even in the dim light it looked very much like Kristi, and I wondered if she'd possibly posed for the artist. The name Oscar Callum was carved in the base. The name she had said rang a distant bell. Amazing.

I quietly got dressed and tiptoed out of the room. I cleared the table and brought the hors d'oeuvre platters in from the balcony. I stacked all the plates in the dishwasher. I hand-washed and dried the silverware and the crystal wine glasses. I put the wine bottles in recycling. I walked down the hall to Chandler's office and sat behind his desk. Other than pens and a blank notebook, all the desk drawers were empty. I wondered if Kristi had cleaned them out. The file cabinets were locked.

I walked into the kitchen. The clock on the stove said 5:50 am, and I toyed with the idea of getting undressed and climbing in with her, but I'd already had enough disappointment for one day, and it wasn't even six in the morning. On my way out the door, I happened to glance at the end table. Along with a set of car keys and what looked like a garage door opener, there were a half-dozen dog leashes, red, black, green, blue. There was no other evidence of a dog in the unit, and at the moment, I was too tired to give it much thought, so I headed home.

Morton, my supposed watchdog, remained asleep on the couch and didn't bother to wake up when I came in the front door. He must have learned that from Kristi. I went into the kitchen, got the coffee going, then headed upstairs and took a shower. I changed into a clean shirt and jeans, headed up the block to the bakery for a cara-mel roll, and went back home. Morton was still asleep on the couch.

I checked the news online then Googled Malcolm Webster, the guy who did the painting above Kristi's fireplace. Chandler's mentor was how Kristi had de-scribed him. The Wikipedia article had a picture of a guy I pegged as mid-sixties, maybe seventy. He was wearing a suit and tie and standing outside a large building that looked like it could have been on a college campus. A number of museums around the world were listed as dis-playing works he'd done. It went on to describe his painting style, gave a brief history, and concluded with the line that Webster had been reported missing in 2016.

I heard Morton jump off the couch and stretch. A few minutes later, he wandered into the kitchen and bonked his head a couple of times on my leg, indicating it was all right with him if I gave his head a scratch. I did just that then opened the backdoor and let him out. By the time I filled his food and water dishes, he barked at the backdoor, reminding me he had a breakfast to eat. I

finished up my caramel roll while Morton devoured everything in his food dish and we headed down to the office.

Twelve

I'd just poured my first cup of coffee in the office. "Whoa, late night?" was how Louie greeted me when he arrived.

"I didn't sleep very well."

"Everything OK? Hey, wait a minute. Weren't you going to meet up with that beauty queen, Katie?"

"Kristi, actually, and yeah, I went over there for dinner last night."

"And? Come on, Dev, details. I need details," Louie said as he poured himself a coffee.

"Unbelievable."

Louie's eyes widened as he settled in behind the picnic table and set his mug down. "So good? What's she into? Really crazy?"

"Really crazy doesn't begin to cover it." I went on to tell him about the night. The fruit hors d'oeuvres, the vegan chili, the three bottles of wine, and the icing on the cake, did I want top or bottom.

He looked at me and laughed. He laughed at me for what seemed like a couple of minutes until he was red-faced and began coughing. I was almost ready to get up and give him the Heimlich maneuver when he settled down.

"You know, Dev, I warned you, but I had no idea things would end up taking this direction. Beautiful, absolutely beautiful."

"Thanks, Louie. Plus, I got the name of another painter who disappeared. The name Malcolm Webster mean anything to you?"

Louie seemed to think for a long moment and eventually shook his head. "Just like this woman's husband? All of a sudden, he disappears?"

"What about the name Oscar Callum, lived up north outside of Duluth?"

"Another painter?"

"No, this Oscar was a sculptor, but an artist, none the less."

"And he's missing too?"

"Sounds that way. I'm about to call Diane at Find Art and see if she knows anything."

"All these guys disappearing, you ever think it might be aliens?" He said and started laughing again. This time, he was a little more controlled.

"Very funny, not. Although there does seem to be a common denominator, they're more or less reclusive. Even though Chandler was married to Kristi from the little bit she described, it sounded like he pretty much did what he wanted. Worked some very early and very late hours. Then the fact that the guy has been missing for over half a year, and she's just now getting around to looking for him? She still hasn't reported it to the cops."

"You think you should maybe give your pal LaZelle a ring?"

"That's gonna be my second call, right after I talk to Diane."

Louie shook his head.

"What, you don't think I should call Diane?"

"No, she sounds sane. But I think you should ditch this Kristi person and tell LaZelle the little that you know. Maybe there's a pattern there. Maybe it's just the way these people operate, but I don't see a win for you anywhere. You ever bother to discuss payment with her?"

"With Kristi?"

"Yeah. Did you mention rates, expenses, you know, how you want to get paid?"

"Well, not exactly."

"I'll take that as a no. You've already spent the better part of two days mousing around with this, and now instead of just this Chandler character missing, you've got two other guys. That's a total of three, Dev. I'm telling you, drop this thing. Back out. It's got all the earmarks of nothing but problems."

Thirteen

Ignoring Louie's advice was a daily occurrence for me. I phoned Diane at Find Art. "Good Morning, Find Art. This is Diane."

"Hi Diane, Dev Haskell."

"Oh, hi Dev. Why do I think you're probably not calling to place a bid on Chandler Hancock's 'Season Opener'?" Fortunately, she laughed.

"Like I said, I'm out of that demographic. I did have some questions for you. Mind if I stop by?"

"What kind of questions?"

"I just need some general info on a couple of other artists. Information maybe a little more specific than the PR version I'm reading online."

"Yeah, sure. I mean I'll tell what I know, which isn't going to be particularly unique, but it's probably a step up from what you have already."

"You got any plans for lunch?"

"Actually, I have to be here, but if you want to come down over the lunch hour, we can certainly chat. It's a roll of the dice if I'll have any walk-ins. Late in the week, like today, there might be one or two, but please feel free to stop by."

"Okay, I'll be down there around noon, and I'll pick up lunch."

"Don't worry about it. I brought a sandwich so—"

"Good, you can stick the sandwich in the fridge and save it for tomorrow. I'll see you around noon."

"Looking forward to it," she said and hung up.

I phoned Aaron LaZelle next and left a message. At 11:30, after doing nothing for most of the morning except yawning, I drove over to City Salsa House, a Mexican restaurant not far from my house. With the limited parking on the busy street, I had to park a half-block away.

As I rounded the corner, I passed a bus stop. There was a fat guy sitting on the bench. He had an orange beard in desperate need of a trim and he could have used a shower. As I walked past, he eyed me in a way that didn't encourage conversation. I thought he looked familiar, maybe, but I kept going and entered the restaurant. I ordered spiced chicken soft shell tacos and, for dessert, two Mexican Flans. There were just two booths occupied, and I was sitting at the bar, sipping an ice water and waiting for my take out when the door opened. I was the only guy seated at the bar, and I looked at the reflection in the mirror.

It was the guy from the bus stop. He was big, maybe six foot two. His tangled ginger-colored hair looked like it hadn't seen a comb, let alone shampoo, for quite some time. His orange beard looked even worse. He wore shorts, sandals, and a grimy t-shirt that said, 'Beer Me.' The t-shirt almost, but not quite, covered his hairy navel.

The woman working behind the bar said, "Oh no," under her breath and hurried into the kitchen

"Hey. You say something to me?"

I didn't turn around but kept watching him in the mirror.

"I'm talking to you. Is your name Haskell? You some bullshit detective?" Not that there was a lot of conversational chatter in the place to begin with, but things suddenly went dead quiet.

I turned around on the barstool, leaned back against the bar, and stared at him. After a long moment, it came to me. "Gerry Berk, when did they let you out?"

"It's been seven months, no thanks to your ass."

"Maybe next time you won't try to force yourself on little high school girls riding the city bus."

Two guys stepped out through the swinging kitchen door. One was dressed in white and carried a wooden mallet, the kind you use to pound meat. The other guy was mean enough looking without the mallet. They were at least as large as Berk, only younger, fit, and there were two of them.

"Sir," the guy with the mallet said, "I think it would be best if you left." He began to slowly pound the mallet into his open hand, leaving no doubt he would be more than willing to use it.

"I'm just coming in here to get a drink."

"We're not going to serve you, so you might as well leave."

"You can't do that. It's against the law. I got rights, and I—"

"Gerry, it's gonna be three on one, and we're gonna kick the shit out of you and toss you in the dumpster, so just get your worthless ass the hell out of here," I said.

He looked at me for a moment then at the two guys who had now come around from the back of the bar. They had spread apart and stood maybe eight feet away, each with a table between them and Berk. I had the feeling they may have done this once or twice before.

"You got lucky today, Haskell. That ain't gonna happen next time. I'll find your ass," Berk said then turned and limped out the door.

A moment after he walked out, two women stepped in and headed for a booth. "Oh, my God, did you smell that guy?" one of them said.

The guy with the mallet stepped back into the kitchen. The other guy walked to the door and looked up and down the street then came over to me. "I'm sorry, sir. Are you all right?"

"Yeah, thanks for coming to the rescue. That jerk is all talk and no action. But you don't need him in here."

Three guys walked in and settled into the far booth. One of them nodded at the man talking to me and said, "How's it going, Georgie?"

He gave them the thumbs-up then turned back to me. "Can I get you a drink or something?"

"Thanks, but the ice water's just fine. I should apologize. That jerk wouldn't have come in here if he didn't recognize me. He was sitting at the bus stop out there. I thought he looked familiar, but I couldn't place him."

"His name is Berk?"

"Yeah, Gerry Berk. He was arrested for assaulting a fourteen-year-old girl on a city bus some years back. The kid was the daughter of a friend of mine. I'm a P.I. and tracked him down. That limp he's got, I'm proud to say I gave it to him. Figured it would help me spot him from a distance, although I was looking right at him when he was on the bus bench, and nothing clicked in this thick skull of mine."

That seemed to bring a smile to his face. "A P.I.? Private Investigator?"

"Yeah." I held out my hand. "Dev Haskell's my name."

He shook hands with me and said, "George Estrada. Nice to meet you. You got a business card?"

I took out my wallet and lo and behold I actually had a business card in there. I pulled it out and handed it to him. He glanced at it for a moment then said, "I may give you a call. Let me check on your order. It should be up by now."

As he turned, the woman came out of the kitchen carrying a white plastic bag with two white Styrofoam trays.

"Oh, here it is now. Perfect timing, Carmen." He took the bag from her and handed it to me. "Here you go, Dev. And no charge. This is on us."

"George, thanks, but I insist. Please, let me pay," I said and handed my debit card to Carmen. She took the card and looked at George.

"Really, George, I insist. You and the other gentleman were very helpful. Let me pay."

George shrugged, and we shook hands. "I'll be in touch," he said and headed back into the kitchen.

Carmen walked over to the cash register and ran my card through. I opened the plastic bag and sniffed. It smelled delicious, and I could feel my stomach rumble. It suddenly dawned on me I hadn't eaten anything except a caramel roll for breakfast.

"Um, I'm terribly sorry, Mr. Haskell, but this card has been denied," Carmen said.

"Denied? Can you try it again?"

"Actually, I already did that, sir. Um, three times. It's been denied."

"Oh, maybe the deposit I made this morning doesn't clear until the end of the day," I lied.

"I'm sure that's it, sir," she said and pasted on a worried-looking smile.

"Here, better try this one," I said and handed her another card. "Gee, I hope it's not your system. That could make for a long day."

She flashed a quick smile and punched some keys on the little terminal. A moment later, she grinned and gave the thumbs-up then hurried over with the receipt and a pen. "Just need your signature, and you're good to go."

I quickly signed the receipt, added a four dollar tip, and hurried out the door. Fortunately, Gerry Berk was nowhere to be seen. Hopefully, he'd gone home to take a shower.

Fourteen

I walked into the Find Art Gallery carrying the plastic bag with the Styrofoam trays. There were two couples looking at the abstract paintings on the walls. One of the guys wore a Green Bay Packers jersey. Diane was seated behind a small counter near the door.

"Hi, Dev. Oh, you didn't have to do that but thanks. You want to bring that in back and set it in the cubicle?" She lowered her voice, "It shouldn't be too much longer."

"I'll see you back there," I said and headed for the back room. I set the Styrofoam trays next to the laptop and took a seat. After about five minutes, I opened the bag. Along with the Styrofoam trays, there were two plastic containers with Mexican flan and two sets of plastic utensils and napkins. I laid the napkins on the desk counter and arranged the plastic knife, fork, and spoon. I waited a couple of minutes and figured maybe a little taste wouldn't hurt, just to make sure it was good. I opened one of the trays and took a forkful of rice, delicious. I took a second forkful and closed the tray. Another minute or two passed, and I thought a taste of chicken fajita might not be a bad idea. I cut off a piece and ate it. At no surprise, it was wonderful. Then I thought, *'Since that was just an end piece I should maybe have another bite, get the full effect.'*

I suddenly realized I was almost halfway through the meal when I heard the door open, and Diane hurried over to the cubicle. I quickly closed the Styrofoam tray and licked the fork clean before she stepped in.

"Sorry that took so long. Nice folks from Wisconsin."

"Did they buy anything?"

"That's not the way this business works, Dev. Mmmm, this smells delicious. What did you get?"

"We are dining on chicken fajitas from City Salsa House. I've had them before, and they're very good."

"And the rice?" she said and nodded at my t-shirt. Three or four pieces of orange rice were scattered across my chest.

"I just wanted to make sure it was good enough for you."

"Yeah, sure you did. Okay, let's dig in. I'm starving."

She opened the lid on her tray and said, "Oh my, I'm not sure I'm going to be able to finish all of this."

I moved my tray off to the side and leaned forward, more or less blocking her view.

"What are you doing?" she said and pushed me back, so I was sitting upright. "Dev? Oh my God. It's almost all gone."

"No it's not. I ordered a half-order for me."

"Liar pants on fire. You've already eaten most of the rice, and one of the fajitas is completely gone."

"I wanted to make sure it was good enough for you."

She looked at me and started to laugh. "You are a real piece of work. Well, is it?"

"Yeah, I think you'll like it."

She shook her head and said, "Incredible," just under her breath and took a forkful of rice. "Mmm, this is really good. Okay, you're safe, and no, I'm not going to be sharing anything with you."

"I brought dessert, too," I said and nodded at the round plastic dishes with the flan.

"God," she said, shoveling another forkful of rice into her mouth. "I'll have to go on a diet, but it is really good."

"Crazy experience getting it." I went on to tell her the Gerry Berk tale. I didn't embellish it very much.

"Oh, he sounds creepy. What did you say his name was?"

"Gerry Berk, big fat guy with an orange beard. You can't miss him."

"Thanks, if I see him, I'll be sure to go the other way. Okay, so you said you wanted some information on a couple of artists. How can I help?"

We chatted and ate for the next thirty minutes. I asked the occasional question, but mostly I listened to the information Diane had off the top of her head regarding Chandler Hancock, Malcolm Webster, and Oscar Callum. It seemed Hancock was by far the most outgoing of the three, with Webster not quite as reserved as Callum. First off, Webster was married to a nice woman who was younger, and as far as Diane knew, Callum had never married. The other thing was Chandler Hancock lived in the city. As focused on art as he may have been, working in the early morning and late at night, he still had to interact with people and crowds. The other two resided in rural areas where they wouldn't have to see people for weeks if not months at a time.

As far as Diane knew, none of the three would have been labeled as crazy or bizarre. Yes, they were artists and therefore maybe slightly different from the average person who didn't necessarily have their particular set of traits. But they weren't wackos. "And believe me," she said, "there are plenty of crazies in all aspects of this business."

She went on to say, "The only thing I really find strange is this disappearance thing. Suddenly, they're not there, no contact with anyone. Not so much as a phone call or an email to say I'm going to live in the Bahamas or the Amazon jungle for the rest of my life. Their homes aren't up for sale. There's still money in their bank accounts. These guys were successful, but they weren't billionaires. At some point, you have to buy food, gas, pay the light bill. I don't get it."

"Do you think Chandler Hancock was making a lot of money?"

"Making a lot of money? Do you mean like millions?"

"Not necessarily. But was he making enough to live comfortably?"

"I suppose he was, yes. Did he travel to Europe or China on a regular basis? I don't believe he made that sort of income. At least not at this time. His work and reputation were definitely on the rise, and maybe in ten years or so, with a bit of luck, and continuing to produce, who knows? Why do you ask?"

"I was over at his place, going over records and things." I maybe fudged my explanation. "They seemed to have a pretty nice place."

"Think of it like this, Dev; in the industry, we basically double the price. So that painting for fifty grand, he grosses twenty-five. Deduct from that, everything from rent to insurance and the hours he spent creating it. That fifty grand painting is nice, but he's had a number of them that were far less expensive. At the end of the day, he's a small business person. The shows he may have in New York, San Francisco or Tampa? He pays for his flights to get there, as well as hotels and meals. He pays for all expenses. And, the money he makes on the paintings, that's only if they sell. The three paintings we have back here, including the one for fifty grand, we haven't paid him a thing. They're simply here in the hope someone will ask if we have his work and maybe purchase one of them."

She took a spoonful of her flan while I ate the last half of her remaining fajita. As I was finishing up, she reached for my flan.

"Do you really have room for this?" she said.

"Not really, but I was going to try to force it down, all the same."

"Let me put it in the refrigerator and save it for someone more deserving, namely me." With that, she picked up the plastic dish with my flan and walked out of the cubicle. She was back a minute later. "What?"

"Oh, nothing. Just glad you liked it."

"Thanks, Dev. A wonderful lunch, and it was great to see you. I wish I had more specific information, but I don't. Like I said earlier, if you hadn't called me, I would have chalked Chandler Hancock up as just one more talented artist that is operating on a different plane from the rest of us. But linking the three of them together certainly gives one pause. I'm still not sure it's as sinister as you might want to suggest."

On the way back from lunch with Diane, I stopped in at the post office branch to check Chandler's P.O. Box. Now there were two letters sitting in his box, and one of them was the envelope I mailed yesterday with the yellow magic marker along the edge. Tomorrow was the 19th. It would be interesting to see if anyone followed my directions on the letter and showed up at the Depot Bar at 5:00.

Fifteen

The following morning, I was parked outside Kristi's building just before seven, hoping she'd drive somewhere so I could follow her and come up with some answers, any answers. Things weren't adding up. From the comfortable lifestyle to not reporting Chandler Hancock's disappearance to the police, it wasn't making sense to me.

She made an appearance at 11:30. Not the appearance I was expecting. I figured she'd be driving, and I could tail her. There she was, only on foot, with six dogs, each one on a separate leash. The same leashes I'd seen on the table next to her door when I'd left yesterday morning. There was a black lab, a golden retriever, a dachshund, a small poodle, and two little white, furry dogs. She headed around the corner and along the sidewalk. I knew there was a dog park in that direction about six buildings away.

I sat in the car and waited for ten minutes watching her through my binoculars. The dogs seemed to be well-behaved. None of them were straining at the leash or snapping at one another. They eventually walked up a small rise; the dog park, a large fenced area where they could run, was at the top of the rise. When it looked like they were about to enter the park, I started my car and slowly headed in that direction.

I parked just below the small rise then climbed out and headed up to the dog park. Kristi was the only person up there, but she had the six dogs with her, so the place looked more or less crowded. The dogs were all off the leash. She had one of those Chuckit ball launchers, and she was tossing an orange tennis ball to the pack of dogs. She launched the thing over their heads, and one of the dogs would leap in the air and grab it on the first bounce, usually the lab or the retriever. The dachshund was the slowest in the group. By the time he turned around and got moving, he didn't take more than a half-dozen steps before one of the larger dogs had already grabbed the tennis ball. The two little white furry dogs seemed more interested in chasing one another around than going after the ball.

Kristi's back was to me, and I stepped into the area and closed the gate behind me. She launched the tennis ball again, and I called, "Kristi."

She turned and placed her hand on her forehead to shield her eyes.

"Oh, hi, Dev. What are you doing here?" The lab ran back with the ball and dropped it at her feet. She moved the Chuckit launcher to grab the ball then turned and gave two fake throws before she sent the ball sailing over the pack of dogs. They all seemed to be enjoying themselves.

"I was just going to stop by, see if you were home. I thought it might be you walking up the street, but I wasn't sure. Where'd all these guys come from?"

"This is what I do. I walk dogs," she said and indicated the pack heading back toward her. Once again, the lab had the orange ball.

"How long have you been doing this?"

"Oh, a while, I guess."

The lab dropped the ball at her feet, and just as she was about to grab it with the launcher, one of the little white furry dogs raced in and took off down the field with the ball in his mouth. The other five took off after him.

"De Gaulle, get back here with that. De Gaulle, do you hear me?"

"Maybe he doesn't understand English."

"He does that every time. It's part of the game. Now they'll share and chase one another around. Eventually, they'll get tired. Once three or four of them are lying down, it's time to head back home."

"What if they don't want to head home?"

"They always do. They know there's a treat waiting for them back in the building."

"They're all from your building?"

"Yep. Three are right on my floor. I like it, well, unless it's twenty below. Then it's not so fun. When winter comes, we usually do a quick walk around the buildings and go back inside. It's a race to see who can get back inside first, them or me. So, what did you want to see me about?"

"Well, first off, thank you for the other night. The vegan chili was excellent."

"Still some left. Stop up when we head back, and I'll give you a container full."

"I wondered if you had any financial records on Chandler's art sales over the years."

"Probably. If we do, they'd be in his office."

"In the desk?" I asked, wondering how she would reply.

"No, he doesn't like to keep anything in the desk. In his own way, he's a bit of a security freak."

Once again, she was speaking in the present tense. Like she'd just been with him at the breakfast table this morning.

"If there are any records, they'd probably be in the file cabinet or maybe on his computer. Unfortunately, I don't have his password, so I can't get in there."

"Yeah, if you wouldn't mind, I'd like to check it out this morning."

The lab dropped the ball between the two of us then walked a few feet away and stretched out. The retriever stretched out next to him.

"Shouldn't be too much longer. They're getting tired."

Ten minutes later, she had all the dogs hooked up to a leash. She looked around and said, "Treat. Treat. Who wants a treat?"

Suddenly, they were all up and heading for the gate. "Come on, treat," Kristi called as I pulled the gate open and we headed down the street to her building. She quickly delivered each dog back to its apartment. As the door was answered, she tossed a small dog biscuit into the unit, and the appropriate dog dashed in to get it. None of the others made a move. The last to be dropped off were the two little white furry dogs. They were in the same unit, and like all the others, they hurried in to grab their biscuits.

"How did you ever get into walking dogs?" I asked as we headed down the hall to her place.

"I've always loved dogs, and this way, I can enjoy them and not have to deal with any of the problems. I don't have to take them to the vet. I don't have to clean dog hair off my furniture and clothes. I don't have dog hair all over my car. Plus, with Chandler's work, I've no doubt a dog would end up in his studio sooner or later, which can only point to some impending disaster. Besides, he's allergic to dogs. So walking them is the best of both worlds."

Sixteen

I sat at the kitchen counter while Kristi warmed our coffee in the microwave for thirty seconds. She set the mugs on the kitchen counter and then stared at me over the edge of her mug as she drank. I was hoping for an explanation on the bunk beds, or God forbid the suggestion of a rematch, but she didn't say anything. The coffee was barely lukewarm. She finally set her mug down and said, "Let me get the keys to the file cabinets, and you can take a look at Chandler's records."

I followed her down the hall, and she stopped at her bedroom door. For a half-second, I thought, *It's about time. She's going to invite me in.'* Instead, she said, "Go on into the office. I'll get the keys, and I'll join you in a minute."

I wandered into the office. Everything looked the same as the last time I was in there. Not that there was really anything to move around. The adding machine was in the same position, and the length of paper tape hanging out the back looked just like it did the other day.

Kristi stepped in and flipped on the light switch. "I'll open the file cabinets, Dev. Why don't you settle in behind the desk? All I ask is that you don't take anything. Chandler's a bit of a control freak when it comes to his files, and he'd know right away if something was missing."

"Are you familiar with how he's organized his files?"

"No. This was his job. He didn't share any information with me, ever. And to be honest, I really didn't want any."

She slipped the key into the lock in the upper right-hand corner of both four-drawer file cabinets. The lock unit immediately extended out, and she pulled the top drawers open maybe a half-inch. "There you go. Help yourself. I've never been in them, so I'd be absolutely no help at all." She walked around to the front of the desk and headed toward the door. "Just give me a call if you need anything," she said and hurried out of the office, closing the door behind her.

Maybe the idea of going through Chandler's files seemed like a violation to her. Maybe she didn't want to come across information that suggested he was into drugs or had a secret affair. Maybe she had to use the bathroom. Whatever it was, she couldn't get out of the room fast enough.

I pulled the top drawer of the first file cabinet open, grabbed a handful of files, placed then on the desk, and sat down. By mid-afternoon, I'd been through two cups of cold coffee. I was going through the final handful of files in the bottom drawer of the second file cabinet, and about the only thing I'd learned was that Chandler Hancock, as much as I initially disliked him, appeared to be a fairly squared away individual. I'm not a financial guy by any stretch of the imagination, but at least on the surface, he seemed to keep legitimate records. I finished up with the last of the files, returned them to the bottom drawer, kicked the drawer closed, and pushed the locks in flush with the cabinet frame.

For the first time, I noticed a closet door. I'd been so focused on first the desk and then the files that it had never registered with me. I turned the knob, and the door opened. A string with a little metal end hung from the light in the ceiling. I pulled the string, and the closet light came on. There were clothes hanging on either side of the closet. To the left, what appeared to be raincoats, winter coats, and fall jackets. Two looked like they belonged to Chandler, but the majority were definitely Kristi's. On the right side were five racks of shoes, stiletto heels, sandals, pumps, casual shoes, crocs, oxfords, loafers, athletic shoes, boots, Birkenstocks, flats, clogs, slip-ons, and a pair of combat boots. Above the shoe racks were shelves with piles of tops, shorts, jeans, and t-shirts and then there, hanging on the wall, was a painting.

The image was definitely Kristi, stretched out on what looked like a red velvet antique couch, in all her beautiful, naked glory. Nothing was left to the imagination. In the painting, her left arm was draped along the top of the couch, and her hair was a wonderful blonde color, just the way I remembered it. There was no doubt it was her, no doubt at all.

The actual painting wasn't all that large, maybe twenty inches wide and twelve inches high, although the elaborate antique gold frame gave it the sense of being much larger. The signature in the corner of the painting read Myles Rossler with an exclamation point behind the name. Forget the fact that I knew Kristi. It was an excellent painting of one very hot woman. Funny that it was hung in the closet surrounded by shelves filled with stacks of clothes.

The shelf beneath the painting had a small drawer hanging beneath it. The drawer was no larger than maybe eight inches across and four inches high. I pulled it open, and the only thing inside was a stained white t-shirt. I pulled on the t-shirt, and it was heavy. I took it out of the drawer and unfolded it. It held a .45 semi-automatic pistol. The stains on the shirt were clearly from oil on the pistol. I picked it up and looked; there was a clip. I released the clip, and it was loaded with shells with brass casings. Strange accessory for an artist, but then again maybe not. I wrapped the pistol back up in the t-shirt and returned it to the drawer. I turned off the light, closed the door behind me, and headed back to the kitchen where I assumed I would find Kristi.

I was wrong. She wasn't in the kitchen. She was in the living room. She was seated on a yoga mat in front of the double doors leading out to her balcony. The doors were open, and the screen was pushed to the side. The sun was streaming in, and Kristi was sitting in the sunshine.

She wore a very small pink thong and I presumed a smile, although I couldn't be sure since her back was to me. Her legs were spread wide, and she was leaning forward, placing her hands over her toes with the bright red nail polish. She seemed to hold that position for at least twenty or thirty seconds before she would sit upright and, with her arms outstretched, turn from side to side a dozen times. Once that was complete, she resumed her stretching position for another half-minute.

I stood quietly for a very long time and watched the private show. Eventually, I cleared my throat and said, "Hey, Kristi, I'm all finished in there. I put everything back in the file drawers, locked them, and turned off the light."

She stretched her arms out. "Did you find anything?" She asked, and then began twisting first left and then right.

"From what I could tell, everything seemed to be in order, not that I'm any kind of financial genius."

She asked me another question, but I was more focused on her turning from side to side and the wonderful bouncing it created, so I didn't hear what she said.

"Dev?"

"Oh, sorry, I didn't quite hear you. What did you say?"

She was stretched out again, hands reaching over her toes, perfect rear, tiny pink thong, and large breasts.

"Are you even paying attention?"

"Yeah, yeah, sure, sorry, just thinking of something else for a second."

"What's your next step?"

I felt like saying *'getting rid of your stupid bunk bed.'* Instead, I said, "I'm going to look into a couple of other artists who apparently had everything going their way career-wise and then suddenly seemed to disappear."

"Do you think there might be a connection?"

"Only one way to find out."

She was stretching again. I considered asking if she wanted me to hold her ankles while she did sit-ups for an hour or two but thought better of it.

"Well, I guess I'll take off. Thanks for letting me interrupt your day."

"Not a problem," she said and began with the outstretched arms and the turning from side to side again. "Call. Me. If. You. Learn. Anything," she said. Saying one word with each turn, completely oblivious to the show she was putting on.

Seventeen

I headed back to the office, and for the next hour thought about Kristi doing her stretching exercises on the yoga mat. I put Morton in the car, and we drove across the river to the post office. I went in and checked P.O. Box 457. Chandler Hancock's P.O. Box. It was empty. I got back in the car and headed downtown. I pulled into a parking ramp directly across the street from the Depot Bar. It was almost 4:30, and people were beginning to head home. I was able to get a parking space on the second level. I sat on the hood of my car and looked out at the front door of the Depot Bar directly across the street.

At five minutes before five, who should walk down the street and into the bar? None other than Kristi McKenzie. She looked gorgeous from where I sat, although I much preferred her attire from earlier this afternoon. I wondered for a moment if she still had on that little pink thong. I sat on the hood of the car and waited until she came back out the door forty-five minutes later. She gave a quick look up and down the street then headed back the way she'd come.

Once she was out of sight, I walked down the stair-case and crossed the street to the Depot. The place consisted of one long room. The bar had a green granite countertop and ran along one side of the long narrow room. Eight booths were up against the wall opposite the bar and ran the length of the bar. An open area between the bar and the restrooms was filled with a half-dozen tables. There were six guys and two women seated at the bar. The women were sipping white wine and involved in a conversation. The six guys appeared to be in the bar on their own and simply stared at the half-empty glass of beer in front of them. A couple sat in one booth, and three guys occupied another.

It certainly wasn't what you'd call crowded, and it took all of fifteen seconds to get a look at everyone in the place, including the bartender reading the paper. Kristi must have sat in here for the better part of an hour waiting for, she didn't know who, to walk in with a thousand dollars cash.

It told me one thing. Despite her supposed hands-off policy on Chandler's files, she apparently had no problem opening and reading his mail and then showing up for a meeting with someone who remained anonymous.

Morton and I headed home. I took him for a walk, heated up some chili from the refrigerator for a late dinner, and decided to head up to bed around eleven. I turned off the lights on the first floor and was about to go up the stairs when I happened to look out the front door. It was dark, and the person staggering on the far side of the street was too far away to identify. But, he was large, fat, with unkempt hair and a large beard. Gerry Berk? Maybe.

I washed up, brushed my teeth, and headed to bed, setting my nine-millimeter on the table next to my side of the bed, just in case. Around two in the morning, Morton woke me with a quiet growl. I grabbed the pistol and listened by the bedroom door for a long moment before I opened it. I checked the rooms upstairs then headed down to the first floor and went through the house with the lights off. Everything seemed fine.

When I came back upstairs, Morton was stretched out on the bed and breathing deeply. I closed the bedroom door, set my digital alarm for 6:00 am, and placed a chair below the doorknob just in case. After twenty minutes, I fell back asleep, and neither Morton nor I woke until the alarm went off. I headed for the bathroom, and Morton went back to sleep.

Eighteen

I was on my second cup of coffee when Morton made his way downstairs. He stopped at my stool and bumped his head against my knee a few times until I caught on I was supposed to scratch him. Once I got the message and complied, he headed for the backdoor and waited for me to let him out. It was a clear day, warm, but not humid. I stood out on the back porch for a moment and figured it wasn't going to get any better than this to head up to Warba, Minnesota and see what I could learn about the sculptor Oscar Callum.

I let Morton in, filled his food and water dish, made breakfast, and sent Louie an email telling him we were heading up north for the day. We took off a little after nine, made Duluth around 11:30, then headed north and west on Highway 2 for another hour. The highway ran right through the middle of town, population one hundred and eighty people. There was a liquor store, a grocery store, a community school, a Lutheran church, and some nice looking homes. I pulled in front of the liquor store and went inside. For a small town, there was a pretty decent selection of beer and liquor on the shelves.

"What can I do for you?" the man behind the counter said and gave me a look that suggested I wasn't from around there. He had dark hair and a full beard, and I guessed he might be forty. He was built like he'd done hard labor for a lot of years on a farm or maybe cutting timber.

"Sorry to bother you. I'm looking for someone, but all I've got is a PO Box number. He's a sculptor, and I was hoping to purchase one of his works, but I have no idea where—"

"Oscar Callum," he said.

"Yeah, that's his name. He's the one I'm looking for," I said, suggesting there might be more than just one sculptor in the town.

"Sorry to say you're a little too late."

"Too late?"

"No one's seen hide nor hair of Oscar, oh, must be for over a year now."

"Did he leave town?"

He shook his head. "Not as far as anyone knows. One day he's here, next he's gone. Never any problems as far as I know. He was a nice sort, quiet, but nice. Polite. Always kept to himself. Donated that sculpture in front of the school and never asked for so much as a penny. Did a statue for the church in town, too. Same thing, just told the reverend to keep him in his prayers."

"He have any family around, brothers or sisters?"

The guy shook his head and said, "Nope. As far as I know, he lived by himself. Don't know where he came from originally, but he's been here as long as I can remember. Then, one day, it's just, poof," he snapped his fingers, "and he was gone. Just like that."

"He live here in town?"

He shook his head. "No. Out Highway 2 about a mile then down the county road. Nice enough little place. Has an out-building he does his work in. I think he has sculptures all around the world. You'd never know it to talk to him, quiet, unassuming type."

I shook my head like this was all news to me. "I'd no idea."

"Yeah, we still get two, three folks a year coming through looking for him, just like you. Most of 'em hoping to get their picture taken with him. Like I said, he'd never mention anything like that. Private sort, if you catch my drift."

I nodded and said, "Well, thanks for your time. Guess I'll head out."

"You going back to the cities?"

There was no point in trying to lie and say I wasn't from the cities. Locals can spot city folks from fifty feet. I don't know what it is, but they're rarely wrong about it. "I'm heading over to Grand Rapids; got some cousins over there. Want to stop in and say hi before I head back down."

"Drive careful, then."

"Thanks for the help," I said. I climbed back in the car, reached into the back seat and gave Morton a scratch on the head. I started the car and headed up Highway 2.

I glanced in the review mirror and saw the guy from the liquor store standing out front, holding the door open as he watched me drive off. I checked the mileage and began to slow down when I reached nine-tenths of a mile.

Sure enough, at the one-mile mark, there was a county road off to the right. I made the turn and passed five different places nestled into the woods. Each place was twice as far away as the previous one. I kept driving, went through an 'S' curve, and suddenly there was a weathered mailbox with the name Callum. The paint on the mailbox was faded and chipped in spots, but there was no doubt that's what it said. I slowed to make a right turn and pulled onto a trail that wound through birch trees and the occasional pine. It suddenly opened into a wide area with a single-story house that looked like it was probably built in the late 1940s or early 50s. It was painted a faded burgundy color with peeling white trim. The entire place was in desperate need of a paint job.

Off to the side was a concrete block structure with a garage door and a sheet metal roof. Two blackened metal smokestacks protruded from the roof, one in either back corner of the building. An entrance door was on the opposite end of the building from the garage door, and between them were two windows made up of four panes each.

I turned off the car and climbed out. Morton was suddenly up and looking out the window excitedly. No doubt examining all sorts of possibilities to get into trouble. I looked around. Even without knowing the situation, the place gave off that greyed look of vacancy. Weeds were growing in front of the garage door and, indeed, all over the dirt trail I'd taken through the trees. There was nothing like a trimmed bush or a pot of flowers that suggested an inhabitant. My car had left the only tire marks on the dirt trail, the open area in front of the house and the block building.

I walked over to the building and tried to look in the window, but it was so dirty I couldn't see in. I went back to the car, pulled some Kleenex out of the glove compartment, and wiped off one of the window panes. It was a little better. At least I could see in, kind of.

There wasn't much to see. Equipment, shelves, sheets of metal, and pipes were scattered around with propane tanks and a lot of tools. Parked inside was an ancient-looking grey pickup truck, so old it had vent windows. I walked over to the house, knocked on the front door, and tried the doorknob. The place was locked. There was a small vehicle with a snowplow mounted on the front of it parked alongside the house. Based on the leaves and branches underneath and the weeds around it, the thing hadn't been moved for at least a year.

I walked around the rear of the house and tried the backdoor. It was locked, too. There was a picnic table and a gas grill sitting out on a concrete pad. The grill was up against the back of the house and under a black polyester cover. Dead leaves had collected beneath the grill and the picnic table. What had once been a decent grass area around the concrete pad was overgrown with weeds and ten-inch grass that had gone to seed. I continued around the far side to the front of the house. All the windows were covered with shades except for the front picture window that looked like it had an old bed sheet hanging over it.

I wasn't sure what I thought I'd find up here, but I'd hoped it might be something, anything. I put Morton on a leash and walked him around for twenty minutes before we climbed back in the car and headed out to the county road, empty-handed.

Nineteen

We didn't get very far. There was a county sheriff's car pulled across the entrance to the county road. A deputy with a badge on his chest and a gun on his hip was leaning against the side of the car, eating an apple. He looked to be enjoying the sunshine, and he gave a friendly wave as I pulled to a stop.

His car was shiny and white with a gold swoosh running along the front and rear door. Within the swoosh was the image of a gold badge in the shape of a five-pointed star and next to that the words 'Itasca County SHERIFF' in black letters. Along the front quarter panel were the words 'Proudly serving since 1893'. His uniform consisted of brown trousers, a brown tie, and brown flaps on the breast pockets of his tan shirt. He wore a brown baseball cap, and when he signaled me to step out of my car, he smiled in a way that suggested it would be a very good idea to follow his request.

I'd been through this routine enough times to get the message. As I stepped out from behind the wheel, I kept my hands where he could see them with my arms somewhat outstretched to the side." How's it going, officer?"

He nodded and seemed to consider my question for a moment. He tossed the apple core off to the side before he said, "Can I ask what you're doing here?"

"I'm a private investigator from Saint Paul. I've got a client whose husband disappeared about six months ago. He was an artist. I know Oscar Callum disappeared about a year or so ago, and so did another artist down in the cities. I'm trying to figure out if there was something that tied these three situations together. So far, I'm coming up empty-handed."

"So, you're not up here to buy a statue?"

"I told that to the gentleman at the liquor store to see if he knew Oscar Callum was missing. The folks I've talked to about my client's husband were under the impression he was maybe taking time off. No one suspects foul play, including his wife."

"You have some identification?"

"I do. It's in my wallet in my front pocket."

"Why don't you show it to me, you know, slowly."

I pulled out my wallet, took out my driver's license, and my P.I. License, and handed them to him.

"Haskell. And you live in the cities?"

"Yeah, Saint Paul."

"Okay," he said and handed the cards back to me. A branch snapped off to the side, and I looked over to see another uniformed deputy step out of the woods. He was carrying a rifle with a scope.

No doubt, it was the surprised look on my face that caused his response. He smiled and said, "Just playing it safe, P.I." He walked past me and opened the trunk on the squad car, returned the rifle to its rack, and closed the lid on the trunk.

"You guys know anything about Oscar Callum's disappearance?" I asked.

They both shook their heads, and the one who'd had the rifle said, "No sign of intrusion. No activity on his bank account. No history of a confrontation with anyone. The man kept to himself, never caused any problem, and was very private."

"And also generous," the cop who'd been leaning against the car said. "He donated a sculpture to the school, another one to the church."

"Donated money to the church in Warba, too, but to my knowledge never attended," the rifleman said.

"And to the VFW over in Grand Rapids, but same thing, he never even entered the place."

"The man at the liquor store said Callum didn't have any family around."

They both nodded, and the rifleman said, "The thought up here has been that he was out in the woods somewhere, maybe had a heart attack or a stroke and died. It happens from time to time, and sometimes they're found, and once in a while, they simply disappear."

"Your story's the first we've heard about any other artists disappearing. Standard practice, we send information to several departments, haven't heard jack shit from Minneapolis or Saint Paul," the one cop said.

"Or anywhere else, for that matter," the rifleman said.

"To be honest, I've more or less put this thing together on my own. It's tentative at best. I talked to the homicide section in Saint Paul. They basically said to keep them posted, but they don't have the time or the budget to put anyone on my theory. At least not yet."

"We can identify with that," the rifleman said and looked at his partner. "So what'd you find at Callum's place?"

"Not much other than it seemed to confirm what you guys have said. He's disappeared, no sign of any activity, certainly none this summer. He's got a snow plow parked next to his house that hasn't been moved for quite some time. I think I made the first set of tire tracks around the place this summer. The house is locked up, no sign of a break-in. Hell, there's a gas grill just sitting on a back patio that someone could take, and no one would even know. If I put some of my thoughts down on paper, could I send it to someone in your department? Not that I have anything concrete at this point. It's just a theory."

The rifleman took a business card out of his pocket and a pen from his breast pocket and wrote something on the back of the card. "Department email address is on the card, and I wrote Joel Nikolic's name on the back. He worked the investigation on Callum's disappearance. The case is cold and still open."

"Thanks, guys, I find anything out, I'll copy him." We shook hands, and they climbed into the squad car, made a U-turn, and drove down the road. They stopped maybe a quarter mile down the road. The rifleman got out and stepped into a separate vehicle parked alongside the road. A moment later, they both disappeared around the bend. I climbed back into my car, gave Morton a heavy scratch, and we headed back down to the city. I stuck to the speed limit all the way to the interstate.

Twenty

It took an hour longer to drive back down to the cities. I ran into rush hour traffic thirty miles from town. I debated going home but thought I'd better check in the office. Louie was sitting at his picnic table desk, reading a file with his stocking feet propped up on the table. He lowered the file and looked up as we entered. "Oh, hey, I didn't expect you guys back today. Everything go okay?"

"Depends on who you talk to. Apparently, I remain the only person who's trying to link Chandler Hancock's disappearance to other missing artists." I went on to tell Louie about Oscar Callum's place and meeting the two Itasca County Deputies. "They basically said the same thing Aaron LaZelle told me. If you find out anything, let us know. They seemed to be of the opinion Oscar went for a stroll in the woods and suffered a heart attack. To be honest, it sounds a hell of a lot more logical than someone killed him and ran off with statues and sculptures."

"You talk to Katie about what they said?"

"Katie? You mean Kristi?"

"Yeah, her too."

"No, there's really nothing to tell her. I didn't even tell her I was going up north. Although one of the reasons I went up there was because she had a statue in her bedroom done by Oscar Callum, and it looked like her. Exactly like her. I meant to ask her about it yesterday before I left, but I had some other things on my mind and forgot," I said, recalling Kristi's erotic stretching in the sunlight.

I didn't see any point in telling Louie about Kristi showing up at the Depot Bar yesterday evening. The more I thought about it, the dumber my idea seemed. If I got a letter from someone saying they had a thousand bucks for me and they wanted to meet in a public place to pay me, what was the downside? All that did was waste more time and didn't get me any further ahead. I made a mental note to ask her if she posed for the statue on her dresser, but then, so what if she did? There was no crime in that.

"You got something planned, or are you free to join me over at The Spot for a libation?" Louie asked.

"Yeah, I s'pose. Why attempt to accomplish anything at this stage?"

Morton had been standing at the door looking at me since we stepped into the office, and a one-watt light bulb suddenly blinked on in my thick skull, reminding me he'd been in the car for over four hours and probably could do with a potty break.

"Tell you what, let me give Morton a quick walk around the block, and we'll meet you over there." At the sound of his name and the word 'walk', Morton's tail began to wag. I put him on the leash, and we headed out. It turned into a three-block tour before Morton did his business. Fortunately, tomorrow was trash pickup day in the area, so I bagged his deposit and tossed it into a trash bin lined up at the curb for the pickup.

We walked back past the office and waited for the light to change before we crossed the street. A city bus pulled away from the curb and began to head up Randolph Avenue. Suddenly, a hoarse voice shouted my name. I glanced at the bus just as a meaty forearm hung out the window and gave me the finger. A disheveled figure with an orange beard and an extended middle finger waved his hand back and forth as the bus climbed the hill. Gerry Berk. I hadn't seen that lowlife piece of crap since his sentencing over ten years ago. And now, in little more than twenty-four hours, I'd seen him twice, possibly three times, if that had been him in the middle of the night staggering down the street. Nothing seemed to be going my way of late.

We crossed the street, and I headed for my car. I unlocked the passenger door and opened the glove compartment. I untucked my shirt, took my nine-millimeter in the sticky holster and shoved it in my belt, then pulled my shirt over the weapon. I looked up the street but didn't see anything remotely resembling that fat piece of shit Gerry Berk heading in my direction. I locked my car, and we joined Louie in The Spot.

Mike was tending bar, and he nodded at me as we walked in. He was filling four glasses at the beer tap, and I said, "Hi, Mike. I'll take a Summit IPA when you have time. No rush." He gave me a nod in response.

Louie was seated at the end of the bar, and I took the stool next to him. He had an open bag of pork rinds in front of him, but it didn't appear he had eaten any of them. As I took up a position on the stool, he pulled a couple of chips from the bag and reached down to Morton.

"You're gonna spoil him, Louie."

"You kidding? I'm the only source of sanity the poor guy has. Hey," he said and nodded at my untucked shirt. "You expecting trouble?"

"Hopefully not." I went on to tell him about my run-in with Gerry Berk at City Salsa House the other day. "He's probably blowing a lot of hot air, but the way my luck has been running this week, I thought it might be a wise idea to at least hedge my bets."

"Yeah, I guess I don't blame you. Fat guy with an orange beard, I'll keep my eyes open."

"Just don't approach. The bastard's a nut case. Listening to a reasoned thought is not in his genetic makeup."

I stayed for only one before I drove home. I drove past my place and went around the block, keeping an eye peeled for Gerry Berk, thankfully, I didn't see him. I pulled into the garage, got Morton out, locked the car, lowered the door, then made my way down the driveway, all the while looking from left to right. Two newspaper circulars and a citywide notice about something at the public library were in my mailbox. I pulled them out, stepped into the house, and locked the door behind me. I flipped on the porch light, and we headed into the kitchen.

For dinner, I had the choice of two remaining pieces of pizza supreme from the week before or a container of chicken curry from I don't know when. I decided on the curry, but when I opened the lid, there was a fuzzy growth on the surface, so I decided against it. Instead, I made a grilled cheese sandwich with pepper jack cheese. It tasted so good I made another and ate all of that one, too.

After cleaning up the kitchen, I hit the lights and went upstairs to read. When I plugged in my cellphone to recharge it, the screen lit up and announced I'd missed a call from Aaron LaZelle. I returned the call and ended up leaving a message on his office phone. "Hi, Aaron. Dev Haskell, returning your call. Sorry I missed you. Call me back at your convenience. Tag, you're it."

I stretched out on the bed and started reading. I woke up at about 1:30 in the morning. I brushed my teeth, then went downstairs in the dark and checked all the windows and doors to see if I might spot anything unusual. Fortunately, I didn't. I went back up to bed, placed the sticky holster with my pistol on the table next to my bed, and went to sleep.

I woke a little after six the following morning. Morton was stretched out next to me, still sound asleep, so I climbed out of bed and hit the shower. I got dressed and headed down to the kitchen, put the coffee on, and fired up my laptop. Morton arrived in the kitchen right on time, just after my second cup of coffee. I gave him the usual scratch on the head and let him out the backdoor. A moment later, my phone rang.

"Haskell Investigations."

"Hi, Dev. Aaron. Hey, this missing painter you're looking for, you said he was married?"

"Yeah, to a woman I knew in high school."

"Her name wouldn't happen to be Kristi McKenzie, would it?"

"As a matter of fact, it would. Why, what's up?"

"Probably nothing, but the name rang a distant bell. I'm heading into a meeting, but if you could be down here later this morning, say around ten, I can show you what we have. It's tenuous at best, but I think you'll find it interesting."

In a muffled voice, he apparently said to someone in his office, "Yeah, I'll be there in just a minute." Then clearly addressing me, "I gotta fly, Dev. Hope to see you at ten."

"I'll be there, Aaron. Thanks for calling," I said, but I think he had already hung up.

Twenty-one

Aaron had said he'd be finished with his meeting by 10:00. Just in case, I arrived at the station twenty minutes early. At 10:30, the desk sergeant called my name. As I stood, he pointed to an unsmiling woman in jeans with a badge attached to her belt and her blonde hair tied in a tight bun. Humorless Detective Rogers.

I'd had the distinct displeasure of riding up in the elevator to the homicide section with her a couple of times before. As I walked toward her, she turned on her heel and headed toward the elevator just around the corner. No smile, no nod, no greeting. By the time I caught up with her, she was on the elevator holding the door open. She removed her hand from the elevator door as I was about to step on. The doors suddenly closed quickly and bounced off my shoulders before they slid back. Her eyes seemed to sparkle for half a second, satisfied with her minor success. She pressed the close button and shook her head.

Since a code had to be entered on the keypad next to the door to the homicide section, there was no point in stepping off the elevator before her. As the doors opened on the floor, I smiled, stepped back, and extended my hand. "Please, Detective."

She stormed past, apparently upset that I had canceled whatever assault she planned from behind me. I caught up to her at the entrance to homicide just as the buzz sounded alerting you that the door was unlocked for the next fifteen seconds. As I stepped inside, she grumbled, "He's in his office." She gave a slight nod toward the end of the room then immediately took a left turn and headed for her desk.

I nodded at a couple of people as I made my way to Aaron's office. Fortunately, Detective Norris Manning was nowhere to be seen. The guy hated me and never missed a chance to try and lock me up. I was sure bitchy Detective Rogers was his fan.

Gino Bendetti was on the phone when he smiled and gave me the finger.

Dermot smiled and waved.

Charlie Paulden waved and called, "Hey, Dev."

The door to Aaron's office was open, and I knocked on the doorframe. He was on the phone with a mug of coffee in his hand. When he looked up and saw me, he said, "Sorry, but I have to go. My appointment just arrived." He hung up the phone, glanced at his watch, and then held his hand off to the side, palm up. "So where you been? What took you so long?"

"What took me so long? I've been waiting for you for almost an hour. Soon as the desk sergeant called my name, I hurried onto the elevator with eternally unhappy Detective Rogers, and here I am."

"I sent someone down to get you twenty minutes ago."

"Twenty minutes? Aaron, I've been cooling my heels down there for the better part of an hour. I'm not kidding, man. An hour."

"Hmm, maybe something came up."

"Maybe she stopped in the cafeteria and had a coffee and a couple of doughnuts."

He shook his head and reached for a pile of manila folders on his desk. He slid them over and arranged them on his lap. He fanned through the first four folders, pulled out the next one, and set it in front of me. "You remember this case? It was back nine years ago?"

I opened the file and looked at a black and white photo of a body lying against the street curb. It was winter, snow on the street, and a light dusting on what looked like the leather jacket of the victim. The victim's name was Joseph Lauer. He was more or less curled up in an almost fetal position. I lifted the photo, and there were a number of other photos, six in all, 8x10 black and whites. They were basically shots of the same scene from a variety of different angles.

I shook my head. "I was probably still in Iraq, getting ready to come home."

"He was hit by a car on a snowy night," Aaron said, stating the obvious. "The driver was questioned but never charged. Lauer's blood alcohol concentration was one point eight."

I glanced at the top photo again. "One point eight? He was shit-faced. Was he thrown from his car?"

"He wasn't driving. He was walking."

"Kristi hit him?"

"No."

"So what am I missing here? You said on the phone this had something to do with Kristi McKenzie?"

"Look at that last photo."

I pulled out the last photo. There was a tag in the upper left-hand corner that listed the file number and the photo as number six. The photo was taken maybe eight feet away from the body. The photographer had been standing on the sidewalk facing the street.

"I'm not picking up anything, Aaron. If she wasn't driving, was she a passenger in the car or something?"

"She's suspected of pushing him off the sidewalk and into the oncoming vehicle. Check out the footprints on the left. That large pair of footprints matches the size eleven shoes Lauer was wearing. There was a sole imprint identical to Lauer's. The smaller pair, behind him and then tracking down the sidewalk, are a size five. It's speculation, but she pushes him into the oncoming car and runs away."

"And why do you link her to this guy? Were they married?"

"Engaged, living together but not yet married. She was the sole beneficiary of his life insurance policy, one point five million."

"One point five million?"

"Yeah. The family was from St. Michael and into real estate in a big way. Ever hear of the Ham Lake airport proposal?" My blank look must have given me away. "Yeah, it was maybe fifteen years before our time, although bits of it still occasionally surface in the legislature. Back then, there was a proposal to build a second metro airport about thirty-five miles out of town up in Anoka county, in the Ham Lake area."

"I've never heard of it."

"It never really went anywhere, groups going pro and con on the deal. Lauer's family, his grandfather and his old man, put together a group that purchased all the land for the Ham Lake site. I'm talking years of preparation, and in the end, the thing goes bust. They've got all this land; what better way to use it than housing. They build a shitload, come out wealthy beyond their wildest dreams, basically divest themselves of everything in 2007, at about the peak of the market, right before the crash and the great recession. Young Lauer is sitting pretty and slated to marry a beauty queen."

"But Kristi? Was she at the scene?"

"She says no."

"So why don't you believe her?"

"Because apparently, there was a tape showing her at Costello's bar that evening with Lauer. Buying him drinks, whiskey shots as a matter of fact."

"Costello's? Isn't that where the Red Cow is to-day?"

"It is."

"But that doesn't prove anything."

"No, it doesn't. In the tape, she's sipping a coke and lining up shots for the kid. Pouring whiskey down him like there's no tomorrow. They leave, it was snowing, and she's got a white jacket with a fur lined hood, white fur."

"Still doesn't prove anything, Aaron."

"Yeah, I know. They lived down in that area, actually not far from your place, on MacKubin Street. He's hit two blocks away, in the opposite direction from where they lived."

"So why the suspicion? What about the driver?"

"An elderly couple. It's snowing. They think Lauer stumbled out in front of their car. They never even saw him. They heard a big bang, stop, get out to look, and there he is in the ditch. No one else around. Response time is six minutes after the first report. The driver takes a breathalyzer maybe ten minutes later, comes up clean. He's a diabetic and hasn't had a drink in over twenty years. Autopsy confirms Lauer's blood alcohol at one point eight."

"And Kristi said she wasn't with him?"

"Yeah."

"But there's the tape. What happened when she was shown that?"

"Therein lies the problem. There is no tape, as in, it's missing. It was logged in, and now it's missing. The system they had back then was nothing like today. The evidence room has since moved twice and then the massive move into the new location. So Kristi's involvement becomes mere speculation."

"A bartender didn't recognize her? I mean, she's a real beauty. How could you forget someone like Kristi?"

"It was during the Winter Carnival. The street is closed off. You've got two hundred thousand people coming to watch the Crashed Ice jumpers down in front of the Cathedral. It's shoulder to shoulder customers, and Costello's is the closest bar, only three blocks away. We'll never know for sure, but I'm thinking perfect timing on the part of your friend Kristi. And now we find out her current husband has been missing for five or six months, and the only person who contacted us is you."

Twenty-two

I was heading back to the office when my cellphone rang. There's a new law in Minnesota, no driving while talking on cellphones. I pulled over, put the car in park, turned down the radio, and answered, "Haskell Investigations."

"Dev Haskell, please."

"Speaking."

"Oh, hi, Dev. I wasn't sure if that was you or not. This is George from City Salsa House. I hope I'm not interrupting anything."

"No, George. Just on my way back from a meeting. What can I do for you?"

"Well, a bit of a personal matter I'd like to discuss with you. I'd prefer not to meet here. Is there someplace we could get together? I promise not to take up too much of your time."

"How about my office? It's maybe a ten-minute drive from the restaurant."

"I could do that. What does your afternoon look like?"

"What time you thinking?"

"Maybe three this afternoon, once things slow down here and we're getting ready for the nighttime crowd."

"That'll probably work. I'll have to move an appointment," I lied. "But I don't expect a problem."

"You sure, I mean I could—"

"Don't worry about it, George. You have my card?"

"I do. Your address is over on Randolph, right?"

"It is, Randolph and Victoria."

"I'll see you at three, Dev, and thanks for making time for me."

"Looking forward to it, George."

I pulled away from the curb and drove to the office. When I arrived, Louie was out, and apparently I woke up Morton because, when I unlocked the door, he slowly rose off his bed and stretched.

I opened a file cabinet, pulled out a half-dozen files, and placed them on my desk. I took a yellow legal pad from my desk drawer, pulled back some blank sheets, and wrapped them over the top of the tablet, so it looked like I'd written several pages. I emptied both coffee mugs, rinsed them out, and started a fresh pot. I grabbed my binoculars off the desk and quickly checked the apartment across the street. It was the middle of the workday afternoon, and none of the women appeared to be home, so I stashed the binoculars in a desk drawer. I tossed the grocery store circulars and the three envelopes with credit card offers into the trash. I picked up the two beer cans from Louie's picnic table and ran the trash bag outside to the bin.

At ten minutes before three, I Googled a crime scene tape from Western Kentucky and had it up on my computer screen, then I sat and waited, looking out the window. At five minutes after three, a white sports car screeched to a stop across the street. There were four pipes hanging out the back, and the windows were tinted so dark I wasn't sure they were legal. The door swung open, and George Estrada climbed out.

The car was so low I didn't think I could even get in, let alone climb out of the thing. George stretched and rolled his shoulders a couple of times before he walked across the street and entered the building.

I clicked play on the video I had lined up on my computer. It was a four-minute video. Immediately, an ad for disposable diapers came on. In the lower right-hand corner, the countdown began at ten seconds before I could skip the ad. I heard the stairs start to creak at the five-second mark, four, three, two, one. I clicked on SKIP THIS AD. The video began, security camera footage of an office burglary. Two idiots were riffling through file cabinets and desk drawers. I heard footsteps at the top of the stairs, and I picked up my cellphone and pretended to talk into it as George opened the door and smiled.

"Yes, they're in there. The camera I set up has them recorded. No masks, it's obviously the two I suspected. We can go to the police."

George stood in the open doorway carrying a white plastic bag. I waved him in and said, "Arthur, I have a client who just stepped into my office. Let me get back to you on this. I've already alerted the police. They're waiting for my go-ahead before they make an arrest. Yeah, it's a complete success. Thanks. Talk to you soon." I set my phone down, pushed pause on the video, and clicked on the screen to turn it off.

"Hi, Dev. Sorry. I didn't mean to interrupt. Was that a burglary?"

"Not a problem, George. Yeah, but nothing we didn't suspect. I'm just getting things in order for a case I've been working on. With the evidence we have, there's every chance there'll be a major out of court settlement. Things are looking good. Please, take a seat. Any problem finding the place?"

"No, I knew right where to go." He pushed the white plastic bag between the stack of files and the yellow legal pad. "Little something for you, Dev. I appreciate you making time to see me today."

"George, thank you, but you didn't have to do this. This is so kind of you."

"Dinner for two and I tossed in two flans. I think you said you liked them, didn't you?"

"Like them? No. I love them."

"Well, you and some hot young thing can have dinner tonight. It's our special for tonight, a White Chicken Enchilada Skillet. You're going to love it."

"Oh, thanks so much. God, you keep this up, I'm going to have to go on a diet. That souped-up thing out there on the street, is that yours?" I said, pointing out the window at the white sports car.

"Yeah, one of my weaknesses is cars. That's a Corvette Grand Sport. Ever ride in one before?

"No, never."

"Four hundred-and-sixty-horsepower from an LT one V-8 engine. Carbon sixty-five, Michelin Pilot Super Sport tires. It comes with a removable roof panel. I love to rev the engine high in each gear and hear that sweet muscle car sound."

"You lost me. I'm one of those boring folks who just think of a car as something that takes me from point A to point B."

"Oh, sorry to hear that," he said, sounding like I'd just told him I had a month to live.

Twenty-three

I said and placed the plastic bag over on the far edge of my desk." So, you mentioned you had a bit of a personal item to discuss. Tell me about it,"

"Well, it's not all that complicated. It looks like someone is ripping off the restaurant. Unfortunately, it almost has to be an employee."

I nodded and said, "Do you have someone in mind?"

He shook his head. "No, and that's part of the problem. I have no idea. Obviously, a number of people have access to the cash. Servers and bartenders, and occasionally even our hostess is cashing someone out."

"Do you have cameras on the premises?"

"Yes, and one is focused on the cash register to eliminate this exact problem. I've spent hours going over the tapes. I'm not seeing anything. I collect the receipts at the end of the evening. Lock them in a safe along with the cash drawer. Only me and the owner have access, but we're losing somewhere between fifty and hundred bucks a day. That may not sound like much, but round it up, and it's close to a grand a week. Over the course of the year, we'll be out twenty or thirty grand."

"Thirty grand, ouch! Let me ask you some questions and please don't be offended, George."

"No, please, ask away."

"The owner has access to the funds. Any chance the owner is giving themselves a daily cash bonus."

"To be honest, I didn't want to think that, but I had to eliminate the possibility. The owner is my aunt. She just turned eighty-two and still works every day. I have a camera targeted on the safe. She hasn't opened it in weeks, and the last time she did, I was with her. So, she's out as a suspect. Thank God."

"So the funds are disappearing at some point in the evening, and you can't determine when."

"I think so," he said and nodded. "I don't catch it on a daily basis. I mean, the funds add up and all, but at the end of the week, when I total everything up and balance against expenses, our deposits aren't matching up with expenses. Been going on for nine weeks."

"Is the cash register behind the bar the only place for transactions?"

"Yeah, cash and credit."

"Most of your transactions are credit cards?"

"Most, meaning maybe sixty percent, but an awful lot of cash still comes across. Smaller bills, folks paying cash on dinners for two, maybe a couple of beers or glasses of wine. Of course, a good portion of the drinks are paid for in cash. We have a lot of folks at the bar in the evening. Maybe a drink or two before they're off to somewhere else like a play, a movie, or even home. They toss a twenty on the bar, and leave a tip."

"You ever think about maybe standing behind the bar and ringing up everything yourself?"

"That would be a last resort, but yeah, I've thought about it. It would make for a very long day. It's not unusual for me to be in there at eight in the morning, getting things ready. The cleaning crew is in around seven. Staff begins to arrive at ten. We open at eleven, serve until nine-thirty at night, and usually close around ten-thirty. That's seven days a week. I couldn't keep that up for long. I'm gonna be forty-eight next month. The days of working those kinds of hours are pretty much behind me, and I to be honest, I don't want to."

"Tell you what. Why don't I show up tomorrow morning and have lunch at the bar? Just to get a handle on how things go. Would that be all right with you?"

"That would be great. I'll get a special meal for you. You're gonna love it."

"Actually, George, I'd like you to ignore me. Let me order off the menu. I'll pay in cash, sit there for a while, pretending to read the paper or something. You start doing nice things for me, and whoever is involved in this is going to tread lightly. Sound like a plan?"

He smiled and reached across the desk to shake my hand. "You enjoy that dinner tonight, Dev. You and that special someone."

"I will, George. Thank you for stopping by. I'll see you tomorrow."

"Thanks, Dev," he said and hurried out the door. I watched him cross the street and slip into the Corvette.

A moment later, he fired it up, revved the engine three or four times, and headed up the street.

Twenty-four

Dinner with someone special? Against my better judgement, I called Kristi, thinking maybe a rematch, and this time, if I brought dinner, when she asked me if I wanted top, she'd be in a better frame of mind. I ended up leaving a message.

I called Diane. She answered on the fourth ring. "Hi Diane, it's Dev."

"Hi, Dev, what's up?"

"Calling to see if you've got time for dinner. A client of mine—"

"Oh, I'd love to Dev. Thanks for thinking of me. Unfortunately, I've got other plans for this evening."

The way she said it suggested the other plans were with somebody, probably a male somebody. "Okay, my fault. I should have gotten in touch earlier. Maybe some other time."

"Maybe," she said in a tone that suggested maybe not.

I called Heidi next. She was always willing to do anything that didn't involve her having to cook dinner. I left a message, and she called back five minutes later. "Hi Dev, sorry I couldn't take your call. I was on another line."

"Not a problem. Just checking in to see if you have time for dinner tonight. A new client of mine is so pleased with my work that he—"

"Tonight? Oh, Dev, I'd really love to, but I'm, um, otherwise engaged for the evening. Until pretty late," she added, which probably meant until tomorrow morning. I was immediately jealous.

"You sure? I was going to prepare a White Chicken Enchilada Skillet for dinner. I've got a special sparkling white wine," I lied, pulling out all the stops. Heidi loved sparkling white wine.

"Oh, I'd love to, Dev, but I'm already committed, and like I said, it's probably going to be a late evening. I'm sure I'll be exhausted."

I was sure she would be, too, and not just from talking. My loss. "Okay then, Heidi, some other time."

"Thanks, Dev, maybe another night."

What was with this maybe routine? How about a little appreciation for your man bringing over dinner and telling you nice things so you'd take him to bed? My phone rang. It was about time, Kristi. I decided I would invite her over to my place and avoid the whole bunkbed debacle. I thought I should make sure to take pictures and send them to Diane and Heidi, remind them what they missed out on.

"Hi Kristi, thanks for calling back."

"Hey, Dev, sorry I missed your call. I was out for my run. What can I do for you?"

"I'm preparing a very special dinner this evening, a white chicken enchilada skillet. Thought it might be fun having you over to my place for dinner, and we could—"

"Oh, Dev, can I take a rain check? I'm booked for this evening. Besides, I think I mentioned I'm a vegan, so chicken is out anyway, it's really not my thing."

Shit. Shit. Shit. Why hadn't I remembered that? "You sure? I know you're a vegan, Kristi. That's why I prepared a special rice dish I'm sure you're going to enjoy. I was thinking of picking up some wines I thought you might like to try. What kind did you say you liked?"

"You know me, just about any kind. Thanks for the invite, but I'm going to be tied up tonight. Maybe some other time. I'd love to try the rice dish."

"Yeah, some other time then. Enjoy yourself."

"Oh, I will, Dev."

She hung up, and I was convinced she really was going to be tied up. Literally. For just a moment, I thought about calling her back and asking if I could watch. It had been a while since I'd been out with Denise. She talked incessantly about things I wasn't the least bit interested in, but under the circumstances, dinner, just enough wine to eliminate any inhibitions, yeah, I could deal with that.

Her phone rang eight times before she answered. She was probably on another line, boring some poor soul out of their mind. "Hello?"

"Hi, Denise. A voice from the past, Dev Haskell. Calling to see if I could bring you over some dinner tonight, or you're welcome to come over to my place if you feel like it. It's been way too long since I saw you, and I was thinking this would be the perfect time to—"

"You're, you're kidding me, right? I suppose you've been drinking."

"Drinking? No, as a matter of fact, I'm in my office. At my desk, to be honest. Remember?" We'd had a torrid night at The Spot a year ago and hurried over to my office after close to 'use' my desk.

"Unfortunately, I do remember, although I've been trying to forget ever since that person you share your office with walked in on us the following morning."

"Oh, yeah. Guess I kind of forgot that part. I was so—"

"Well, if you forgot that part, you apparently also forgot me telling you to never, ever call me again. I'm in a wonderful relationship with a very nice guy. So please, Do. Not. Ever. Call. Me. Again. Ever!" She shouted that last word and slammed down the phone.

Carol was always up for a good time. A little on the crazy side, but I was at the point where I could put up with that. Crazy could be good, and Carol was certainly energetic. I dialed her number. After one ring, a recording came on. "The person you have contacted is not receiving calls from this number at this time. Thank you. Message two-twenty-nine."

Great. Carol blocked my calls. That did it. I hung around the office another forty minutes hoping someone might call back with a change in plans, but it never happened. Morton and I headed home.

Twenty-five

Once home, I warmed one of the white chicken enchilada skillets in the microwave, settled down in front of Netflix, and proceeded to inhale the meal. I ate one of the delicious flans and then, just to punish the almost half-dozen women who already had somewhere else to go, I ate the second flan. I headed up to bed around eleven and tried not to think about what they were all doing at that moment. I could only hope it involved something like changing a flat tire on their car, and they were all wishing they hadn't turned me down.

It was around 2:30 when Morton woke me. He was standing on the bed, staring at the bedroom door and growling. Heidi had a key to my place, and for just a second, I wondered if maybe she decided life would be a lot more fun snuggling next to me. I heard what sounded like a noise from downstairs and got out of bed. I quickly pulled on my jeans. I took my nine-millimeter out of the sticky holster and cautiously opened the door. Nothing.

I left the lights off and hurried downstairs. I didn't see anyone on the front porch. The front door was still locked, and the empty wine bottle I'd placed in front of the door in case someone opened it was still in place. I hurried back to the kitchen. Pretty much the same. No sign of anyone entering, let alone on the back porch or in the yard. I'd pushed a chair against the door just under the doorknob. It was still in place. I didn't see anything out the side windows in the dining room and the two front rooms. I sat in the dark for another hour waiting, but fortunately, nothing happened.

I went back upstairs to bed a little before four. Morton was stretched out in bed and didn't wake when I climbed in. My alarm went off at seven, and I got up.

Morton came downstairs an hour later, and I let him out. I walked around the back of the house. Everything appeared to be in order. I walked down the driveway to the front of the house, checking the basement windows along the side as I went, everything looked fine.

I climbed the steps to the front porch. The chairs had been moved. It wasn't a big thing, but they'd been moved. I have a long wooden table on the porch that seats eight with plastic chairs arranged around the table. Three of them were stacked and pushed in front of a window next to the front door. The screen on the window had been cut. A horizontal slit just long enough to slip a hand through. Theoretically, you could take a hammer or even something like a rock, smash the pane of glass in front of the brass lock on the inside of the window, unlock the window, raise it, and break into the house.

Clearly, the screen had been cut, but no one had slipped their hand through to break the glass. In fact, if the chairs hadn't been stacked and pushed in front of the window, I wouldn't have noticed the slit screen. This seemed almost too slick an operation for a bumbler like Gerry Berk, but then, maybe I'd underestimated him. Ten years in the slammer was a hell of a finishing school for criminal behavior.

I stacked all eight chairs one on top of another, carried them inside, and placed them in the entryway. I went through the first floor and double-checked all the windows. They were all locked and, with the exception of the one slit screen, appeared to be untouched. I let Morton in and suddenly felt famished, so I placed the second enchilada meal in the microwave, heated it up, and devoured the thing. I was hungry enough that I could have eaten the second flan, but I'd done that the night before. I dialed in the public radio station and turned up the volume, hoping it sounded like someone was home. I checked the house once more before we headed down to the office.

Louie was in the process of loading files into his briefcase and about to head out the door. "Morning, Dev. You doing okay? You look kind of tired."

"Didn't get much sleep last night."

"Oh, really. What was her name?"

"I wish. No, just wide awake in the middle of the night. You heading to court?"

"Yeah. I've got an eleven and a one-thirty. Won't be back until later in the afternoon."

"I'm out to an appointment a little after eleven, back sometime after two. Morton will watch things in here while we're gone."

Louie nodded and headed out the door. I left a half-hour later and headed to City Salsa House.

Twenty-six

I entered City Salsa House a little after eleven. Carmen was behind the bar, unloading glasses from a dishwasher rack. She smiled and said, "Back so soon?"

"It was so good I couldn't stay away." Since I was the only customer in the place, I had my pick of bar stools. I chose one in the corner that gave me a clear view of the cash register and sat down.

Carmen strolled over once she'd emptied the rack of glasses. "What can I get you?"

"I think just a glass of tonic and a twist to start. A menu when you have time but no rush. You have a newspaper?"

"Let me see if I can find the paper for you," she said and walked down to the far end of the bar. She delivered my glass of tonic and the newspaper a few minutes later. "Are you going to want a menu?"

"When you have time, I'm in no hurry." After having that second enchilada skillet for breakfast, I really wasn't all that hungry. Or at least I thought I wasn't. That idea more or less went out the window once she set the menu down in front of me. I paged through the newspaper for thirty minutes. By the time I picked up the menu, my stomach was growling as I read through the various items. I decided to go light, so I ordered the grilled quesadilla, a large flour tortilla filled with chihuahua cheese and tomatoes and served with black beans and rice. I figured the tomatoes and black beans would make it more of a healthy meal. Of course, I followed up with a flan. The place was filling up with the noontime trade by the time my meal arrived. There were three other people seated at the bar, all on their own. One guy ordered a whiskey and a beer back, the woman ordered a salad, and an older guy had a beer and sipped it for the better part of an hour.

Staff was coming and going, running up bills at the computer terminal, grabbing cash out of or placing cash into the register. Maybe after a few more hours of watching, I'd have a better sense of how much they were taking, but as of this noon, I had absolutely no idea what was right. They could have been taking a hundred bucks in twenties and stashing it in their black aprons, and I wouldn't be able to tell the difference. I kept watching, trying to look for something not quite right, but never saw anything out of line.

I did enjoy the meal, and the flan was, at no surprise, delicious. I had a total of three tonics with a twist and basically read the paper from front to back, twice. At a little after two, I paid my bill and left.

I woke Morton when I opened the office door. He got up, stretched, and then stood at the door. I attached his leash, and we headed out for a walk. After my breakfast and lunch, I probably should have done three miles. Instead, we walked three blocks. When we got back to the office, Louie was seated at his picnic table typing on his computer keyboard.

"There you two are, busy day?"

"I spent the noon hour at City Salsa House."

"Who'd you meet up there?" he asked and ran his fingers across the keyboard in a final motion before he sat back.

"Actually, working a case. They're worried about someone pilfering cash. I watched for the better part of two hours, but I couldn't pick up on anything. How'd things go for you?"

"Oh, the usual, both clients mortified, embarrassed, and worried sick about what this is going to mean for their jobs. They'll be fine, as long as they behave, but it's a real yank of the chain. Nothing all of us haven't done before. They just happened to get caught and learned the hard way. What's the latest with the artists?"

I shook my head. "I'm up against a wall with nothing definitive to show for it. To be honest, they're artists, and they disappeared. Nothing else really ties them together." As if on cue, my phone rang. It was Kristi. "Oh, I gotta take this. Haskell investigations."

"Hi, Dev, Kristi. I hope I'm not interrupting anything."

"No, Kristi." I nodded at Louie. "Just reviewing a file. What can I do for you?"

"I feel so bad about having to turn you down last night. I wondered if maybe we could get together later tonight."

"I'd love to, but unfortunately, I have to work, and I probably won't be finished until nine or so."

"Nine? That would work perfect for me. I have a yoga class at five, and I wanted to do a little shopping after that. You want to come over oh, say around half-past-nine? You can always stay the night, you know."

Yeah, top bunk, no thanks. "I'd love to do that. Can I bring something?"

"No, no, just bring yourself. I feel like I haven't seen you since forever. Oh, this will be fun," she squealed and hung up.

Twenty-seven

I must have dozed off because the next thing I remembered was Louie shaking me by the shoulder. "Hey Dev, I'm heading over to The Spot. You want to join me?"

"What? Huh? What time is it?"

"It's just coming up on four-thirty. Figured, if we headed over now, we'd have a better choice of bar stools. Man, you must have had quite the workout last night. You were snoring away for over an hour."

"I told you before, Louie. I just didn't sleep well. I was home all night, just the two of us. Me and Morton."

"So, you gonna join me at The Spot?"

"Oh, man, I'd love to, but I'm on the job over at the City Salsa House tonight, although to tell you the truth, I don't feel much like eating. Big breakfast, big lunch, what I should be doing is taking Morton for about a ten-mile walk, but that's not going to happen. Afraid I'll have to take a rain check."

"Okay, your loss, buddy. Stop down after you're done. I'll probably still be there."

I raced home, let Morton out in the backyard, filled his water dish, and checked the windows for any sign of someone attempting to break in. Everything looked good. I let Morton back in and headed out to the City Salsa House. I had to park around the corner again, but fortunately, I didn't see any sign of Gerry Berk.

It was a quarter after five when I walked into the restaurant. It was a little more crowded than when I had arrived this morning, but I was still able to grab the same stool at the corner of the bar, giving me a perfect view of the cash register drawer. Fortunately, Carmen wasn't working. Not that I didn't think she was nice, on the contrary, she seemed very nice. I was afraid suddenly showing up for lunch and dinner every day might get her thinking something wasn't right with this picture.

The guy behind the bar looked to be about thirty. He was dressed all in black and wearing a short sleeve button-down shirt, which gave him the perfect opportunity to show off muscular arms and about ten grand worth of tattoos.

I have a thing about needles. I hate them. I once told a nurse who was giving me an injection that I was fine with a gunshot wound, but if I saw a needle, I might faint. She just hit me on the shoulder and called me a big baby. All that said, I had to admit it was some pretty impressive artwork. A skull, snakes, a couple of hearts, some flowers, and a sunrise.

"Hi. What can I get you, sir?" the walking canvas asked as he set a menu down in front of me.

"I think for now, just a tonic with a twist."

"Coming right up."

There was a steady stream of folks heading in the door. All but one of the booths were occupied and maybe half the tables. A girl who looked to be high-school age was acting as the hostess, seating folks, and dishing out menus.

My tonic water arrived, and the walking piece of artwork asked, "Interested in ordering dinner?"

"Yeah, but if it's okay with you, I'm going to wait a bit. I'll give you a wave when I'm ready to order."

"Not a problem. Take your time, no rush," he said and walked over to a couple who had just sat down at the bar.

I watched people come in for the next twenty minutes. Now the booths, the tables, and the bar were all full. Three couples stood near the front door, waiting for a seat. I thought it might be best if I ordered. I still wasn't all that hungry, at least until I glanced at the menu and then thought maybe chicken fajitas couldn't hurt. The order arrived fifteen minutes later, marinated chicken with bell peppers, tomatoes, lemon, and onions. There was a side of guacamole, sour cream, lettuce, pico de gallo, Mexican rice, beans, and a stack of flour tortillas. I dug in, thinking I'd get half of this to take home and eat at a later date. The next thing I knew, I was using the last of the tortillas to wipe the plate clean.

"You must have been hungry," the bartender said when he delivered another tonic with a twist and cleared my plate. "We won't even have to wash this. I'll just put it back in the stack. You thinking about a little dessert?"

I was going to be there for another two and a half hours and had to do something. "Yeah, I'll have a flan, when you have time. No rush."

"Coming up," he said and carried my plate to the end of the bar, where a plastic tub was filling up with glasses, plates, and silverware. He waited on three more couples before he stepped into the kitchen with the tub and came out a minute later with my flan. I'd like to say I nibbled at it over the course of a half-hour, but I'd finished the thing in about five minutes and was debating licking the dish. With no one to talk to and nothing to read the only activity I had was eating.

I sat for the next hour-and-a-half sipping tonic water. The place was gradually thinning out. There were eight others besides me at the bar. Half of the booths were empty, and only three of the tables were occupied. The night trade was definitely slowing down. When the bartender brought me my bill, it came with two chocolate-covered mints, which I immediately inhaled. I paid, lingered for another fifteen minutes before I left with absolutely no indication anyone was stealing funds.

Twenty-eight

I walked out of the restaurant and around the corner to my car with no problem. No one, or thing, remotely resembling Gerry Berk was anywhere to be seen. I settled in behind the wheel and drove over to Kristi's. After three large meals today, I couldn't think of a better way to wear off some of those calories than an all-night wrestling match with her.

I was able to find a parking place just in front of Kristi's building and stepped out of the car. I felt a momentary twinge in my stomach but chalked it up to anticipation and excitement.

"Hey, good looking, it's about time."

I looked in the direction of the voice and there was Kristi, three stories up, leaning over her balcony railing in a purple Vikings jersey. She held a glass of red wine and took a sip. "Go on in. I'll buzz you up," she called and disappeared from sight.

When I stepped into the lobby, the door was already buzzing, and I hurried over to open it before it stopped. I took the elevator up to the third floor and walked down the hall to Kristi's unit. She opened the door when I was ten feet away, smiled, and took a sip from her wine glass. I felt another twinge. God, the excitement.

She was barefoot, and tonight the toenails were done up in what looked like a version of a French pedicure, pink with a silver stripe and then above the stripe, purple. The toes next to her big toes had silver rings with a shiny stone. A diamond? The Vikings jersey was the best I'd ever seen. It hung down just below her hips, and I was pretty sure she didn't have anything on underneath.

She wrapped her left arm around my shoulder, planted a big wet kiss on my lips, and held it there for a long moment. Not a complaint on my part. When she pulled away, she said, "What do you say to a glass of wine? Get you in the mood."

"Oh, believe me, Kristi, I'm in the mood. But a glass of wine couldn't hurt." I followed her into the kitchen.

She poured me a glass of wine, emptying the bottle. She reached down below the kitchen counter, opened a small refrigerator door, and took out another bottle of wine. She twisted off the cap and filled her glass almost to the rim.

"Come on. It's such a gorgeous night, let's sit out on the balcony." We headed out to the balcony. Lights from across the river reflected on the water, adding a sur-real sense to the evening. She had arranged two of the wicker chairs side by side, facing out toward the river. She sat down in one and then turned sideways, curled her legs up onto the chair and said, "So, you were working late?"

"Yeah. Not on Chandler's situation. I expect some information tomorrow on your case," I lied. "Tonight I was at a restaurant. They're worried about someone stealing from them."

"Did you make an arrest?"

"No, I can't do that, only the cops can. And I didn't see anything illegal. Looked to me like a bunch of hard-working people."

She nodded and took another sip. "Have you seen your friend, Diane, lately?"

"Diane? You mean from Find Art?"

"Yeah."

"No, I haven't. Why do you ask?"

"Well, I thought maybe since I couldn't see you last night that maybe you asked her over. You seem to like her."

"That might be too strong a term. I mean, she's nice, and she's helped me in the investigation as far as getting me to understand some of the business aspects of the art world. But she wasn't with me last night."

She smiled and took another sip of wine.

"Kristi, I'm looking at your toenails. Is there a name for that design?"

She turned a little in the wicker chair and stuck her legs out, moving her feet from side to side as she did so. "It's called a Twisted French Pedi. Do you like it?"

"Yeah, it's really nice. What size shoe do you wear? You have lovely feet."

"I wear a size five. Oh, don't tell me. Do you have a foot fetish too?" she said and giggled.

"A foot fetish? No, I just thought your feet looked really nice." I laughed at her suggestion and felt another twinge, this one just below the stomach.

"Just got the nails done today. When you told me you could come over, I thought that was the perfect excuse. Glad you like them."

"Yeah, they're lovely." We talked on for the better part of an hour. I refilled Kristi's wine glass twice. I didn't have more than a sip or two, it didn't seem to be sitting right, and I certainly didn't want anything to interfere with the later activities. I asked a couple of general questions about Chandler, which, despite all the wine, she dodged expertly.

I was just getting around to bringing up her former fiancé, Joseph Lauer, when she took my hand and said, "You know what I need right now?"

"More wine?"

"No, silly." She giggled. "You. I want you all to myself tonight. Come on," she said. She took me by the hand and led me into her bedroom. Being the perfect guest, I thought it would be impolite to argue. I felt two more twinges, this time much stronger, but I ignored them.

Just like before, when we stepped into her bedroom, the blue light came on. Only tonight, she didn't tell Alexa to turn it off in two minutes. She turned around and faced me and then giggling she pulled the Vikings jersey over her head and tossed it into the corner. I'd been right. She didn't have anything on underneath.

"You like?" she asked and took a staggering step back and forth just as a violent spasm signaled a ninety-second warning. My body was going to do something terrible, my choice where, I had ninety seconds to decide.

As I stared wide-eyed she reached for my belt, unbuckled it like a pro, and then knelt down in front of me. My body sent a distinct tremble, a warning. I now had sixty seconds before it did something terrible.

"Would you hold that thought and excuse me for just a moment?" I said as I hurried out of the room holding my pants and picking up speed on the way to the bathroom.

Twenty-nine

Maybe ten minutes later, I heard a noise out in the hall. Fortunately, I'd locked the bathroom door. No one but me needed to be exposed to this particular disaster, and if there had been a way for me to flee the scene, I would have taken it. Kristi tried to turn the doorknob then knocked softly. "Dev, honey, are you all right?"

"Yeah, Kristi, everything is fine. I should be out in a minute or two."

"Okay," she said, not sounding all that sure.

Fifteen minutes later, she knocked again. "You still in there, Dev?"

"I'll be fine. Just a couple more minutes, I think."

"Okay, hurry up, or I'm going to start without you," she said, sounding like she was only half-joking.

I didn't know how long I'd been seated in the bathroom. All I knew was Kristi had knocked on the door twice to ask if I was all right. I hadn't heard from her in the last half-hour, but every time I thought it might be okay to stand, my lower tract suggested otherwise.

All was quiet in the place, and I leaned back and closed my eyes for just a second. When I finally woke, for a brief moment I wasn't sure where I was. Unfortunately, the truth flooded back to me. The toilet paper roll was empty, and I cautiously stood and shuffled over to the vanity with my jeans around my ankles. I opened the cabinets beneath both sinks and then pulled out all four drawers. No toilet paper, anywhere. I picked up the box of Kleenex and hurried back to sit down.

Eventually, I was able to tiptoe into the bedroom and peek at Kristi. I'd heard her snoring from out in the hallway. She was sound asleep, unfortunately, and the sheet was pulled up to her chin. What looked like a large, purple, battery-operated appliance was on the floor next to the bunk bed, which explained the smile on her face. It was still buzzing. I picked it up, turned it off, and put it in the open dresser drawer. There was absolutely no point in trying to climb in with her. Besides, I was pretty sure I was in need of a shower.

I hurried out of the place, took the elevator down to the ground floor, and drove home. I pulled into my garage, locked the car, lowered the door, and then glanced from left to right as I made my way down the driveway. I closed and locked the front door behind me and climbed up to my bedroom. Morton, my watchdog, didn't so much as open an eye. I quietly got undressed, took a long hot shower, and crawled into bed just as a hint of pink sunrise appeared on the horizon. My phone on the nightstand next to the bed woke me at nine-thirty. Morton was nowhere to be seen.

"Haskell Investigations."

"Hey, Dev," Kristi said. "Woo-hoo-hoo. What a night. You are really something."

"Yeah, sorry about that. Must have been something—"

"Sorry? Listen to you. Are you kidding? That was something. I had a little too much wine to actually remember, but I can still feel the results. Lord, save me. Oh my God. Never in my life."

Maybe there was an opening here. "Yeah, we both got a little crazy there, Kristi. Sorry I had to leave so early, but I didn't want to wake you. What do you say to a rematch tonight?"

"Oh, my God. You are really something. A rematch, are you kidding? It'll take me a week to recover. I've never had anyone . . .well, just wanted to call and say thank you. Hey, sorry, but I've got to go and get ready for the dog walk. Thank you. Thank you. Thank you," she said and hung up.

Well, I guess that was something. I'd take the credit if she wanted to give it to me. I slipped on a pair of boxers and headed downstairs. Morton was waiting for me at the backdoor, and I let him out. I filled his food and water dish, picked up the papers from the wastebasket he'd knocked over, and put a slice of bread in the toaster. I thought it might be best if I took it easy on the food intake today.

Once we ate, we headed down to the office. Louie was nowhere to be seen, but maybe that was just as well. I really wasn't up to answering any questions about the previous night's activity. I placed a call to Aaron LaZelle and left a message. I told Morton he was in charge and headed over to City Salsa House. Carmen was behind the bar when I walked in.

"Well, what do you know? You're getting to be a regular. Can't get enough, I guess."

"Yeah, something like that," I said and settled onto the same stool at the bar.

"Tonic with a twist?" she asked.

I nodded. At least I wasn't feeling any stomach cramps. She set the drink in front of me and placed a menu and a newspaper next to it. "Just let me know when you want to order."

I sipped tonic water and read the paper for the better part of an hour before I waved Carmen over. By this time, the lunch crowd was in full swing.

"What can I get you?"

"You know, not to sound boring, but I think just a bowl of chicken soup will do me."

"Chicken soup, yeah, okay. You want a side of re-fried beans or maybe some cilantro beer rice with that?"

"No. I think just the chicken soup."

"Okay, coming up."

I sat and slurped soup, read the paper, and kept my eyes on the cash register, but I was no further ahead than I was yesterday. If someone was stealing funds, it was impossible for me to catch it. I decided I'd give it one more try tonight, but if that didn't work, I planned to sit down with George and see where we go from there. I paid my bill, left Carmen a tip, and headed out. I was back in the office at two-thirty. Louie wasn't around, and I took Morton out for a walk. We did three blocks, and actually, I was feeling pretty good. Maybe it was a combination of the chicken soup and staying off the heavy-duty food. Whatever it was, I wasn't about to complain.

Thirty

y phone rang just as Louie stepped into the office. He was red-faced from climbing the stairs and simply gave me a nod as he headed toward his picnic table desk.

"Haskell Investigations," I said, answering the phone.

"Hi, Dev, Diane at Find Art. Just checking in to see how your investigation is going."

"Oh, nice of you to call, Diane. I seem to have hit a bit of a wall. Chandler Hancock is still missing, and there is absolutely nothing to indicate where he might be. A big fat zero."

"The wife has no idea?"

"No, she doesn't, and beyond that, there is nothing out there to indicate foul play. No body. No one is using his credit cards. His car is in the underground garage exactly where he left it last January. His wife—"

"The McKenzie woman."

"Yeah. She has no idea where he might be. They don't own a lake place or a small farm, somewhere that he would, or even could, have gone off to. I don't know what to think."

"Is there anything that would link him to the other missing artists?"

"You mean Oscar Callum or Malcolm Webster?"

"Yes."

"In a word, nothing. All I've come across is that they were artists, living and working here in Minnesota. I suppose they could all be together somewhere, laughing as the price of their work slowly rises every day that they're gone. But that seems more than a little far-fetched."

"And Myles Rossler?" Diane asked.

"Rossler?"

"Myles Rossler. He paints a lot of contemporary nudes. Quite good, actually."

I thought back to the nude painting of Kristi McKenzie that was framed and hanging in the office closet. "I'm not familiar with him. Who did he paint, models?"

"Interestingly, he found a unique niche, women who wanted to be painted, not necessarily models. Rumor has it he charged upwards of twenty grand for a painting. Most of his work is obviously in private collections. The few that do enter the market sell for an exorbitant amount. It's interesting, the painting is good, very good, but that isn't what commands the price."

"Then what does?" I asked.

"The subject."

"A naked woman? I can watch a year's worth of triple X videos online for free. Why would I pay that kind of money for a painting of someone I don't even know?"

"Because in the couple of cases where the paintings actually came on the market, the subject was someone you did know or knew of."

"I'm not following."

"In one case, he painted a Republican congress-woman from out east, in another the mayor of some city down in Kansas. Think about it. The sale immediately becomes a real bidding war between political operatives, one side wishing to expose the individual in the painting. The other side is hoping to keep the whole thing under wraps."

"So why not just take pictures? Wouldn't that be faster?"

"The painting, actually the portrait, would do much more damage. Photographs could always be tossed off as the unfortunate result of a peeping Tom or some other pervert. But a painting, where the subject posed naked for hours while he painted her, one brushstroke at a time, that could end up changing the outcome of a national election."

"Well, there you go," I said. "Politicians are the largest criminal class outside of an institution."

"Yes, but you can see how a painting of that type, in the wrong hands, could cause some real problems, and that's exactly why the two that have gone to market sold for such an outrageous amount."

"Do you have any of Rossler's paintings in the gallery?"

"I don't believe so. I'd have to check to be sure. Even if we did, due to contractual arrangements we wouldn't be allowed to sell them without the express approval of Myles Rossler, and given the potential complexity of the situation, it would probably be a good legal move to get an okay from whoever modeled for the painting."

"So what you're saying is I should add this Myles Rossler to the list of missing artists."

"Yes, unless you can come up with a logical explanation as to why he's missing. I think these incidents have been ignored and kept quiet for far too long. If there's any hope of finding out what's going on, it would seem to me their disappearance should become public knowledge."

'Yeah, and at the same time raise the value of the artwork you have in storage,' I thought. "Sounds like a good idea, Diane. As a matter of fact, I have a call into a friend on the police force. I'll mention it to him."

"What the police should do is call a press conference and mention it to the world. If for no other reason than to alert other artists. It looks like there's a serial killer out there going after talented artists."

"Well, we don't actually know that anyone has been killed, yet. But, I will mention it to my pal."

Thirty-one

So much for naked portraits. The more I thought about it, the more it seemed completely normal that Chandler Hancock would keep the naked portrait of his wife hanging in a private place. Kristi wasn't a mayor or a congresswoman. She was a model with a figure that had been surgically enhanced. Big deal. She was gorgeous. Still, Myles Rossler was a fourth name I could add to the list of missing artists. I Googled him to see what I could learn.

The image that came up was of a guy who looked to be maybe sixty with a handlebar mustache. In the online image, he wore a white coat and a beret. He was standing in front of an easel with a canvas mounted on it, although you couldn't tell what, if anything, was on the canvas. He held a traditional paint palette in his left hand and a thin brush in his right. The article mentioned three museums that had his work. One was in Minneapolis, the other two were in L.A. and San Francisco. It mentioned that he lived in Stillwater, Minnesota. Just thirty minutes from my office.

I looked him up on Facebook. His last post was over a year ago, although there were a number of posts on his site from three months back wishing him a happy birthday. Under the 'About' heading on Facebook, an address was listed on Minar Avenue North. I Googled the address and came up with an image on google maps. It looked like an old farmhouse that appeared to be in reasonably good shape. I wrote down the address, left Louie a note, then Morton and I headed out to Stillwater.

We were just ahead of the rush hour, although the traffic was still heavy. We took Highway 36, turning off at Manning Avenue North. We passed the St. Croix Vineyards and turned onto Highway 12. We drove about two-and-half miles on 12, and suddenly, there was Minar Avenue North and Rossler's place, just off the road and sitting on maybe four acres of land. What had probably been a hundred and sixty acre farm up until the 1960s was now a well-established housing development.

I pulled into the gravel driveway and parked alongside the house. The house was three stories. The third-story had a small paned glass window at the peak of the roof. Yellow fiberglass insulation ran along the bottom six inches of the window, clearly an attic. The lap siding on the house was painted an olive green color with dark green trim. The front door was actually a set of double doors that looked to be oak.

I got out of the car and climbed the four concrete steps to the front porch that ran across the front of the house. There was a large picture window and, above that, a stained-glass window of flowers and a hummingbird. The stained glass looked to be original to the house.

I rang the doorbell twice and heard it chime inside, but no one answered. There was a brass knocker on one of the double oak doors, and I knocked a couple of times but still got no answer. I walked around to the back of the house, where a three-car garage was situated. The roof on one side of the garage was all glass panels, and I figured that was probably Rossler's studio. The entrance door was padlocked, but I knocked anyway. No one answered. I walked all around the garage, but there were no windows.

I headed back toward the house, climbed the four steps leading to the back door, and knocked. At no surprise again, there was no answer. A wooden door led down to what, at one time, had been the coal cellar, but it was padlocked.

I walked around to the front, went up the steps and over to the picture window. I peered in with my hands against the glass and my head resting on my hands. It appeared to be a living room with an elaborate antique fireplace that was most likely original to the house. A brass chandelier hung from the center of the ceiling, and a table lamp rested at either end of a red velvet couch. The couch looked exactly like the velvet couch in the painting of Kristi. I counted nine framed nude paintings hanging on the three walls that I could see.

"Can I help you?" a woman's voice said from behind.

I turned to see a woman standing on the lawn. She was wearing shorts and a grey t-shirt with red letters that said Stillwater High School. She had thick grey hair, cut short, and blue eyes. Her arms were crossed, and she had a look on her face that suggested she was talking to a misbehaving ten-year-old.

"Hi, I was looking for Myles Rossler," I said, and immediately, memories of the two Itasca County Deputies up at Oscar Callum's place flooded back in my mind. I gave a quick glance around, and at least there didn't appear to be someone in the bushes aiming a rifle at me.

"Myles isn't here at the moment."

I thought about lying to her, but she didn't look like the type who would buy whatever tale I told. I walked down the front steps and said, "My name is Dev Haskell. I'm a private investigator in St. Paul. I'm looking for a painter who's been missing for maybe seven months. While I've been looking, the names of three other artists have surfaced with similar circumstances. They've all gone missing, simply disappeared. No sign of violence. No sign of financial problems. Their bank accounts remain untouched. They've just disappeared. Myles Rossler is one of those names."

"You have some ID you can show me?"

I pulled out my wallet. "Here's my driver's license and my PI License. Myles painted a portrait of the woman I'm working for. Her husband is, or rather was, an artist of some renown. I believe he and Myles probably knew one another."

She studied my driver's license for a long moment, turned it over, gave a quick look, then handed it back to me. "My name's Joan Landell. We live next door. We've known Myles for twenty-five years. My husband still cuts the grass here once a month, just in case he comes home."

"Can you tell me anything about him being missing?"

"No, is the short answer. We're not even sure when it happened. Carl, that's my husband, noticed the grass needed cutting last summer right around this time. He called Myles three maybe four times over the course of a couple of days. At my insistence, he finally came over and knocked on the door. No answer. We figured maybe he up and took a trip and didn't tell us. After a few more days, we were worried and called the police, afraid he might be dead inside. They went in, looked around, everything was in order, thankfully, no body. But the place has been empty ever since."

"How did they get inside?"

"The police? They picked the lock."

"No sign of him or where he might have gone? A note or an invitation or something?"

"No. There was dirty laundry in the basket in his bedroom. Coffee still in the pot. Silverware and a plate in the sink. Two suitcases were still in the closet, and it looked like he hadn't packed anything, clothes were still in his dresser and closet. Food was in the refrigerator, only some of it had spoiled. It was very out of character for him, and we kept hoping he might return. We still do, although we know it's probably wishful thinking at this point."

"Did you try his cellphone?"

"We would have if he had one, but he didn't believe in them."

"What did the police say?"

"Well, they agreed it was strange, and they said they'd keep an eye on the place. They drive past every now and then, but I haven't seen them for at least the better part of a month. You on any kind of schedule?"

"Schedule?"

"My husband will be home, oh probably in the next half-hour. I know he'd like to talk to you. We live just over there." She pointed at a grey rambler with an attached garage and a large oak tree in the front yard.

"Yeah, I'd like to talk to him, talk to both of you. I've got my dog, Morton, in the car. Let me give him twenty minutes of exercise, and I'll knock on your door if that'll be okay."

"I'll put the coffee on. Come on around to the backdoor when you're ready," she said and headed over to her house.

I grabbed a tennis ball from under the back seat and tossed it toward the three-car garage. Morton took off after it. We played fetch for a good twenty minutes. When I led him back into the car, he curled up on the rear seat and closed his eyes. I walked over to the Landell house.

There was a concrete patio and a glass-topped table with an umbrella and four chairs at the rear of the house. The back storm door was open, but the screen door was closed. I stepped onto the back stoop and rang the doorbell.

"Be there in just a minute," Joan called. I heard what sounded like an oven door closing, and a moment later, there she was. She unhooked the screen door and said, "Come on in, Dev. I was just taking some blueberry muffins out of the oven."

The kitchen looked vintage 1980s. A pan of a dozen blueberry muffins sat on the cooling rack resting on a chopping block. The cabinets were oak, the countertops were white Formica, and the floor was grey linoleum. The refrigerator had a number of pictures of three little girls, and I guessed they might be grandchildren.

Joan took a plate from a cabinet and quickly picked up four muffins, one at a time, and half-tossed them onto the plate. "Yikes. Just out and they're hot," she said, shaking her hand. "How do you take your coffee?"

"Black is just fine."

"Come on and join me at the table. Carl should be home any minute." She handed me a steaming coffee mug, and we sat down beneath a framed print of the 'Last Supper.'

I would say we chatted, but actually, I just listened to Joan wax on about what a wonderful neighbor Myles Rossler was. During the monolog, she switched back and forth from present to past tense while describing him. I was on my second cup of coffee when the door opened, and Carl stepped in carrying two grocery bags. He had grey hair, a neatly trimmed grey mustache, and sparkling blue eyes.

"Did they have the chicken thighs?" Joan asked.

"Yeah, I got three packages, six each."

"I only wanted one."

"We can freeze the other two."

"You know I don't like to do that."

"Okay, I suppose we could throw them out then."

"All right, we'll freeze them."

"Hi, Carl," I said, standing and holding out my hand. "My name is Dev Haskell."

"He's a private investigator," Joan said, "from St. Paul."

Carl gave my hand a solid handshake. "An investigator? What's this about?"

"He's asking about Myles."

Carl nodded and said, "Get me a coffee, will you, Joanie, while I put this stuff away. So, Myles Rossler, you have some information on him?"

"No," I said maybe a little too quickly in an effort to answer before Joan jumped in. Carl began to unpack the two grocery bags and align the various items on the counter while I told him the same thing I'd told Joan. That I was looking for Kristi's husband, and from that investigation, I'd learned about three other artists who had been missing, Myles Rossler being one of them.

"I'm not with a police force. Joan tells me you've been in touch with the Stillwater Police, but they haven't been able to come up with anything."

"I wouldn't say they've been trying all that hard," Carl said. He was at the refrigerator now, putting away red peppers, milk, and butter. Then onto the freezer, where he placed the two packages of chicken thighs, one on top of the other.

Joan was up, handed him a mug of coffee, and then opened the package of chicken he'd left on the counter and proceeded to run the thighs under the water tap.

"Let me tell you what I know about Myles. Joan, you fill in the blanks," he said and then winked at me.

Thirty-two

Carl and I settled in at the kitchen table while Joan prepared the chicken thighs in a baking pan. Carl took the last remaining blueberry muffin from the plate and peeled away the paper muffin cup. "You want one of these. Joanie makes the best."

"Yeah, I know. I already had two. As delicious as they are, I'm one over my limit. So tell me about Myles."

"Great guy, wonderful neighbor. Never a problem, quiet, pretty much kept to himself."

"Although if you invited him over for dinner, he'd be here a half-hour early and always ask for seconds," Joan said.

Carl chuckled. "Yeah, one of those lean fellas that ate like a horse. Course, cooking his own dinners, he probably finished them in ten minutes. You can just imagine what he cooked, hot dogs, TV dinners, ice cream."

"Sounds like you've been peeking in my kitchen windows."

"Well, we're having chicken, roast potatoes, cauliflower with a sauce tonight, and you're more than welcome to stay," Joan said from the kitchen counter. She was in the process of sprinkling spices over the chicken thighs.

"Oh, thanks, that's very kind of you, but I've got a five o'clock appointment back in town." I turned back to Carl. "So he was pretty quiet, no wild parties, no naked women painted outside."

Carl smiled. "No, you'd never know that was his business. He never mentioned it."

"You'd never peg him as an artist," Joan said as she opened the oven door. "If you didn't know any better, you'd think he was maybe an accountant or a banker or something."

Carl nodded. "Other than the people he painted, I really can't remember anyone showing up for dinner or a visit over there in twenty years."

"Twenty-five," Joan said.

"Occasionally maybe a UPS or Fed Ex delivery, I'm guessing more artist materials. I'll give him this much. He was dedicated to his work. Painted seven days a week, wouldn't you say Joanie?"

She had just poured herself a mug of coffee and joined us at the table. "Yeah, he was always painting. All day, every day. Wasn't uncommon to see the lights on in his studio until nine or ten at night. Next morning he'd be there bright and early, working away."

"Always painting someone?"

"Yeah, business was always good as long as we've lived here." Carl got up from the table and headed for the muffin pan.

"Carl, no. You'll ruin your appetite. Now no more. I just put dinner in the oven."

Carl smiled, grabbed a chunk of muffin that had overflowed the muffin cup, and quickly tossed it in his mouth. "Myles always had a list of people lined up to be painted."

"A list?"

Joan nodded. "He wrote your name down on the list, and then he'd call you when your turn came up. If you couldn't come, he just went on to the next person, and he'd put your name at the bottom of the list."

"Did he do a painting of you?" I asked.

Joan nodded and said, "Yes, but not what you're no doubt thinking. Carl, why don't you get it and bring it in here?" Carl got up and headed into another room. "As far as I know, most of his notoriety centered on the naked lady paintings. But he did others as well. He did portraits of children occasionally. One time, he did a wedding couple."

Carl came back into the kitchen, carrying a framed painting. He turned it around and held it in front of him. It was beautiful. It was Joan in what looked like a very silky wedding dress. She was seated in an antique-looking gold chair. Behind her was a reddish drape with gold designs. Her shoulders were bare, and there was a see-through veil around the upper portion of the dress. She wore a double strand of pearls and dangling pearl earrings. Her legs were crossed, exposing one ankle and a foot wearing a white high heel. She held a red flower on her lap.

"He did this for our fiftieth, a surprise," Carl said and suddenly choked up.

"It was Myles' idea. That's my wedding dress. If you can believe it, I had packed it away for fifty years, and God bless him, he talked me into posing for this painting," Joan said. Her eyes were suddenly moist.

"It's beautiful. Museum quality," I said.

"What do you think it cost me?" Joan said.

"I don't know. I've heard he charged upward of twenty thousand dollars for some of his work, and from what I understand, they only increase in value."

Joan grinned and said, "A pot roast dinner."

"And the rhubarb pie, two pieces," Carl said.

"I'm not kidding. That is really gorgeous. It looks like it should hang in a museum."

"Remember Joan? We had that one woman take a look at it. She was going to give us an appraisal, you know for insurance, but when we told her we didn't want to sell it, we never heard back from her. She never did give us the appraisal figure."

"Different sort of woman. At least twenty-five years younger than Myles."

"I'd say he fancied her. Or maybe it was just her fancy red pickup truck," Carl said. "She hung around for a bit, but after being single all those years, he wasn't going to put up with all the nonsense, and she eventually disappeared."

Joan frowned at the nonsense remark and said, "You can hang that back in the living room, Carl."

"You know I'm right," he said and hurried out of the kitchen.

We chatted for another ten minutes, and I had to get going. I said thanks, complimented their painting again, and promised to keep in touch if I learned anything. I drove home, let Morton out the back, dumped the mail into recycling, and headed over to City Salsa House.

Thirty-three

The bartender was stacking clean glasses on the shelf behind the bar. He smiled and nodded when I came in. With the exception of one woman on her cellphone, the bar was empty. Unfortunately, the woman was sitting on my stool. I left a stool between us and sat down. The view was going to be lousy from this angle.

She had her purse resting on the bar. She gave a look that suggested, 'What the hell?' and glanced down the length of the bar at all the empty seating. She pulled her purse off the bar, set it on the empty stool in the corner, and half-turned her back to me. She continued her conversation only now in a much quieter tone.

"Don't tell me, tonic and a twist?" the bartender said.

"That'll do and a menu, when you have time," I said loud enough so the woman on my stool got the message I was going to be sitting here for a while.

He returned with my tonic water and the newspaper. I made a show of opening the paper, which brought a disgusted sigh from my neighbor. I began to read the same articles I'd read at noon.

The evening crowd was beginning to build. The place was maybe half-full. With the exception of four women laughing and talking over each other in one of the booths, everyone appeared to be relatively well-behaved. Two women came in, and one of them called out, "Mandy." The woman next to me looked up from her cellphone screen, grabbed her purse, and hurried over.

"Oh, you guys, creepy," she said as they were led back to one of the tables. As they sat down, both of the new arrivals looked over their shoulders and gave me the once over. I slid off the stool I'd been relegated to and took up my rightful position.

Just like the previous three times, a lot of servers were in and out of the till. George had said about sixty percent of his business was credit cards, and that seemed about right. Over the course of the evening, three different servers put a hundred dollar bill in the cash register, but then again, it was coming up to the weekend, so maybe folks had stopped at the ATM before they came to the restaurant.

The three women who knew me as creepy left about seven-thirty. The woman who'd been on my stool stared straight ahead and made for the door. When her two friends looked at me, I gave a little wave and raised my eyebrows. They picked up the pace and joined their friend out on the sidewalk.

I ordered crispy fried chicken and a salad, staying away from the rice and beans. Just to be different, I ordered flan for dessert. I left the restaurant a little after nine and headed home, once again no wiser than before on, not only how, but even if, someone was stealing cash.

I let Morton out, checked the windows for any sign of someone trying to get in, and then settled in front of the TV. I awoke to the Netflix image on my TV. It was close to three in the morning. I turned off the TV and the light and headed upstairs. I was just coming out of the bathroom when I heard a noise downstairs. I hurried into the bedroom. Morton was stretched out on the bed softly snoring. I grabbed my pistol from the night table and slowly made my way downstairs in my stocking feet. My ears were strained in an attempt to pick up any noise.

Suddenly, there it was again, a loud thump. I looked out the window next to the front door. The front porch light was on, and I heard another thump, although I couldn't see anyone yet. Then, two more thumps, one right after the other. I slowly unlocked the front door and took hold of the doorknob, holding the pistol in my left hand. There was another thump, and I tore the door open. As I stepped outside, something dark and furry rushed past me, a dog or maybe a small coyote. Either way, it wasn't Gerry Burke. I watched for three or four seconds as it dashed across the street and disappeared in the darkness.

I looked under the table at the far end of the porch. There was a bone, a hambone by all appearances. I walked over and picked it up. Whatever animal it was, he must have stolen the bone from someone's yard. I know Morton didn't currently have one out in the back.

I gave a quick glance around, tossed the bone into the front yard, and stepped back inside. I locked the door and headed back up to bed.

Morton hadn't moved, and he was still snoring. I climbed into bed, thought about giving Morton a shake to stop the snoring, but instead fell asleep.

Thirty-four

espite the hambone incident, I woke ten minutes before my alarm went off, feeling somewhat rested. I turned off the alarm, showered, and went down to the kitchen. I was reading the paper online, having my second cup of coffee when Morton decided to make his appearance. I gave him his morning scratch and let him outside.

I watched him for a moment, and it reminded me of last night. I walked to the entryway and stepped out onto the front porch. I couldn't see the hambone anywhere, so the culprit must have returned to retrieve it.

I went back inside, filled Morton's food and water dish, and let him back in. I scrambled up three eggs, adding tomatoes, feta cheese, and black olives. After breakfast, we headed down to the office. Louie was already there, going over a file.

"You two are in early."

"Well-rested and looking at a full day," I said.

"What have you got going on?"

"Lunch and dinner at City Salsa House."

"Sounds like a nice gig. I must be in the wrong line of work."

"Yeah, well, nothing's happening there, at least that I can see. If someone is stealing funds from the cash register, there is no way I'm going to catch them. I can't detect anything. I'm gonna have to sit down with George today and tell him I'm not picking up on anything. I don't know what the amount of the check is that they're ringing up, so when they take a bunch of cash and stick it in the receipt holder, I have no way of knowing if it's legit or not."

"And he said they're losing about a hundred bucks a day?"

"Yeah, give or take."

"Is he sure it's cash?"

"What else could it be? They can't debit the credit card payment."

"What about liquor, cases of wine, or food? He probably buys liquor by the case. Maybe someone's ripping off a couple of bottles every day. If they've got high-priced whiskey, and vodka, and stuff, someone could be grabbing two or three bottles, and they could easily be at a hundred bucks. Hey, I know, why don't you offer to show up at everyone's house for a drink and see what their liquor cabinet looks like."

"Yeah, thanks for the advice, but I don't see that as a very viable alternative." I filled my coffee mug and settled in behind my desk. I called Diane at Find Art and left a message. Next, I phoned Aaron LaZelle and surprise, he actually answered my call.

"Yeah, Dev, what's up?"

"You have time to talk, Aaron?"

"I can give you a minute or two. What's happening?"

"I got a couple of things. First of all, you mentioned Kristi McKenzie the other day and the accident where that guy was pushed into the car."

"You mean Joseph Lauer, her fiancé at the time. The guy who just happened to have a one-point five million dollar life insurance policy and gorgeous, young Kristi was the sole beneficiary."

"Yeah, anyway, I was talking to her the other night, and she wears a size five shoe." It was my most recent night from hell. Kristi's in the mood, answers the door damn near naked, and I get the shits.

"You're talking shoe size with this woman?"

"In a roundabout way. She mentioned her shoe size when I commented on her pedicure." I didn't think it was important to bring up the fact that she wondered if I had a foot fetish.

Aaron chuckled and said, "Huh. Interesting. Who knew you had a foot fetish?"

"Yeah, right. Hey, there's a couple of other things I should mention. I told you that along with Kristi's husband, Chandler Hancock—"

"Common law husband, right?"

"Yeah, but along with him, there are these other artists I've come across, all from Minnesota and all missing under similar circumstances."

"And what are the similar circumstances, again?"

"They just disappear. One day everything is normal, and the next day they're gone. No indication of violence or that they left on an extended trip. The Stillwater folks I talked to yesterday said the cops checked their neighbor's house, and everything looked fine, but the food in the refrigerator was spoiled, and it sounded like he was the kind of guy they interacted with on a neighborly basis."

"Stillwater? And what was this guy's name?"

I got the impression Aaron was going to write it down. "Myles Rossler," I said and spelled it out for him. "The other two are a guy named Malcolm Webster and another fella named Oscar Callum."

"Okay, got them. And no signs of foul play in any of these?"

"No, nothing. I haven't really checked into Malcolm Webster, but I talked to two Itasca County Deputies the other day. That's where Oscar Callum is from. A little town called Warba. Anyway, same deal, no indication of violence or anything. The cops up north were thinking maybe he took a walk in the woods and had a heart attack or something, and his body is out there in the wilderness somewhere."

"Yeah, possible, it's all still a bit tenuous, Dev."

"Yeah, believe me, I know. So then here is the next thing, tenuous at best, but check this out. Kristi McKenzie has a piece of artwork from each one of these guys."

"Yeah, but Dev, her husband was an artist. He probably knew these guys. Maybe they have one of his paintings. It wouldn't be unusual for them to trade a work. It's kind of like a plumber having a pal who's an electrician and they work on each other's house."

"Yeah, maybe. Add this to the list. Oscar Callum, the sculptor, made a small statue maybe ten inches high. It looks like Kristi was the model for it. I know it doesn't prove anything but just saying. Then get this, Myles Rossler, talented guy that he is, does portraits."

"Okay."

"He's known for doing nude portraits of women. He did one of some republican congresswoman and another of some mayor down in Kansas that I guess ended up selling for thousands, like fifty thousand, just to keep the things under wraps."

"Yeah, interesting, but so what?"

"Rossler did a nude of Kristi. It's hanging in the closet of what was, or is, Chandler's office."

"Hmm, bit by bit, Dev. But nothing that would allow us to question her or ask for a warrant."

"Yeah, I know. You know what you might do?"

"What?"

"Just do a search through state records. See if anything comes up on Kristi. Maybe she has a conceal and carry permit or something."

"I suppose I could do that. But it might be a while before I can get to it."

"No rush. Actually, it would be great if she came out clean. Let me know what you find out."

"Okay, and Dev, keep me posted on any other tenuous information you find."

Thirty-five

I pulled up in front of the City Salsa House just before eleven. As I came around the corner, a car was just pulling out, and I was able to grab the parking spot. I climbed out and locked the car. I had nothing in my car of any value, and there was no sign of Gerry Berk, but why take the chance?

When I stepped inside, Carmen was the only person in the place. She was busy placing silverware rolled up in black napkins at each one of the tables. "Hi Dev, be with you in just a minute. You want the usual?"

"Yeah, that would be great. No rush."

I took up a position on my stool. A newspaper was already sitting on the bar in front of the stool. Carmen stepped behind the bar, filled a glass with ice, squirted tonic into the glass, and ran a wedge of lime around the edge. "Here you go," she said, setting the glass down in front of me. "How's your day going?"

"Good. I remain the most boring guy in town."

"I doubt that," she said.

I glanced at the headlines in the paper. More news out of Washington I wasn't interested in. I took a sip of tonic, turned sideways on the stool, and casually glanced out the door just as Gerry Berk walked past headed in the direction of the bus bench. From where I sat, I couldn't see my car, and I immediately panicked, thinking he did something like slit all four tires or shoved a burning rag into the gas tank. I hopped off the stool and hurried over to the door.

Two guys were just coming in, and I stepped back so they could enter then looked out the door. My tires looked okay, and I didn't see any flames from the street side of the car. I looked in the opposite direction, but since the bus bench was up against the building next door, I couldn't see it without opening the door and looking out. That would just be looking for trouble.

Another guy came in, and I stepped aside so he could enter. He nodded thanks as he walked past. A bus came around the corner and stopped. The bus destination, Rosedale, was illuminated above the windshield along with the route number sixty-five. I watched as Gerry Berk suddenly appeared and stepped onto the bus. Today, he wore sandals and was dressed in camouflage shorts with the same grimy t-shirt that said 'Beer Me.' Like before, the t-shirt left his navel exposed. I pitied whoever had to sit near him on the bus.

I stepped back from the door as the bus pulled away from the curb and into traffic. The last thing I needed was Berk the jerk getting off at the next stop and waddling back to give me a hard time. When I returned to my stool, Carmen had left a menu on top of the newspaper. I spent the better part of the next hour searching for an interesting article to read and chugging down two glasses of tonic. The place was busier than usual at the noon hour, but I chalked it up to being Friday. I ordered chicken fajitas and rice for lunch and asked Carmen to hold the refried beans. After my Kristi experience, I was still playing it somewhat careful about what I ate.

I had no better luck watching the cash register, and I made a mental note to give George a call once I got back to the office. I was thinking Louie's suggestion of people stealing bottles of alcohol held some promise, and I planned to bring that up.

It was close to two when I paid my bill, left Carmen a tip, and headed back to the office. Morton was asleep on his bed, and Louie was just getting off the phone when I walked in.

"You working that restaurant gig again?" Louie said as he tossed his cellphone on top of a file.

"Yeah. As a matter of fact, I'm going to call George now and tell him I'm not coming up with anything. I've been thinking your idea about someone ripping off bottles of wine and liquor holds some promise."

"Yeah, although if you owned a restaurant or a bar, wouldn't you keep that stuff under lock and key?"

"Yeah, but George said his eighty-two-year-old aunt actually owns the place. I don't know. Maybe she's more trusting?"

"Or she could be a hell of a lot tougher. You never know."

I settled in behind my desk and called George Estrada. He answered on the second ring. "Hi, Dev. I was hoping to hear from you. What have you found out?"

"I have to level with you, George. I got a big fat nothing. Your servers could be taking the cash right in front of me, and I'd never know. They put a wad of cash in those little black receipt holders, and since I don't know how much the bill was, I don't know if it's legit or if they're ripping you off. Let me ask you something."

"Go ahead, shoot."

"Could the funds you're losing actually be from someone pilfering stock. A couple bottles of the right whiskey or wine, and you could easily be out a hundred bucks. Do you have a secure place where the liquor is stored?"

"You kidding? With my aunt? I'm lucky she doesn't have some armed guard standing over the storage room. It takes two keys to get in the storage room. Only my main bartenders have one of the keys, that would be Carmen on the day shift and Eddie at night. My aunt and I have the second key. No one gets in there and removes anything without either my aunt or me standing right at the door."

"Carmen stocks the bar at ten-thirty in the morning. Eddie stocks it every afternoon at four. On the odd occasion when we're out of something, either my aunt or, more often, I will head downstairs and get whatever is needed."

"So pilfering liquor is out."

"Yeah, I'd say so. But now you've got me thinking about the meat cooler."

"The meat cooler. You mean a refrigerator?"

"No, it's a walk-in cooler, a freezer actually. Chicken, steaks, sausage, and a whole host of other things. I suppose it's possible someone could be ripping us off in there, but let me think about it for a bit. You going to be in tonight?"

"I can if you want me to, but I wanted to be upfront with you on what I have, or rather don't have so far."

"Yeah, let's have you do one more night. In the meantime, I'll think about the food angle. Anything else?"

"Nothing other than what I have seen, and that is, you've got a really nice staff. Fun folks, all good servers. Carmen and Eddie have taken good care of me behind the bar."

"Glad to hear it. Let's talk tomorrow," George said.

Thirty-six

Morton and I headed home about 4:30. I figured, since it was my last night staring at servers at City Salsa House, I might as well celebrate a little. I let Morton out into the backyard, took a shower, pulled on a clean shirt, and stepped into reasonably clean jeans. I let Morton back in and headed to the restaurant. It was 5:45 by the time I got there, and parking was at a premium. I had to park at the far end of the block and around the corner. The house on the corner had a neatly trimmed hedge all around the yard. As I parked my car, a number sixty-five bus drove past, turned at the corner, and stopped.

I was a little cautious walking up the block and wasn't sure what I'd find when I turned the corner. Fortunately, all I saw were two high school girls waiting at the bus stop. No sign of fat Gerry Berk. I smiled and said, "Hi," as I walked past. The girls must have been pretty street-smart because they both ignored me.

The place was jammed inside. All the booths and tables were filled. Four people stood around the hostess area, all sipping what looked like Margaritas. Amazingly, my stool was open at the bar. Eddie, the tattooed bartender, was pouring beers at the opposite end of the bar. He smiled and gave me a nod as I took up my position on the stool. When he was finished with the beers, he headed down toward me.

"Hey, look at you all dressed up. Hot date tonight?"

"Not unless someone calls me in the next hour or two."

"Yeah, I know how that goes," he said and laughed. "Get you the usual?"

I shook my head and said, "No, I think tonight I'll celebrate and start off with a Corona."

"A Corona, coming right up," he said and headed back down the bar to one of the coolers. He returned a minute later with the bottle of Corona and a chilled mug. "Are you going to want to see a menu?"

"Yeah, but no rush."

He reached back and grabbed a menu off a stack in front of the whiskey bottles. "Just give me a wave when you're ready to order."

I casually watched the servers at the cash register and didn't notice anything that looked out of line. The placed remained full, and just about the time one of the tables or booths emptied out, another couple or group came in the door. There were a number of people at the bar who appeared to be there just enjoying the drinks.

I ordered another Corona, got a freshly chilled mug, and perused the menu. I ended up ordering Enchiladas Suizas, corn tortillas layered with chicken, Swiss cheese, and covered with tomatillo sauce, topped with feta and Colby cheese, sour cream, onion, and cilantro and all served up with Mexican rice. I was still playing it cautious when it came to the refried beans.

I sipped my beer and recognized a couple that came in. The guy was a lawyer, and I'd appeared on the witness stand in an assault case against his client. He had cross-examined me in court for no more than five minutes and got me out of there as fast as he could. I didn't remember his name, but his wife was named Eileen or Aileen, I couldn't remember which. He pretended to ignore me or maybe didn't see me. She gave a little wave as they headed back to a table.

My dinner arrived on a huge platter and smelled delicious. My stomach growled as I took in the wonderful scent. At the moment, it smelled even better than Kristi's perfume. I ordered another Corona to celebrate dinner and began to attack my meal.

I tried to take my time and not inhale the meal, but in what seemed like just minutes, the platter in front of me was clean. It was so good I had to stop myself from licking the platter.

"Oh, man, you must have been starving," Eddie said as he grabbed the empty platter and my silverware. "Can I get you anything else? Maybe a flan?"

"Actually, that sounds like just the thing I need."

"Coming right up."

I took my time eating the flan. Really, I did. When I'd finished that, I ordered another Corona and sipped it over the course of maybe twenty minutes, and then, just to top off the night, I ordered one more. Fortunately, with five beers under my belt, I didn't have too far to drive.

Thirty-seven

I paid my bill, shook hands with Eddie the bartender, then walked over to the table with the lawyer and his wife and said hello. A couple of beers always makes me a little friendly. Five beers probably makes me close to obnoxious.

I headed out the door and looked up and down the block for any sign of Gerry Berk. Fortunately, I didn't see his fat ass anywhere. It was after nine and dark, but the occasional car driving past illuminated the sidewalk ahead of me. As I walked down the street, I glanced into the lighted living rooms of the houses I passed. Two places had large TV's playing. Another one looked to be in the middle of entertaining, with a number of people standing around talking and drinking glasses of wine. I made my way down to the end of the block and turned the corner. I clicked the fob on my car key that flashed the headlights and unlocked the driver's door.

I heard something snap behind the hedge and caught a quick glimpse of Gerry Berk just before everything went black.

Thirty-eight

I heard a voice that sounded somewhat familiar. At first, it seemed very distant but gradually grew closer. I blinked my eyes open and couldn't recognize my surroundings. The room was painted white with a window that looked out at a red brick wall. The window was modern and slid from left to right rather than pull up like the ones in my house.

"A pretty serious concussion. I want to keep him here for another night just to monitor him. I'm not expecting any problems but just to play it safe."

"Okay, thanks, doc," another voice said, it echoed in my head, but I recognized it as Aaron LaZelle's.

I turned my head, and a lightning bolt of pain shot through my skull. "Hey, what the hell happened?"

Aaron and a guy in burgundy scrubs with a stethoscope draped around his neck looked over at me.

"Oh, so you decided to join us. How's the head?" the guy in the scrubs asked. He stepped alongside the bed I was in and seemed to study me. "You banged your head on the sidewalk and hurt your jaw in the fall, Mr. Haskell. Fortunately, someone found you and called 911. You have a concussion, but the good news is you're going to be all right. With any luck, the next twenty-four to forty-eight hours should make a big difference, as long as you rest. Now, I'm going to check your eyes," he said and pulled out a small flashlight. "I want you to try to follow this as I move it around, okay?"

"Yeah."

He kept the flashlight off and moved it from left to right. I followed it with my eyes, although there was some pain when my eyes moved to the far right.

"Okay, good, now I'm going to turn on the light and examine your pupils." He clicked on the light, and I immediately felt a sharp pain and squeezed my eyes shut. "That feel uncomfortable?"

"Yeah, it really hurt, like something just stabbed me in the eye."

"Okay, that's normal. I'm going to have you spend another night here, just to be sure you're okay. I'll leave you two alone. If you need anything," he lifted a cord that was wrapped around the bedrail on the side of the bed, a little white unit with a button dangled on the end. "Just press this button, and it will alert the nurse's station. I don't want you getting out of this bed unless you have to use the bathroom. Okay? The longer you just lie here and take it easy, the faster your recovery will be."

"Okay," I said and attempted to nod, but pain immediately shot through my skull again.

"Yeah, try to keep that head still. It's going to be uncomfortable for a day or two, but you're already on the road to recovery. Any questions?"

"Yeah. What the hell happened?"

"It looks like you fell and hit your head on the sidewalk. You, ahh, had an alcohol level of one point five. Maybe your friend can give you more information," he said and nodded at Aaron standing at the end of the bed. "I'll check on you a little later. For now, just remain in bed and take it easy." He nodded at me and headed for the door. He said, "Nice to meet you," to Aaron as he walked out of the room, closing the door behind him.

"Way to screw up my weekend off, Dev. Hope you're happy."

"Yeah, that's right, like I did this on purpose."

"Fortunately, that couple found you. Ed Gilbert, a lawyer and his wife."

"Yeah, and his wife is Eileen or Aileen or something. I remember I saw them in the restaurant. I couldn't think of his name."

"Their word to the EMTs was you seemed to have had a lot to drink."

"Yeah, some beers, I guess. I can't remember how many. But more than one."

"You were walking home?"

"No, no, my car was there. I remember flashing the lights and unlocking the door and nothing really after that."

"Well, you're awfully damn lucky it's not winter and twenty below zero."

"I just can't remember much. I remember parking, walking up to the restaurant. I ordered something with a lot of cheese. I think it was good. Hey, can I ask you a favor?"

"No, I'm not going to pay your hospital bill. So don't bother asking."

"Very funny. But if you would just grab my car keys. They're probably in my jeans. Can you go to my place and let Morton out in the back for ten minutes and fill his food and water dish?"

"Yeah, I can do that," he said, taking my jeans from a hook on the side of a wardrobe cabinet. "Let me just check and… Humf, no keys. Did you have a wallet last night?"

"Yeah, of course."

"Well, it's not in your jeans, just a cellphone in here." He pulled the wardrobe open and looked inside. "No, nothing here. Let me go out and check with the nurse's station. Maybe they've got a secure place where they lock up that stuff."

Aaron stepped back into the room a couple of minutes later. "They don't hold any of those items," he said, referring to my car keys and wallet. He pulled the cellphone from my jeans and placed it on the table in front of me.

"Oh, great."

"I'll swing by the restaurant. You were at City Salsa House?"

"Yeah, parked on Grand Ave at the opposite end of the block. The corner house has a hedge, and I parked next to that." Suddenly BOOM! There it was. The image of Gerry Berk coming through the hedge. "Holy shit."

"What?"

"It just came back to me. Gerry Berk. The son-of-a-bitch hit me over the head."

"What?"

"Gerry Berk. He's a fat-assed guy with an orange beard. Catches the sixty-five bus on the corner. He was hiding behind the hedge when I walked to my car, and he hit me over the head. I bet that bastard took my wallet and car keys."

"How do you know this guy?"

"He did ten years up at Saint Cloud. He saw me a couple of days earlier and threatened me at City Salsa House, but they kicked him out. Bastard was waiting for me. He had to be." I went on to explain my relationship with Berk, his assault on a friend's daughter, and the permanent limp he now had, along with a ten-year prison record.

"I'll call it in. Let me see if we can find him. I better get going."

"Okay. Hey Aaron, don't forget Morton. I've got a spare set of house keys attached to the drainpipe on the back of the house."

"Got it," he called and hurried out of the room.

Other than a trip to the bathroom, I was in bed for the rest of the morning. The one time I did get up, I was slightly dizzy, and any fast movement only seemed to increase the dizziness. I had a chicken sandwich for lunch, but two bites were more than enough. Along with my wallet and car keys, I seemed to have lost my appetite as well.

Thirty-nine

I drifted off to sleep in the afternoon. At some point, someone had come in the room and removed the tray with the chicken sandwich and replaced it with a bottle of water. My cellphone ringing woke me.

"Hello?" is how I answered, and then I had to clear my throat a couple of times to get my voice back.

"Dev? It's Kristi. How are you?"

"God. You won't believe it. I'm in the hospital."

"Hospital? What happened, heart attack?"

"No. Some jerk clubbed me over the head. Attacked me from behind," I added.

"Oh my God. Are you okay?"

"They're keeping me overnight, but just for observation. I hope to be going home tomorrow."

"Oh, you poor thing. What hospital are you in?"

"I'm down at United, just off West Seventh and Grand. But don't do anything crazy, you don't have to come down and visit me," I said, hoping she'd rush down. With any luck, there'd be some stress release if she was just as frantic as the other night when she was wearing the Vikings jersey.

"Well, I've got dinner plans, but maybe I could pop in for a second after that."

"Thanks, but don't worry. Besides, I'm sure their visiting hours here close at eight or something."

"I'll see how it goes, just meeting a couple of girlfriends. Oh, Dev, I'm so sorry to hear this. Did it have anything to do with your investigation of Chandler?"

"No, a completely different case I'm working on, and I was just in the wrong place at the wrong time."

"Okay, well, I'll try to get down there this evening. I better run. Catch you later," she said and hung up.

I thought about checking in with George Estrada but decided against it. I drifted off to sleep again, and when I woke, a woman was entering the room with a food tray. She smiled, said, "Hi," and set the food tray on the table in front of me. She laid a bottle of mineral water on the side of the tray and left.

The plate on the tray had a metal cover over it. I pulled off the cover and set it off to the side. The plate had a mound of penne pasta with a thin red sauce. The sauce was lukewarm and tasteless, but I ate it anyway. A small bowl of red Jell-O with a dollop of something on top that looked like whipped cream but wasn't apparently served as the dessert. I couldn't remember the last time I had eaten Jell-O. It wasn't half-bad.

I occasionally moved my head, and the headache seemed to have disappeared. I could move my eyes from left to right without any pain. I thought about watching TV, but I didn't want to have to figure out the remote and decided against it.

A young guy in scrubs came in maybe an hour later and took my food tray. By then, it was dark outside, and a nurse came in and checked on me. She took my blood pressure and temperature.

"How am I doing?"

"Pretty good, fine as a matter of fact. You keep this up, we're going to have to kick you out tomorrow."

"That would be just fine with me."

"Yeah, I know the feeling. I'm going to turn a couple of these lights off so you'll be able to get some sleep tonight. Right now, that's the best thing you can do for your recovery."

"Thanks, much appreciated."

"Sweet dreams," she said, turning off two of the three lights in the room. The only light left on was over the bed, and she dimmed that one way down. She closed the door on her way out.

I drifted off to sleep for a bit and was vaguely aware of the door opening and closing. I started to fall back asleep when a hand slowly ran up my thigh and remained on my chest, lightly moving back and forth across it. "Dev," a voice seemed to whisper. I thought I must be dreaming, but then I heard the voice again. "Dev, honey."

I opened my eyes and stared into Kristi's face about three inches from mine. "How are you feeling?"

"Kristi? How did you get in here? What time is it?"

She smiled and said, "Don't worry, it's late. I'm going to spend the night," she said and stood up. She was dressed in light blue scrubs and had a stethoscope dangling around her neck. "See." She shrugged, put the stethoscope in her ears, and proceeded to listen to my heartbeat. "Oh, well, you must be alive. Cool, I can actually hear your heart."

"Where did you get all that stuff?"

"You like? My friend, Karin. She's a midwife. I have to have this back to her by nine tomorrow morning," she said and indicated the stethoscope. "Why don't you move over so I can get next to you?"

She kicked off her clogs and slipped in the bed next to me. She kissed me a number of times and giggled in between. At any other time, I would have considered it a great opportunity, but at this precise moment, I wasn't up for it. Literally. I drifted off to sleep.

"Oh my God," a voice shrieked, and suddenly, I heard the door slam, and there was shouting out in the hallway.

Kristi was suddenly awake and jumping out of bed, "I gotta run," she said, slipping on her clogs, grabbing the stethoscope, and hurrying out of the room. I listened to her footsteps fade down the hallway.

Maybe a minute later, I heard a commotion coming down the hall, and I closed my eyes and pretended to be asleep. Three people suddenly burst into the room, two women and a guy, all in hospital scrubs. I slowly opened my eyes, suggesting they just woke me up.

They did a quick look around the room, and one of the women said, "She must have just left," causing all three of them to hurry back out of the room.

"We better check the other rooms," the guy said out in the hall, and I heard three sets of footsteps quickly disappear.

Forty

No one came back and questioned me about Kristi. One of the nurses stepped in while I was eating breakfast. A bowl of oatmeal, by the way. She asked me how I slept and then asked if I had a friend who worked at the hospital. She said someone had mentioned my name, but she couldn't remember who. I thought she was trying to figure out what happened. I just played dumb, which wasn't hard to do.

Aaron arrived just as my breakfast tray was being carried away. He was dressed in jeans and a t-shirt, clearly his day off. "How you feeling?" he asked as he came in. I had a small plate on my tray with a couple of cookies on it. He grabbed them off the plate and said to the woman carrying the tray out, "No point in letting these go to waste."

"I'm feeling pretty good. Amazingly, I've been following the doctor's orders and stayed in bed. I've got one hell of a lump on the back of my head. But the dizziness has disappeared. I'm ready to get the hell out of here."

"Well, I checked at the nurse's station. The doc will be making his rounds later this morning. If he sets you free, why don't you give me a call and I'll drive you home. As a matter of fact, once he sees you, give me a call either way and keep me updated."

"You find that Berk bastard?"

"You want the good news or the bad news first?"

"Give me the bad news."

"The short answer is no. I've got a BOLO out on him, so with any luck, we'll grab him. The other bad news is he probably has your wallet and your car. Did you stop payment on your credit cards?"

"No. I didn't even think of that. I don't have the card numbers or the eight hundred number to call. I can get them once I get home, but I'm screwed until then."

"Mmm, not quite. Let me make a phone call," he said as he pulled out his phone. "What is it, Visa? Mastercard?"

"I've got two Visas and an American Express."

"Yeah, sergeant," Aaron said, "I'm at United Hospital dealing with the victim of an assault. I need to have someone cancel his credit cards. Yeah. Two Visas and one American Express. Yeah, first name is Devlin. Last Name is Haskell." He spelled out both names. "Date of birth, Dev?" I gave it to him. "Just a second. What's your address?" I told him. "Yeah, and that's a five-five-one-zero-two on the zip code." He glanced at me, and I nodded. "Last four numbers of your social security?" I gave him that. "Yeah, call me with any problem. No, thank you, much appreciated."

He disconnected and said, "Those should be canceled. If we call, they'll get the card numbers and shut them down, send us any recent activity. But let's check to make sure when you get home."

"Thanks again, Aaron. So is there any good news?"

"Oh, yeah. Morton's fine and he didn't shit in the house."

"Thanks for letting him out, Aaron."

"Not a problem."

We chatted on, and Aaron had a little more information on Gerry Berk. He'd be going back to prison if the police got ahold of him before I did. "So knowing that, Dev. Unfortunately, there's a good possibility he may have fled the state. We've sent the BOLO to the Dakotas, Wisconsin, Iowa, and Illinois. I pulled a release photo that was taken less than a year ago, so it's relatively recent. Tell me again how he found you."

"Just bad luck. He was sitting at a bus stop, and I walked by. I didn't recognize him. He's ten years older than when I last saw him. He's put on about a hundred pounds and grown a beard. Unfortunately, he's just as stupid as he was before, maybe even more so. I was sitting in City Salsa House, minding my own business, when he came in looking for trouble. George Estrada and another guy who works there kicked him out. They'll attest to that, and so will the bartender. Her name's Carmen. He was riding the sixty-five bus the other times I saw him. It heads out to Rosedale. I can't believe someone would hire that fat fuck. Last time I saw him, he was wearing camouflage shorts and a t-shirt that didn't cover his big hairy gut. The t-shirt said 'Beer Me' on it."

"Beer Me?"

"Yeah."

"Well, we'll find him sooner or later. Just a reminder, if he's got your wallet, and he's got your address. You want to crash at my place for a couple of days?"

"Oh, thanks, man, but that's not necessary."

"You sure? It's no problem on my end."

"Thanks, Aaron, but I'll be okay."

We chatted for a bit about nothing in particular. Aaron begged off, saying he had to run some errands and reminded me to call him with an update once the doc came by.

Forty-one

The doc came in as I was attempting to eat lunch. Another white bread sandwich, this time with packaged meat and two pickles next to the sandwich. I didn't touch the sandwich and was just finishing up the little dish of green Jell-O with a slice of radish on top, when he strolled in.

"How are we doing today?"

"Feeling pretty good. Ready to go home."

He nodded and said, "Okay, let's see how you do. Can you turn sideways and sit up on the edge of the bed for me, please?"

I pulled the sheet back, moved to the edge of the bed, and hung my legs over the side.

"Good, how's the head?"

"No problem. I've got a lump on the back of my skull, and I definitely know it's there, but it's not throbbing."

"Dizziness?"

"No."

"I want you to stick your arms out to the side. Good. Now close your eyes and touch your nose with your right hand. Okay, and now with the left. Okay," he said and pulled out the flashlight. "Remember this? I want you to follow it around as I move it. Okay, good, and now let's go in this direction. All right, good. Now let's turn it on and see how you do. Okay, good. Good. Have you been out of bed at all?"

"Followed your directions so only to use the bathroom."

"And how did you sleep last night?"

"No problems, in fact, I was sound asleep, slept through the entire night," I said, figuring there was no point in mentioning Kristi's appearance.

"Didn't wake once?"

Now I knew he was searching. "I had a couple of nurses, two women and a guy, come into the room early this morning. I think they must have had the wrong room because they left right away. But until they came in, I didn't wake up once. Slept like a baby."

He nodded like he wasn't sure he believed me then took the best approach for me and the hospital. "Okay, Mr. Haskell, I think you're good enough to go home. I'll leave a list of things you should and should not do for the next week or so. No alcohol is number one, and we'll list some moderate exercises you can do. It's been a pleasure meeting you. Just keep doing what you've been doing yesterday and today, and you'll be as good as new by the end of the week."

"Thanks, doc. So, I can call my pal to come and get me?"

"I'll let the nurses know. There's a brief check out procedure and some paperwork, then call your pal, and you're free to go."

One of the nurses was back in my room five minutes later. She was nice and very pleasant, but once again, I had the feeling she could not wait to see the backside of me. I signed some insurance paperwork, folded the exercise directions a couple of times, and slipped them into my back pocket. Then I sat on the edge of the bed and waited for Aaron to show up.

Forty-two

Aaron arrived about a half-hour later. They wouldn't allow me to walk out. Apparently, it was policy I had to be rolled out of the building in a wheelchair. A nurse pushed me down the hall to the bank of elevators, and we got off on the first floor. She wheeled me outside, where I sat with her standing next to me until Aaron pulled up in his car.

Just before he pulled out of the parking ramp, she leaned toward me and said, "Hopefully, you had an enjoyable stay."

"Oh, yeah. Under the circumstances, very pleasant."

She smiled as Aaron pulled into the round-about in front of the entrance. "So I heard. Okay, well, here's your ride. Have a pleasant rest of the day. It's certainly been interesting, Mr. Haskell," she said.

Aaron hopped out and hurried around to open the passenger door. "Your ride awaits." As I got up and slid into the passenger seat, he called, "Thank you," to the nurse pushing the wheelchair back into the hospital.

"Our pleasure. Definitely one for the books," she said.

Aaron looked at me and said, "What'd she mean by that?"

"You got me. Maybe they don't deal with a lot of concussions on that floor."

It was less than a ten-minute drive to my house. "You sure you don't want to crash at my place?" Aaron said at least three separate times as we headed up the hill and past the Cathedral.

"No, thanks for the offer, but I'll be fine. I plan to just take it easy for the next couple of days." He pulled into my driveway and stepped out of the car. I thought he would just drop me off, but then I remembered I didn't have any house keys. Aaron cut across my front lawn and walked up onto the front porch. Being the proper guy I am, I walked up the front sidewalk. As Aaron opened the front door, Morton met us in the entryway with his tail wagging.

"Hi, Morton. So good to see you, boy. Not to worry, I wasn't going to leave you in Aaron's care for too long. It's good to be home," I said and gave him a long scratch behind the ears. "Aaron, can I talk you into a beer? I'm just gonna have a water."

"Yeah," he said, checking his watch. "I got time for one."

We headed into the kitchen. Nothing seemed out of place in the house, and it didn't look like Gerry Berk had broken in. I grabbed a dog biscuit out of the cookie jar and tossed it Morton's way. It bounced off the wall, and he caught it before it hit the floor. I opened the refrigerator and said, "Aaron, name your poison. I've got a Summit, a Surly, or an Able, all IPA's."

"I'll take the Able," he said.

I pulled out a can, opened the freezer door and took a chilled mug off the door shelf, and handed both of them to Aaron. I reached back in the fridge, pulled out a container of garlic hummus, and set it on the kitchen counter. I took a package of crackers from the cabinet and set them next to the hummus.

"Since when did you become the perfect host?" Aaron said.

"I appreciate all you've done for me, man."

"A ride home from the hospital. It's the least I could do. A lot of nice people are in there either as patients or staff, and I figured it was just my civic duty to get someone like you out of there as fast as possible."

"Yeah, that too. But I meant putting the BOLO out on Gerry Berk. Looking for my car. Getting my credit cards blocked. Feeding Morton. I know how hard you work, and this has screwed up your time off, so, it's very much appreciated." I filled a glass with water and raised it toward him in a toast.

"Forget it. You'd do the same for me. So what was it the nurse was referring to out on the sidewalk when I picked you up?"

"You got me. Yeah, I thought that was a little strange, too."

He studied me for a moment but didn't say anything else. We discussed Gerry Berk for a bit. Aaron was of the opinion that he had probably fled the state, in my car, and that if he had any sense, he would clear the five-state area as soon as possible.

"We couldn't determine any form of employment. Up until a month ago, he was in a halfway house for recently released offenders. We've alerted the family of the young girl."

"Bobby Thompson and his wife?"

"Yeah, he sends his regards, by the way. Say's he still owes you. Anyway, their daughter is out of the country. Over in the UK at the moment, just beginning to earn a master's degree in IT. A squad car is going to drive past their house occasionally and yours too for the next week or so. Just to keep an eye on things."

"Thanks, Aaron, much appreciated." I shook my head. "Should have killed that bastard Berk ten years ago when I had the chance."

"Yeah, there you go. And then I could spend my days off visiting you in Stillwater Prison, and they wouldn't be giving me beer. By the way, I'm almost empty here."

I grabbed another beer from the fridge. Aaron said he didn't need another chilled mug. We chatted on for another half-hour about people we knew as kids, and then he left.

Since I'd been eating at the City Salsa House for the past few days, I didn't have any leftovers to eat. I pulled a chicken breast from the freezer, thawed it in the microwave, and tossed it in the oven.

I went upstairs, took a quick shower then put on a clean pair of jeans and a t-shirt. I stuck my sticky holster in my belt and headed back downstairs. The doctor had said I could take ibuprofen if I felt a headache coming on, but I felt okay and so didn't take any.

I slathered the chicken breast in bar-b-que sauce and ate it while watching a series on Netflix. By ten, I was feeling tired, and after double checking all the windows and doors, placing a chair beneath the doorknob on the backdoor, and setting Aaron's empty beer cans up against the front door, I went upstairs to bed.

Forty-three

I purposely left the bedroom door open when we went to bed. Morton's growling woke me just after three in the morning. He was staring at the open door and not about to get off the bed. My sticky holster was tucked under my pillow, and I immediately grabbed it and pulled out the nine-millimeter. Morton's growl grew a little louder as I walked to the open door and peeked out. There was definitely someone out on the front porch.

When I'd gone up to bed, the porch light had been on. Now it was off. The odds of it burning out on the night I was released from the hospital were pretty much slim to none. Either whoever was out on the porch had broken the bulb, or they had unscrewed it. I closed the bedroom door behind me, went halfway down the staircase, crouched behind the banister, and waited. Light from the streetlight illuminated the entryway slightly, enough that I could make out a figure at the front door. Whoever it was, they were large. For a brief moment, I considered calling 911, but my cellphone was upstairs in my bedroom resting on the nightstand. Besides, it was too late for that. I heard a key being inserted in the lock.

A moment later, there was a click as the door was un-locked.

The door remained closed for what seemed like an eternity. I heard the key being slowly pulled back out of the door lock. I actually heard the doorknob begin to turn and then watched as the door opened no more than an inch. It gradually opened but so slowly that the two beer cans I'd placed in front of it were quietly pushed back rather than clattering onto the wooden floor.

Inch by inch, the door opened, slowly pushing the beer cans across the floor. I heard a soft whine from Morton upstairs in the bedroom. The front door was now three-quarters of the way open, and a large figure stepped inside. It was Gerry Berk, and he'd changed clothes. He was wearing dark pants and a dark, long-sleeve shirt, maybe a sweatshirt. He had a balaclava pulled over his head, but the dumb shit's orange beard stuck out all around the bottom.

He looked into the front room then stared down the hallway to the kitchen for a long moment before he focused his gaze on the top of the staircase. He took a couple of steps and looked around then turned toward the staircase.

That's when I shouted, "Move and you're dead, ass-hole."

I fired as he jumped to the side.

He fired three quick rounds as he backed up and waddled out the front door. I saw the muzzle flashes, but I couldn't tell where the rounds hit. I hurried down the staircase and cautiously glanced out the front window. I saw him for just a second or two as he headed across the street and disappeared into the darkness. I ran out onto the front porch, ready to shoot, and felt sharp stabbing pains in the sole of my barefoot. I hopped back into the house, slammed the door, locked it, and crouched down against the wall.

My foot was killing me. I cautiously felt the ball of my foot and pulled out a piece of glass and then another. No doubt from the light bulb that had been in the front porch light fixture. I peered out the corner of the front window for the next few minutes but didn't see anything that suggested Berk was still around. I hobbled back up to my bedroom, staying off the ball of my left foot. Morton was now under the bed and not about to come out. I grabbed my phone and punched in the three numbers.

"911."

"Yeah, someone just broke into my house. I shot at him, and he shot back. I don't know if he's still outside. I can't see him."

"What's the address?"

"I don't know if he's still out there."

"What's your address, sir?"

I gave him my address.

"Are you injured?"

"He broke the damn light bulb on the front porch, and I've got shards of glass in my foot."

"Were you shot, sir?"

"No, he couldn't aim worth shit. But I don't know if he's still out there."

"I'm dispatching units now. I want you to go back in your house."

"I'm inside now."

"Stay away from the windows and doors. Do not answer the door until the police arrive and knock on the door. Police are on their way."

"Okay."

"I want you to stay on the line with me until they arrive. Can you do that, sir?"

"Yeah, I can, but I'm all right. I can just let them in when they get here."

"I'd like you to stay on the line with me, sir. That way, if the individual is still around, we can communicate this to you, so you remain safe. Will you stay on the line, sir?"

"Yeah, yeah, I can do that."

I hobbled out to the hallway with my nine millimeter and laid down facing the front door with the cellphone in my left hand and the pistol in my right aimed at the front door. The 911 operator continued asking me questions. 'Did I know who the intruder was? How many shots were fired? Had I remained in the house? Was the intruder actually in the house?' And on and on. I knew he was doing his job, and he was good at it, but I just wanted the cops to get there.

It seemed like an hour, but after just a couple of minutes, I heard a distant siren, and maybe a minute later, two squad cars pulled up in front of the house with lights flashing. They aimed one of their spotlights at the front of the house and another alongside the house going up my driveway.

I saw two figures hurry up the driveway. It looked like one of them was carrying a shotgun. Sometime after that, I heard footsteps on the front porch.

"They're on my front porch now," I said.

"Okay, just wait for a moment until they knock before you open the front door," the 911 guy said. No sooner did he say that then there was a knock on the front door, and I could see an officer through the front door window. I laid my pistol on the carpet, got on my feet, and reached back to turn on the light in the entryway. I thanked the 911 guy, told him the cops were at the front door, and he rang off.

Forty-four

When I opened the front door. The officer said, "Mr. Haskell?" I was just wearing jeans, no shirt or shoes. The cop was blonde with a crewcut, maybe six feet tall and solid looking. He wore a protective vest underneath his shirt. Another squad car pulled up in front of my house.

"Yeah, thanks for coming. You guys find anything? I think I shot him. I saw him running across the street." I pointed down the street in the direction Berk had headed.

The cop shook his head. An officer behind him had a flashlight out and was running it back and forth across the porch floor then down the steps and on the sidewalk. "Blood. Looks like he took off this way," he said to three other cops out front. Two more flashlights immediately came on, and they headed down the street.

"Tell them he's armed," I said to the cop at the door.

He nodded and said, "They know. We got the word shots were fired. You injured?"

"No. I cut my foot on some glass out on the front porch. Bastard broke the front porch light so I couldn't see him out there. There's a BOLO out on him. His name is Gerry Berk."

"You got a look at him?"

I nodded and said, "Yeah. He was dressed all in black. Had on a black balaclava, but his orange beard was sticking out beneath it. He's a fat fuck."

"We'll see if we can get him. Let me just give them that general description. You said he has an orange beard?"

"Yeah, red hair. He's fat, and his beard is orange, maybe this long," I said, holding both hands away from my jawline to indicate the length of Berk's beard. "He's armed with a pistol, fired three shots inside. I'm guessing a forty-five, but I can't be sure."

He stepped back and talked into a small microphone attached to his shoulder. A moment later, he got a response that I couldn't understand. I glanced down the street, and the three figures seemed to be gathered around a spot. I could only hope it was Berk's body. Another squad car pulled over to the curb opposite the three cops. The flashing lights were on but no siren. Someone got out on the driver's side and walked over to them.

"Hey, do you want to come in, and I'll put some coffee on?"

He seemed to think about that for a moment then shook his head. "Let me just check out the back again. I'm pretty sure this individual is gone, but let's be sure. If you'll lock the door, please, I'll be back. We'll need to take a statement from you."

"Yeah, sure. Thanks for being here. You guys are great." The emotion of the night suddenly hit me, and I felt like giving him a hug. Speeding over here into God knows what to make sure I was okay, and they didn't even know me. A tear suddenly ran down my cheek.

"Let me check around out back," he said and headed off the porch as another squad car pulled up in front and parked across the street.

I locked the door, went upstairs, slipped on a t-shirt, and gave a quick look at the sole of my left foot, three small bloodied areas. I looked for glass but thankfully didn't find any more. I pulled on a pair of white athletic socks and a pair of shoes and headed downstairs. My left foot was still sore, but the padding of the sock seemed to help. I went into the kitchen, made ten cups of coffee, and looked out the back window. Three flashlights were working their way across the backyard.

There was a knock on the front door about five minutes later. I hurried out to the entryway and opened the door. Three cops were at the door. Two squad cars in front were just pulling away.

"Come on in, guys. Can I get you some coffee? I just put a fresh pot on."

"Yeah, that would be nice," the guy I'd spoken with earlier said.

The cop next to him was the biggest of the three and black. He glanced over my head and said, "Those from your visitor?"

I turned around and looked at three bullet holes in the wall above the staircase. Two of them were maybe a foot apart, and the third one was about ten feet further up the wall. None of them were anywhere near where I had been crouched.

"Did he see you coming down the stairs?" the black cop asked. I noticed he had sergeant stripes on his shirt.

"No. I heard a noise. Actually, my dog heard it and woke me. The lights were off here, and I thought maybe I heard something on the porch, so I was coming down to investigate when I saw him at the front door. I ducked down on the staircase." I pointed to the approximate area where I had crouched down and aimed at Berk.

"He unlocked the door and slowly opened it. I had those beer cans in front of the door." I nodded at the two empty cans still on the floor, close to the entry into my front room. "But he opened the door so slowly that the cans never fell over. Once he stepped inside, I shouted I was going to call the police, and that's when he started shooting. So, I shot back. Once."

"You had a gun? And it sounds like you knew this guy."

"Yeah, I'm licensed to carry. I shot him with a nine-millimeter. This guy attacked me a couple of nights ago, put me in the hospital for two nights with a concussion. He did ten years for attacking a fourteen-year-old girl on a bus, and I was instrumental in getting him sentenced. He got out almost a year ago and was in a halfway house for recently released offenders up until last month. When he attacked me, he stole my keys, my car, and wallet. There's a BOLO out on him."

"Well, if it's any consolation, you hit him. There's a trail of blood leading down the street that disappears. It looks like he climbed into a vehicle and drove off. You remember what the license number is on your vehicle?" the sergeant asked.

"I do. It's a Jeep Cherokee, by the way, dark green." I gave him the license number and said, "How about some coffee, guys? Just made." They nodded and we headed back to the kitchen. The sergeant radioed in that they were in my house.

"So, you said you had a dog?" one of the cops said as I handed him a mug of coffee.

"Yeah, he's probably still upstairs hiding under the bed."

They all laughed, and the sergeant said, "That makes him smarter than the rest of us."

Forty-five

I gave them my statement. I went upstairs and got a Xerox of my Conceal and Carry permit since fat ass Gerry Berk stole my wallet. One of them went out to the squad car and brought up the image of Gerry Berk along with the BOLO information. If there was anything positive about the incident, it was that dumb shit Berk was still in the city, and every cop in the state would be keeping an eye peeled for him. With any luck, we'd be able to move this latest incident to attempted murder, and he'd be off the streets and locked up for good the moment they found him. The cops did another walk through the bushes out back before they headed out to their next call.

Someone pounded on my door a little after nine. I was on my computer in the kitchen with my sticky holster tucked into my belt. Morton was out in the backyard. I pulled out the nine-millimeter, and rather than walk directly to the front door, I went through the dining room then peeked out the window in the front room just as whoever it was pounded on the door again.

Aaron was standing at the door with his cellphone out. I tucked the pistol back into the holster in my belt and pulled my shirt over it. As I stepped into the entry-way and opened the front door, my cellphone rang.

"Don't answer that, it's me," Aaron said and turned off his phone.

He stepped inside and glanced at the wall along the staircase. "Yeah, heard you had an interesting night."

"Thank God for your guys. They were here and checked things out. Made sure Berk was nowhere around. Nice bunch of guys."

"Yeah, you met Benson?"

"The sergeant? Yeah. Nice guy."

Aaron nodded. "Yeah, he runs a tight ship. We're blessed to have him on the force. So tell me about it. You're convinced it was Gerry Berk."

"Yeah, it was him. He was wearing a balaclava, but his orange beard was hanging out on all sides, plus he was a fat ass. As if that isn't enough, thankfully, he was a lousy shot. I was behind the banister down there." I said and pointed to the lower portion of the staircase. "He had no idea where I was and fired three rounds up there."

Aaron stepped over to the staircase and looked up at the three bullet holes in the wall.

"You said he was firing a forty-five?"

"Yeah, at least, that was my guess, but I can't be absolutely sure."

"And you shot him."

"I fired once, and he ran out the door. I aimed for body mass and think I hit him. There's a trail of blood on my front porch and the sidewalk. The guys here earlier said it stopped down the street, and he probably climbed into a car and drove off. I only wish I would have killed him."

"Well, he's stupid enough not to have left town. We'll see how long he's out there before we spot him. If he tries to go to any of the ERs we'll get him. Where's your gun now?"

I patted my waist. "Can I talk you into a coffee?"

Aaron glanced at his watch and said, "Yeah, don't mind if I do."

We'd been talking for fifteen minutes. Me telling Aaron about Berk's visit. Aaron telling me that, basically, they hadn't gotten a report on Berk's whereabouts. They were checking all the hospitals and clinics, which was standard procedure.

"I don't know, Aaron. I can only hope he's hiding out in some rat-infested cave or out in the woods somewhere, and the wolves will get him. I figure three or maybe four days from now, with any luck the infection will start to take hold and save everyone the time and money it would take to send him back to jail."

Aaron's phone rang. He pulled it out, looked at it, and took the call. "LaZelle. Oh. Really? When? Hum, interesting. No. I'm at the victim's home now doing a follow-up. Yeah, shouldn't take more than fifteen minutes. See you shortly." He hung up and looked at me. "They got him."

"Berk? They got the bastard?"

"Yeah, and your car. You want to come along?"

"I wouldn't miss it. Let me just get Morton inside." I hurried over to the backdoor and called Morton. He'd been lying in the shade working on a stick for the last forty-five minutes. He gave me a look then glanced at the stick, trying to decide which of us was the better option.

"Treat," I said. "Come on in, Morton, treat." That seemed to settle things, and he got up and hurried inside. I tossed him a biscuit from the cookie jar. He caught it in midair then hurried to a corner so he wouldn't have to share with us.

Forty-six

I closed the passenger door and buckled the seatbelt as Aaron sped away from the curb." Where the hell did they find him? Some sleaze ball motel over in Minneapolis?"

"No, the stupid idiot was still in town, actually not too far from here," Aaron said.

"Was he hiding in someone's bushes? I thought they said it looked like he got in a car and drove away."

"Yeah, apparently, that's exactly what he did. He's parked down by the old power plant along the river."

"The old power plant? Down there on Shepard Road?"

"Yeah, not too far from the Upper Landing apartments."

The Upper Landing apartments. Where Kristi's unit was on Mill Street looking out over the river. I suddenly thought of the night when she answered the door wearing that Vikings jersey and a smile. She was all ready for a hot night, but then…oh yeah—that night.

"What's wrong?"

"Oh, nothing. Nothing at all, I was just thinking. Wondering what he was doing down there."

"Who knows? Maybe he wanted to see the sunrise on the water. Maybe he was thinking of doing some fishing. Maybe he decided to be a responsible citizen and was just waiting to turn himself in."

"Yeah, right. Don't hold your breath. Have they arrested him yet?"

Aaron looked at me like I was nuts. "Arrest him? Dev, he's dead."

"Well, why the hell didn't you tell me that? I thought this was some big standoff or something."

"I'll just attribute that to the blow to your head a couple of days ago."

"You never told me he was dead, Aaron."

"You think I'd bring you with me to some ongoing situation? God, that's the last thing we'd need." We drove past the Ramsey house and turned onto Eagle Parkway. We took a right at the light, just across from Kristi's apartment, and we headed up Shepard Road. I decided I wouldn't mention Kristi's place to Aaron just now. About a quarter-mile beyond the dog park at the apartment complex, Aaron took a left and drove around a highway sign that said, 'Road Closed Do Not Enter.' I counted nine squad cars, a BCA van, and a paramedic ambulance. The rear doors to the ambulance were open.

Aaron pulled up, over the curb, parked on the grassy boulevard, and we got out. The paramedics, there were three, two guys and a woman, were all standing around the gurney talking to a couple of cops. A black body bag, minus a body, was laid out on the gurney. No one seemed to be in a hurry.

I saw my car parked about twenty-five feet beyond, at the end of the road. The area was cordoned off with black and yellow tape stretched across the road. The tape read, "POLICE LINE DO NOT CROSS." Two guys in white hazmat suits were standing around my car. One was taking photographs, and the other was dusting the door handle on the driver's side with a brush. No doubt looking for fingerprints.

I looked around but didn't see any of the officers from earlier this morning at my house. They were all third shift and probably home heading for bed right about now. We walked over to two cops, and Aaron struck up a conversation.

One of the cops said, "Some early morning jogger reported it just a little after six. He'd gone past the car maybe a half-hour before heading downriver, and then on the way back home, he decided to take a closer look. He got close enough to see the body in the driver's seat and put in a call. He just left about thirty minutes ago. There was a BOLO out on this perp and the vehicle."

"Yeah, I know. I put it out there," Aaron said. "Any idea when these BCA guys are going to be finished?"

"Shouldn't be too long. They've been here for a couple of hours."

"Well, I got a guy with me who can give a positive ID. Give me a yell when the paramedics head down there to remove the body. I'll talk to them too, but we can wrap this up pretty fast once the BCA is finished."

"You got it, L.T."

Forty-seven

It wasn't thirty minutes later when the BCA team headed back to their van. One of them was carrying a cardboard box with evidence bags. Aaron headed over to the van, and I followed.

"Hey L.T., how's it going? Looks like they found your man," the BCA guy said.

"Yeah, that was fast. I guess an early morning jogger found him and called it in. What'd you see?"

I'd met the guy before but couldn't remember his name. Jim or Jack, something like that. He sat down on the front bumper of the vehicle and pulled off the white shoe booties then stood. He dropped his latex gloves on top of the shoe covers and pulled open the Velcro on the upper portion of the hazmat suit and stepped out of it. He placed it all in what looked like a laundry basket resting on the running board that led up to the driver's seat.

"Didn't see an awful lot. A wound on the right side of his skull that pretty much blew half his face away. Everything splattered across the windows and dash. If I had to guess, I'd say a hollow point. We may know more after the autopsy. There's a good deal of blood on the seat and console. The blood looks to have happened before the shot to the head. If I had to guess, I'd say three to five hours before. We found two shell casings from a forty-five. One in the front passenger seat, another outside, just under the vehicle."

"Did he take his own life?" Aaron asked.

The BCA guy shook his head. "No. No weapon at the scene. One of the .45 shots was up close, within six inches to the right side of his head. The other one was from a slightly greater distance, four to five feet. Tough to say which one was first. Either one would have killed him. Whoever fired the forty-five wanted to be sure he was dead."

"Any identification?" Aaron asked.

"We found a wallet in the console. It matches the vehicle registration we found in the glove compartment, but neither one matched the individual in the BOLO that's out there."

"Yeah. I think you've met Dev Haskell before," Aaron said and turned toward me. I took a step closer and held out my hand. Aaron said, "Dev, you remember Jamie Solvick."

"Yeah, we've met before Jamie. The individual is named Gerry Berk." I spelled it out for Solvick. "He broke into my house this morning around three a.m. I shot him in the side with a nine millimeter, and he ran out of the house. He assaulted me a few nights back, stole my wallet and car."

"Put him in the hospital for two nights with a concussion," Aaron added.

"Sounds like a charming individual," Solvick said.

Aaron shook his head. "Not much of a loss to society. He did ten years for a sexual assault on a young girl. Hasn't been out for more than ten or eleven months."

Solvick shook his head and looked at Aaron. "We've got the wallet and the car title logged in as evidence. We'll have to hang onto them for a bit, but you could at least set the paperwork in motion. I'm afraid that car is going to need a good deal of work. A lot of blood. The driver's window and windshield will have to be replaced. What's the year, a twenty-fourteen?"

"Close, a twenty-twelve, actually."

"Mmm, you could certainly get it listed as totaled. The blood will never get completely cleaned out of it. I might know of someone selling a Dodge Charger, black. I think it's a twenty-fifteen. Fella like you, the ladies would go for it."

"It'll take more than a nice car to get the women interested in him, Jamie. Hey, paramedics are loading the body on the gurney. We want to make a positive ID. Thanks for your help. Come on, Dev," Aaron said and hurried down to my car.

"Thanks, Jamie. I'll keep that Charger in mind. Take care."

"Aaron's got my number," he called as I hurried to catch up with Aaron.

"I got someone here who can make a positive ID," Aaron said, just as the paramedics were zipping up the bodybag. Even though I knew it was Gerry Berk in the bodybag, I was amazed at how stuffed the bag looked.

I'm sure the paramedics all had sore backs after pulling Berk's dead weight out from behind the wheel and onto the gurney.

"That would save us some time. I should warn you, though, he ain't too pretty," one of the paramedics said.

"He wasn't very pretty before someone shot him," I replied.

He flashed a quick smile and unzipped the bag down to about Berk's chest then carefully inserted his gloved hands and spread the unzipped area open. I looked in and about the only area recognizable was the orange beard, which was largely intact. The head, or what was left of it, rested at an angle. The right eye, the nose, the cheekbone and half of the mouth, basically the right side of his face, was gone. In its place was what looked like a raw, red stew of muscle and brain matter. The remainder of the lips were wavy looking, an impossible position in real life. Berk's head reminded me of some of the things we saw in Iraq.

I nodded at the paramedic and said, "Yeah, that is, or was, Gerry Berk."

He pulled out a pen and grabbed a tag attached to the body bag.

"Gerry Berk," I said and then spelled out the name for him. As they rolled the gurney away, I walked over to the passenger door on my car and peered in. There was a hole in the driver's window the size of my fist and another one in the lower left-hand corner of the windshield. Both the window and the windshield had a large spider web pattern around the holes. Jamie Solvick wasn't kidding. Blood and tissue were all over the place, splattered on the driver's side and across the steering wheel and the dashboard. The car was totaled. Thank goodness.

I looked around outside the vehicle while Aaron examined the interior. There was what looked like a recent path through the grass and weeds heading toward the dog park and the Upper Landing apartment complex where Kristi lived.

Forty-eight

ventually, we climbed back into Aaron's car, and he drove me home. As he turned at the Cathedral, he said, "You're awfully quiet, Dev. That certainly wasn't a pretty sight."

"You kidding? Berk getting what little brains he had blown out. I think it's the best possible ending before he tried to hurt someone else, and he definitely would. It's in his DNA. He was simply an awful person, and ten years behind bars just made him that much worse. No, I'm just surprised he even had any brains to blow out."

He shot me a quick look but didn't say anything else until we pulled up in front of my place.

"Aaron, thanks for the ride, thanks for taking me down there, and thanks for all your help. Really, I appreciate it."

"I'm glad things turned out okay for you, Dev. Now we can all move onto the next crazy thing you do."

"I promise to behave," I said and held out my hand. We shook, and I slid out of the passenger seat. Aaron watched me as I climbed up the front steps, and once I unlocked the front door, he drove off. I noticed the glass from the front porch lightbulb still scattered across the porch, now highlighted by a trail of blood drops across the porch floor, down the front steps, and leading out to the street.

I went inside, and Morton greeted me. Surprisingly, there wasn't the usual mess in the kitchen. I let him out the back door, grabbed a dustpan and brush, and headed back out to the front porch. I swept up the bits of glass, then ran the garden hose across the dried blood. The hose seemed to have a modest effect.

I was sitting at the kitchen counter, thinking about Gerry Berk and where his body was found. Not a half-mile from the Upper Landing apartment complex where Kristi lived. I wondered about the little trail through the grass and weeds no one seemed to notice. It led from the edge of the road where Berk was shot down toward the dog park and the Upper Landing apartment complex. And then, last but not least, I thought about the .45 I'd seen in the drawer beneath the naked painting of Kristi. Did any of it make any sense?

Forty-nine

y phone rang in the middle of the afternoon. I'd been up ever since Berk's visit in the middle of the night, and I'd drifted off to sleep in front of the TV. "Haskell Investigations."

"Oh, Dev, hi. It's Diane. Are you okay to talk?" She almost sounded surprised that I had answered.

"Hi Diane, how are you doing?"

"More importantly, how are you doing? Umm, haven't heard from you for a few days. Has anything developed with your missing artists' investigations?"

"Well, yes and no. Bottom line is, I haven't found out anything that you probably didn't already know. All three men have basically disappeared without a trace, no sign of any violence. I was up in Itasca County and spoke with two deputies. Both were aware of Oscar Callum missing, but they were under the impression that he probably went for a hike in the woods and suffered a heart attack or something out in the wilderness."

"But no suspicions of someone breaking in or foul play or anything like that?"

"No. According to them, there was no indication of anything suspicious. I looked around the place. I was probably the first person to drive down the trail to his house in almost a year. The area was overgrown with weeds, no tire tracks. It's where I talked to the deputies."

"As far as Myles Rossler goes, I met his neighbors over there in Stillwater and had a long chat with them. Nice folks, they miss him, said he was a great neighbor. In fact, they're cutting his grass every month, kind of keeping up the place. Just like the Callum situation, no sign of foul play or violence. He's just up and disappeared."

"And the same with Chandler Hancock?"

"Yeah. I've been in his office, went through his files. Nothing. He had two unfinished works in his studio. Was it you or his wife who told me he finished most of his paintings in one day, trying to be like Vincent Van Gogh?"

"I mentioned that to you when we were viewing his painting, 'Season Opener,' in the viewing booth. Remember? The beautiful lake scene. I'm not sure his wife, or live in, whatever she is, I'm not sure she would even know he completed a good portion of his work in one day." I made a mental note that Diane didn't seem to be a very big Kristi fan.

"About all she told me was that he was always painting. When she woke up in the morning, he was already working in the studio, and it wasn't uncommon for him to be painting when she went to bed."

"As successful as he was, or is, I don't think she's ever understood him. Anything on Malcolm Webster?" she asked, moving away from the subject of Kristi.

"To be honest, no, I haven't really looked into him. I know Chandler Hancock viewed him as somewhat of a mentor. One of Webster's paintings hangs over the fireplace in their apartment. I've seen it. It's very nice. In fact, when I looked Chandler up online, there was a picture of him with that painting in the background. His wife told me that Webster painted it especially for Chandler. She also said she didn't like the painting, but Chandler loved it and could talk for hours about the technique and everything."

"She's out of her element. The few dealings I've had with her, I always viewed her as somewhat jealous of Chandler's notoriety."

"You mean because he was famous?"

"Well, maybe. I'm not quite sure. I know she was involved in the whole beauty pageant world. But you know, in the last few years, that stuff has gone on the outs with a lot of people. It's certainly less popular today than even just a little while ago. I know she was successful and, apparently won a number of pageants. She was Miss so and so, I mean, name the small-town event, and she was probably there competing and oftentimes winning. Strange, she never really transferred that into the business of fashion modeling. You'd think she'd be a natural."

"Yeah," I said. "I've been in their apartment a couple of times. Very few of Chandler's paintings were on display. In fact, now that I think of it, none of Chandler's paintings were hanging anywhere. But if there's one, there's at least a dozen framed photos of Kristi McKenzie from various beauty pageants. I remember when she was homecoming queen at my high school, she even had a framed picture of that."

"Yeah, she was quite the looker, but you know how that can go. Maybe she still thinks she's seventeen and homecoming queen. Anyway, Dev, I would encourage you to check into Malcolm Webster, and hopefully, you could get the authorities involved. Either that or get the news media interested. Don't you think they'd love a story about missing artists? Anything to stop having to listen to the insanity coming out of Washington."

"I'll look into it, Diane. Nice to talk with you. If I come across anything, I'll let you know."

"Thank you, and let's get together sooner rather than later. If I don't hear from you, I'm going to instigate a call."

"I would love it. Talk to you soon."

Fifty

I was convinced I'd picked up some friction between Diane and Kristi. Certainly, Kristi wasn't a fan of Diane's, but maybe that was just the hassle of business dealings. Chandler brings a painting to Diane, and it basically is at the gallery on consignment. It could end up being months or even years before it sells. And all that time, as far as I knew, Chandler wasn't paid anything. The flip side of that was no one was going to buy the painting if they didn't know about it, and what better way to inform folks than to have the gallery feature your work for a couple of months. Doing business with three or four galleries, you could have your work in front of folks all year round.

I guess that was the business but a tough way to make a living. No wonder he cranked out a painting in a day. The more out there, the better the odds of selling. I wondered if the income Chandler and Kristi lived off of was financed by the life insurance payment from the death of her fiancé, Joseph Lauer.

I decided to Googled Malcolm Webster. He was older than the other three, almost twice as old as Chandler. Malcolm Webster was last seen two and a half years ago. He lived in Taylor Falls. A small town on the St.

Croix River about forty miles from the city. There was a picture of him sitting in a rocking chair on the front porch of what looked like an old farmhouse. The way it looked, the photo online could have been taken in 1900. But maybe that was all staged.

Forty miles away. It wasn't like I could walk there, so I phoned Louie.

"Where the hell have you been? Is everything all right?" was how he answered.

I felt like it had been a year since Gerry Berk attacked me and put me in the hospital. God, it wasn't even a week. I brought Louie up to date.

"Oh man, a call would have been nice, dude. You okay?"

"I'm surviving. I would have called, but to tell you the truth, I was either asleep or pretty much out of it. Aaron dropped me off at home yesterday after I was released, and dumbass Berk decided last night would be the best time to break in here."

"A break-in? You okay?"

"As okay as I can be. The headache is gone. The memory is pretty much back. I still have the lump on the back of my head, but that's gone down. I can feel the difference. The good news is, Berk is out of the picture. Dead."

"Anything I can do to help?"

"As a matter of fact, there is. Two things, first, I was wondering if I might be able to borrow your car tomorrow. I want to drive up to Taylors Falls and check out another artist who lived up there and disappeared a couple of years ago."

"That'll work. I don't have a court appearance tomorrow. I was planning to be down here in the office, working. So yeah, go ahead and use it all day."

"Okay, thanks, I'll gas it up for you."

"Works for me. You said there were two things?"

"Yeah, you doing anything for dinner tonight?"

"You kidding? Hell no. Surprise, surprise, I got nothing planned. You want to grab something somewhere?"

"Tell you the truth, I was thinking I might talk you into picking up something and bringing it over here. I'm out of just about everything, and I don't have a set of wheels to get to the store."

"Leave it to me," Louie said. "You on any kind of a schedule?"

"No, not really. I got a phone call that woke me a while ago. I was thinking I might close my eyes again and rest up. Still a little tired."

"An intruder breaking in to kill you, yeah, I guess it's all right if you try to get some sleep. Tell you what, I'll give you a call before I head over. If everything stays quiet on this end, it'll probably be around five-thirty. You can give me an update, then."

"Thanks, Louie, I appreciate the help."

"I'm just glad you're okay, Dev. To be honest, I was beginning to worry."

"See you tonight," I said, and we disconnected.

The more I thought about using Louie's car, the less I liked the idea. First of all, I didn't want to inconvenience him, and second, he drove a piece of shit 2008 Saturn Astra. Originally red, the thing had faded closer to a pink color, and then it had been the unwitting victim of Louie's lack of attention. I wasn't sure it could even make it forty miles, let alone get me back into town without stalling on the side of the road or simply blowing up.

It had been a number of years, and I wasn't even sure the phone number still worked, or even if he was alive, but I did a search on my cellphone contact list for Walter at the Trend Bar. Amazingly, he answered just before I was going to be dumped into voice mail.

Fifty-one

Walter may have answered the phone, but that didn't mean he had to say anything. As always, there was a long moment while I listened to the background noise in the bar. As far as I knew, he didn't own The Trend, although it wouldn't surprise me if he did. He eternally sat at the end of the bar, with a constant cigarette going despite the no-smoking laws. He dealt in everything from jewelry, to cars, to things it was just better I knew nothing about. We'd always gotten along well. I just hadn't needed his services over the last couple of years.

I finally broke the phone silence. "Hello, Walter. A voice from the past, Dev Haskell."

There was a chuckle on the other end of the line. Then it sounded like he took a long drag off his cigarette and said, "Well, Dev Haskell. Been a long time."

I remembered Walter's voice as being deep, even though he had always been soft-spoken. This afternoon it was raspy, and after he finished his greeting, he barked out a cough.

"It's been too long, Walter. I'm calling to see if you might be able to help me out."

"This have anything to do with the activity at your place last night?"

Amazing. There had been nothing on the news I was aware of. No reporter had called me. But here was Walter, not even twelve hours later. He probably knew more about the incident than I did.

"Oh, in a roundabout way, yeah, it does. My car's been impounded. It's basically totaled, anyway. So, I'm wondering if you might be able to help me out with a set of wheels? Sorry for the short notice."

"You looking for something new?"

"Let's just say, new to me."

"Anything's possible. You want anything special?"

"Not particularly. Nothing too old. In reasonably good shape. If it didn't look like I was trying to sell illegal items out of the back seat, that would be a plus."

"I might be able to put something together. What timeframe are you looking at?"

"Sooner, the better. Would later tonight or tomorrow morning be possible?"

"I wouldn't be able," he barked another cough. "Wouldn't be able to do tonight. Might be tomorrow morning could work. Why don't you give me a call first thing."

"First thing. You mean about ten?"

"Dev, you should know better than that. I never sleep."

"Okay, I'll talk to you tomorrow morning. Good to hear your voice, Walter."

"You're still a lousy liar, Dev, but nice to chat. Talk tomorrow," he said and hung up.

I crashed on the couch with Morton on the floor next to me. My phone ringing with Louie's call woke me. I checked the time when I answered. It was after five.

"Hey, Louie, you on your way?"

"Just about to head out of the office. I'll stop at the grocery store and then swing by. Shouldn't be more than forty-five minutes. You got some whiskey there?"

"I do, but I won't be having any. You're more than welcome to help yourself."

"See you when I see you," Louie said and hung up.

He pulled the Astra in front of my place about an hour later and hopped out of the car carrying a grocery bag. It didn't look all that full, which was just fine. I figured he probably picked up a couple of meals to go. I opened the front door as he stepped up onto the porch. If he noticed the trail of blood across the porch and heading down the sidewalk, he didn't say anything.

"Come on in, Louie. Great to see you, and thanks for doing this."

"Glad to help out. Oh, so what the hell? The bastard saw you standing there and fired off a couple of rounds?" he said, walking over to the staircase, looking up, and examining the three bullet holes Berk had left.

I made a mental note to deal with those sooner rather than later. "Well, half-right, I wasn't standing there, and it was dark, but yeah, that was his signature before he ran out the door and disappeared. Good riddance."

"Ahh, the world's a slightly better place without him. Hey, let's go back to the kitchen. I'm gonna make us dinner," he said and held up the grocery bag.

"You don't have to do that, Louie. God, you've done enough just bringing the stuff over. I can cook dinner."

"Not a bother, it'll be a breeze." I followed him into the kitchen. He set the grocery bag on the counter and pulled out a loaf of white bread and a carton of processed cheese. "Grilled cheese sound okay to you?" he asked as he pulled a frying pan out of the drawer beneath the stove.

"It sounds great," I said.

Louie fried up four grilled cheese sandwiches for us. One for me and three for him. Actually, that worked out just fine. I wasn't that hungry, and besides, I'd gorged on lime-flavored tostada chips and salsa while we chatted, and Louie brought me up to date on the current courthouse gossip. I really didn't want to talk about Berk, and Louie steered clear of the subject.

I had placed a whiskey bottle on the counter, and Louie had finished two glasses in the time it took him to fry up the grilled cheese. He cut the sandwiches in half, set them on a plate on the kitchen counter, put an empty plate in front of me and another in front of the stool at the end of the counter. Once he had everything arranged, he poured himself another whiskey and sat down.

I took a bite, and it was just what the Dr. ordered, delicious. I had a puddle of Catsup on my plate and ran the sandwich through the puddle before every bite. Louie inhaled his three sandwiches in the time it took me to finish my one. We chatted on for a few more hours. Louie drained my bottle of Jameson and then cracked the seal on my bottle of Jameson Distiller's Safe, the good stuff. He was way past the point of being able to tell the difference, and it was too late to mention it.

I was still exhausted, even after two naps, and went up to bed around eleven. Louie poured himself one more.

Fifty-two

I came downstairs just before seven. Louie was still in his suit, snoring on the couch in the front room. An image of the Big Lebowski was frozen on the TV screen. I turned off the TV and went into the kitchen. I set the coffee pot for eight cups, figuring Louie would need more than one or two. I tossed his whiskey glass in the dishwasher then went online. I did a search and came up with an address for Malcolm Webster in Taylors Falls. I clicked on Google Maps, and the site brought up an image of the house I'd seen in the photo with Webster sitting on the front porch. A farmhouse with white clapboard siding and white trim. Two large elm trees, looking at least a hundred years old, shaded the front yard.

Maybe forty-five minutes later, I heard Morton coming down the stairs. He took a detour into the front room and checked out our guest in the wrinkled suit asleep on the couch before he headed into the kitchen. I gave him the perfunctory head scratch and let him outside. I checked the directions leading up to the Webster house and then took a deep breath and dialed a phone number.

Once again, it rang five or six times before he answered and then nothing, well, except for the soft music in the background. I knew The Trend opened at 6:30 or 7:00. A holdover from forty years ago when there used to be a factory a block away and the third shift folks lined up every morning after work.

"Hi, Walter. How are you this morning?"

"Couldn't be better, Dev," he said and then barked a cough that questioned his response.

"Just checking in to see if you had any luck finding a vehicle. Sorry for such a short notice."

"It's part of the business, Dev. Fortunately, I've been able to find just the thing for you."

This was how it usually went. One could only imagine what 'just the thing' entailed, not that I was in a position to argue. It was always a no questions asked, cash deal. The idea of a title transfer never entered the picture in transactions with Walter.

"Sounds great, do you have it now?"

"In the usual place. If you'd like to come over, oh say in an hour or so, we can complete the transaction. Cost will be a deuce, the usual stipulations."

The next hour or so. I always figured that meant there was someone busily wiping down any fingerprints and making sure the body in the trunk had been removed. A deuce meant the price was two grand, a real bargain. Then, of course, there were the usual stipulations, which boiled down to no questions asked.

"Thank you, Walter. I'll be by this morning."

As he hung up, I heard Louie out in the front room, groaning. After a bit, he rolled off the couch and headed upstairs to the bathroom. Morton barked at the back door, and I let him in. He headed straight for his food dish and inhaled it in just a couple of minutes. I set a glass of water and the aspirin bottle on the kitchen counter and waited for Louie to come back downstairs.

He arrived twenty minutes later. At no surprise, his grey suit betrayed the fact that he'd slept in it. Actually, it looked like he may have slept in it for the past three or four days. His tie was loosened and hung off to the side, and the tail of his shirt partially hung out in the back. He didn't say 'Good Morning' or even give me a nod. He shook four aspirin into his hand, tossed them in his mouth, and washed them down with a gulp or two of water and a grimace.

"Can I get you a coffee, Louie?"

He simply nodded. I poured him a mug and set it on the counter. He took a seat on a kitchen stool and grimaced again as a mouthful of coffee went down.

"How'd you sleep?"

I got a brief nod in response.

"Hey, thanks for offering me the use of your car. But I don't want to put you out. If you can just drop me off at The Trend, Walter told me he's got a vehicle."

Louie looked up at me and took a moment to focus. "Walter, that gangster guy?"

"Mmm-mmm, that might be a little harsh. But yeah. Don't worry. You don't have to see him. You won't have to go into The Trend. All you have to do is drop me off.

Oh, well, and if you could take Morton down to the office, that'd be great. I'll probably be down there about fifteen or twenty minutes later."

"Yeah, as long as you make it out of there alive. I suppose this is another one of his no questions asked deals."

"You know the drill. All his deals are like that."

Louie took another swallow of coffee, smacked his lips, and said. "You got any jelly? Some toast and jelly might just hit the spot."

Fifty-three

Since Louie cooked dinner last night, I made breakfast. Toast with grape jelly for Louie, and I kept the coffee coming. He ate a half-dozen pieces of toast with enough grape jelly on each piece to feed a cub scout pack. On about the fourth piece, a large glob of jelly fell off the toast, tumbled across the lapel of his wrinkled suit coat, and dripped onto his tie. Louie smeared it across his formerly white shirt in an effort to get it off his tie. He had two more cups of coffee before we headed out to his car.

"Why don't I drive?" I said, figuring his blood alcohol content was still well beyond the legal limit. He nodded and walked around to the driver's side as Morton hopped into the back seat and settled on top of the trash and litter spread across the seat and the area where you used to be able to put your feet. Apparently, Louie didn't hear me, so I said a little more forcefully, "Louie, I'll drive. Get in on the other side."

"Yeah, I know. I heard you the first time, but the door doesn't open on that side, so I have to climb in on the driver's side." He slid into the driver's seat then groaned, swore, wiggled, and finally made it over the console and settled into the passenger side. I climbed in after him.

"You got the car keys?"

"Oh, God. Yeah, hang on." He stretched out and searched both front pockets and came up empty-handed then reached into his coat pocket, smiled, and said, "Found them." He handed me the keys, and the car started on the third try.

I looked at the gas gauge. The needle hung below the empty mark. "You want me to put some gas in? Looks like you're running on fumes."

"Nah, ignore that shit. Thing's broken, been meaning to get it fixed for a year. I just filled the tank a couple of days ago."

"You sure? I could—"

"Just drive, Dev, so I can get to the office and close my eyes. My head's killing me."

So much for my supply of whiskey. I drove to my bank, left Louie and Morton in the car while I withdrew two grand in hundred dollar bills. It was a ten-minute drive from the bank over to The Trend bar. I could have taken the freeway, probably cut the time in half, but didn't want to take the risk in Louie's car. I pulled to the curb around the corner from The Trend.

"Thanks, Louie, I should be down to the office in the next half-hour or so. I'll see you there." I turned the car off and left the keys in the ignition. As I walked around the corner to the front door, I glanced back at Louie's Astra. The car was rocking from side to side as

Louie crawled back over the console and into the driver's seat. God help poor Morton.

I opened the door and stepped into The Trend. A younger guy drifted off a stool just inside the door and said, "Morning. Arms out, just need to do a quick search." He ran a wand over me, searching for metal objects, specifically a knife or a gun. Fortunately, I'd remembered the routine and left my sticky holster at home. "Okay, good to go, have a nice morning," the guy said, and I stepped into the barroom.

At just a little after ten in the morning, there were probably fifteen people seated at the bar. I picked up a number of surly looks from various guys who knew I wasn't a regular. The three women smiled, and two of them raised their eyebrows and nodded. Working girls.

Down at the far end of the bar, seated in a cloud of smoke, sat Walter. Two thugs sat about three stools away from him, so he could conduct business without any interruption. Their sole purpose in life was to keep curious people away from Walter.

I headed down the bar in their direction. About halfway down, a burly jerk put his hand out and grabbed my shirt. "Where you think you're going, boy?"

"Let him pass," one of the thugs guarding Walter said.

He slowly released his grip on my shirt and half-whispered, "Maybe later."

I was going to reply but thought better of it and headed toward Walter. I hadn't seen the two thugs before. Last time I went through this, a guy named Lamar had patted me down, but that was a few years back, and I didn't see him today. He'd always been nice to me, so hopefully, things were going well for him, and he wasn't behind bars.

"Need you to assume the position," one of the thugs said as he and his pal got off their stools. I leaned spread-eagle against the wall while he patted me down. His pal stood a few feet away, casually watching me with his hands behind his back, no doubt a gun in one of his hands.

"Okay," the guy who patted me down said and gave a nod to Walter.

Walter cleared his throat, took a drag on his cigarette, and said, "Well, Dev Haskell, as I live and breathe. I'll be damned."

He looked old. The twinkle was gone from his eyes. His hair had greyed and thinned, and he'd lost weight, a lot of weight. The muscular man I remembered from some years back looked fragile. His arms were thin, his shoulders looked bony, and his face was drawn.

"Good to see you, Walter. You're looking good," I said, and extended my hand.

"And you're a liar," he said and didn't laugh. He shook my hand, but his grip wasn't strong, and I thought I picked up the hint of a slight tremor in his hand.

"Appreciate you helping me out, Walter. I can always count on you."

He coughed a couple of times before he said, "Be two big ones, and your ride is out in the lot across the street." Apparently, he was not in the mood for conversation.

I pulled the bank envelope out of my back pocket and handed it to him. He tossed it down the bar to the two thugs. One of them opened it and quickly counted the twenty hundred dollar bills. He looked up at Walter and gave him a nod.

Walter smiled, and for just a moment, the twinkle was back in his eye. He handed me a car key and said. "Over in the lot across the street. It's green, with Tennessee plates and a special interior."

Fifty-four

I walked past the car twice. I checked out a green SUV and a Cadillac CTS before I remembered Walter's line about the Tennessee plates. Odds were it was the only car in the lot with Tennessee plates, and it was an awfully large lot. I walked around with the key for another five minutes pressing the fob and looking for flashing lights. I eventually found the thing in a distant corner. At least the Tennessee plates looked current with the proper year sticker in the upper right-hand corner. The county name, Shelby, was centered along the bottom of the license plate.

I'd walked past the thing twice because a Volkswagen Golf was not the usual type of vehicle Walter dealt in. But then again, my original call was little more than twelve hours ago, and beggars can't be choosers. The wheel rims were chrome five-pointed stars that looked like a sheriff's badge. The car was green all right, but it wasn't painted. It was more like a velvet cloth finish. I ran my hand over the edge of the roof and then actually pinched a little of it between my thumb and forefinger. Okay, not great, but from a distance of ten feet, it just looked like a dull paint job, and that was passable.

The interior was a different issue altogether. Bright orange shag carpeting covered all the seats. Really? The stuff was about three inches long and covered the two front seats and the back seat.

I checked, hoping it was maybe just a slip-on seat cover. No such luck, the seats were completely reupholstered with the stuff. But what could I do? It's not like I could ask Walter for my money back. Well, actually I could, but he wasn't about to give me the two grand back. I unlocked the driver's door and slid in behind the steering wheel. The wheel was about a half-inch from my chest, and I reached around for a bit, looking for the handle that allowed me to adjust the seat. I finally found it and pushed the seat back.

At least the car started on the first try. I adjusted the mirrors and buckled the leopard skin seatbelt. The mileage was a hundred and five thousand, and the gas tank was half-full. I backed out of the parking space then drove through the lot in the direction of Hamline Ave.

At the corner, I waited for two high school girls to slowly cross in front of me. They were both texting on their cellphones, and then, to make matters worse, they stopped directly in front of my car so they could show one another some image on their phones. That did it. I hit the horn. Of course, the horn played a quick couple of bars of Dixie. Both kids gave me a creepy look and hurried onto the sidewalk. I drove down to Randolph Avenue, took a left, and a mile-and-a-half later pulled in front of my office.

I opened the door to the office and said, "Hey, sorry it took—" Louie was leaning back in his desk chair with his shoes off and his feet up on the picnic table. The big toe on his right foot was hanging out of a hole in his sock. He was sound asleep and snoring. His suit coat with the jelly stain on the lapel was draped across my desk. Morton was lying on his bed with his paws placed over his ears.

"Come on, Morton," I whispered. He didn't have to be told twice. He hurried out of the office. I closed the door behind us and we headed back down the stairs. Once outside, I opened the rear door on the VW Golf. Morton took two steps and stopped. He glanced inside and then looked up at me. "Get in, Morton. Come on."

He whined, but he eventually jumped in. He circled three or four times before he settled down and curled up on the shag carpeting. I got behind the driver's wheel, and we headed off to Taylors Falls.

We took Interstate 35 heading north and grabbed the Highway 8 exit that took us to Highway 95. A few minutes later, we headed into Taylors Falls. Surprisingly, the pimped out car from Walter held its own as far as keeping pace with the traffic. The speed limit was posted at seventy, but everyone was moving five to ten miles-per-hour over the limit.

Taylors Falls overlooks the Saint Croix River and is not a large town. Nice, lovely as a matter of fact, but you'd never call it large. We drove through the center of town, took a left at the stop sign, and headed up to First

Avenue. There it was, the Malcolm Webster house. Not that it was identified, I just happened to have the address and recognized the place.

It looked just like the photograph, with the front porch, the white clapboard trim, and the two large elm trees in the front yard. A white SUV was in the gravel parking area in front of a two-car garage. I pulled in and parked. Morton raised his head and looked around. As I climbed out and shut the door, he stood up and whined. I headed for the front porch, climbed the steps, and rang the doorbell. The front door was oak surrounding a large panel of beveled glass and looked original to the house. Much like Myles Rossler's place, I guessed the house might be about a hundred and twenty years old.

What appeared to be a white-haired woman walked into the hallway and headed for the door. There was a small entry area with a door. She stepped into the entry area and opened the front door. "Yes," she said and smiled.

It turned out her hair was actually a pale blonde that looked almost white from a distance and was pulled back in a ponytail. Her skin suggested a much younger woman than Malcolm Webster, maybe late forties at most, and I feared the place had possibly been sold to a younger family.

Fifty-five

Fortunately, she was Malcolm Webster's wife. Her name was Stephanie Freemann, but she went by Stevie. "We've been married for twenty-two years. Second marriage for me and first for Malcolm," she said. We were seated at the table in the kitchen. The table sat in front of a picture window that looked out onto rolling hills and an apple orchard reminiscent of Malcolm Webster's paintings.

"He told me he didn't care what name I used, just as long as I married him. Said I could call myself little Red Riding Hood if I wanted to. So, I kept my maiden name, besides it was such a pain changing my name back after my divorce, then to go through it again, forget it."

"So how did you meet?"

"Through mutual friends, their wedding actually. I'd heard about him, saw his paintings at an exhibit maybe a year before that. We met at their wedding, and he offered to show me his work if ever I was interested. The way he said it, I think he meant it as a throwaway comment." She laughed. "I called him the very next morning, and I brought over dinner that night. We were married six months later. He's a wonderful man."

I told her about Myles Rossler and Oscar Callum.

"I met Myles once," she said, "some years back at one of Malcolm's exhibits. I don't remember much, other than he and Malcolm had participated in a number of showings together over the years. Nice enough man, pleasant, but quiet. Actually, shy might be a better term. But he seemed very nice. Malcolm asked me if I wanted to pose for Myles, but I wasn't interested. Now, I kind of wish I would have."

"I'm more than a little surprised they're both missing," she said. "To be honest, I just assumed Myles had probably passed away and, well, like I said, I didn't know Mr. Callum. I don't believe I ever met him. Although it's quite possible I may have. Malcolm always seemed to know everyone, no matter where we went. And, if he didn't, he would in the next fifteen minutes. He could be very outgoing when he wanted to be."

"There's another artist missing. In fact, I was hired to try and find him, although that search has taken on a little different tack. I'm to the point where I just want to find out what happened to him," I said.

"Who's that?"

"His name is Chandler Hancock, and I've heard Malcolm described as a mentor to him."

"Oh, no. Chandler? I'm so sorry to hear that. Have they investigated his wife? She can be so mercurial. Chandler was a nice guy. Pity he ended up with the beauty queen. He could have done so much better. Interesting, great conversationalist, always smiling. Gosh, I think Malcolm may have even warned him about moving in with, what's her name. Kylie?"

"Kristi, actually. Kristi McKenzie."

She nodded as she said, "Yeah, that's it, Kristi. Fairly attractive but definitely has some issues."

I half-agreed. The more I learned about Kristi, yeah, there were definitely a few issues. But fairly attractive? No, she was an absolute knock out. "Chandler had a painting Malcolm did hanging above their fireplace, a lovely landscape. Kristi told me Chandler would talk for hours about the techniques Malcolm used. Apparently, he loved the painting."

"Mmm, and let me guess. She was less than enthralled, right? Don't even answer, I just know. As far as she was concerned, the only person who could ever produce anything halfway decent just happened to be her husband. By the way, a point she never, ever failed to mention. Talk about keeping your man on a short leash. Of course, being a man, I'm sure he was oblivious to the fact."

"You don't sound like you're much of a fan."

She shook her head. "Oh, I'm sorry. It's just that I think she was, or maybe still is, basically insecure. It's crazy when you think about it. My understanding is she won a number of beauty pageants. It was a different time, of course, but who wouldn't want to win all those pageants and contests? I mean, it appeals to all of us women, whether we want to admit it or not. But in her case, it only seemed to make her more vulnerable. Well, plus, I mean, at some point, wouldn't you have to go out and work for a living? Although, as far as I know, she apparently never did. Bit of a kept woman, though I'm sure she'd never admit that."

"I'm not aware of her being employed, at least not once she was with Chandler," I said. I saw no point in mentioning the life insurance benefit, that we were high school sweethearts, the Viking's jersey incident, or the fact that, apparently, one of Kristi's hot buttons was dressing in hospital scrubs. "On the other hand, I was more or less led to believe she was his unofficial business or marketing person. He created the work. She arranged to have it shown, encouraged sales, and maybe a following. You can never have too many fans."

"Well, now that's the funny thing. If you're going to hit the big time, at least locally, you have to show at Find Art Gallery. There are others in town that are good, very good as a matter of fact. But Find Art is at the top of the list. The owner of Find Art and Chandler's wife never got along. I've seen her on more than one occasion enter the gallery at a showing, and you could feel the friction increase as soon as she came through the door. It was always something like the description was wrong, the type was too small, the hors d'oeuvres weren't good, or there weren't enough. She could be a definite downer."

"Huh, I never picked that up from her." I was picturing Kristi in the Vikings jersey again.

"That's because you're a guy. She saved the negative attitude for us women."

"Can you tell me about Malcolm's disappearance?"

She paused for a moment and took a deep breath then plowed ahead. "Not much to tell. He was dropping off a painting at the Find Art Gallery as a matter of fact. Then he was going to stop in and see Chandler, something about a new line of paints he'd been working with and liked. They were always comparing notes."

"Did he see Chandler? As far as I can remember, Kristi had never mentioned that to me."

"Although Malcolm and Chandler were friends, good friends, she ultimately viewed Malcolm as a competitor. If someone purchased one of Malcolm's works, Kristi knew they really wanted to purchase one of Chandler's, but somehow Malcolm had talked them out of it. I'm convinced she absolutely believed that."

"Doesn't sound too healthy."

"I'm sorry. I don't mean to speak ill of anyone, but she is not what you'd call a happy person. You know how, if you go to someone's house and they have a lovely painting or maybe a piece of furniture? Your thought is probably, oh, isn't that lovely. That doesn't happen in Kristi's world. Her thought is, I want that. And she really wants it. Or, the same thing only better. You know, lovely chair, I have one just like it, only the Queen of England sat in mine. It's just the way she is, and I, well, or Malcolm, just didn't need it in our life. She's the reason Malcolm and Chandler gradually drifted apart."

"Did Malcolm ever mention it to Chandler?"

She shook her head. "No. What would be the point? She'd just start in on how Malcolm and I didn't like her and probably end up by saying maybe it would be better if they just went to bed, and she could remind him how wonderful she was."

"That's always a pretty persuasive argument."

"Oh, you men," she said, then laughed.

Fifty-Six

I sat in my car for a long minute before I started it. We pulled out of the Webster place and headed back toward the city. We passed a small park and pulled over. I needed time to think, so I grabbed the tennis ball from the glove compartment and took Morton out of the car. There were two other cars parked in the lot, but I didn't see anyone. I figured they must be out on the hiking trails. I walked over to the picnic area. We were the only ones there, and I played fetch with Morton for a good half hour.

He finally chased down the ball and brought it back then settled on the ground about ten feet away signaling he'd had enough of playing fetch for one day. We headed back to the car. Two kids who looked about ten were on bikes standing next to the car. Both of them were rubbing their hands across the back of the car, feeling the velvety green finish.

"Hi guys," I said.

"This your car?" the taller of the two asked.

"It is. Matter of fact, I just got it."

"It's really cool. How come it's fuzzy?" the other kid asked. He was shorter and heavier. Not fat, but more like a fireplug, just solid.

"That's a special finish I had put on. The government is testing it out. That fuzzy stuff is actually millions of small antennas. They track this car by satellite wherever I go and map my travels."

They glanced at one another and said, "Cool."

"Did you check out the interior?"

"We took a picture. I hope that was all right," the taller of the two said and held out a cellphone.

"Fine with me. You want a picture sitting behind the wheel?"

They looked at one another and nodded.

"Come on. I'll take your picture. Let me just put Morton in the back seat," I said then pressed the fob and unlocked the door. Morton hopped in back, circled around three or four times, and then settled in. I opened the driver's door for the kid, and he climbed in behind the wheel and grinned. "Go ahead and buckle up, and I'll take your picture."

He handed me his cellphone, pulled the leopard skin seatbelt across his chest, then grabbed the wheel with both hands and made a series of engine noises. I shot three pictures using his cellphone. As he climbed out, I asked the other kid if he wanted his picture taken. He shook his head no. He'd probably been warned about getting into a car with someone he didn't know. I climbed in, started the car, and shifted into reverse.

Both boys stood astride their bikes and watched as I back up. I lowered the window and said, "You want to hear the horn?" They both nodded. I hit the horn, and when the couple bars of Dixie sounded it brought a grin to both faces. "See you guys," I said and took off.

When we got back to the office, Louie was nowhere to be seen. I settled in behind my desk and started to make a laundry list of Kristi Mckenzie items. Ever since my earlier conversation with Malcolm Webster's wife, a number of thoughts that had been rolling around in the back of my mind had now come to the forefront.

First on the list was the fact that Chandler had been missing for the better part of five or six months before Kristi bothered to mention the fact to anyone. Add to that the suggestion Aaron had planted in my head that maybe she pushed her fiancé, Joseph Lauer, in front of the on-coming car. She had a piece of artwork in her home from each one of the missing artists. I didn't count the two unfinished paintings by her husband, Chandler. Then there was Chandler's mentor, Malcolm Webster. A relationship that Kristi tried to put a stop to. Not to mention posing naked for the statute on her dresser that Oscar Callum created and that classic piece of art from Myles Rossler, naked Kristi on the red velvet couch. Something didn't seem right.

As if he read my one-track mind, my cellphone rang. "Hi Aaron, how's it going?"

"Good, Dev, in fact, very good. Hey, I'm calling to see if you might have some time this afternoon to stop by." It was one of those requests where I knew right from the start that I wasn't allowed to refuse.

I wondered if this had anything to do with my purchase of the car from Walter. Maybe the police were watching him, ready to spring a trap, and now I'd be involved in purchasing stolen goods. Even though I was unaware the car was stolen . . . maybe.

"This afternoon?"

"Yeah, any time before five would be fine," he said, sounding just a bit more like a command.

"I suppose I could do that. Anything special you wanted to go over?"

"Just a few questions. Trying to get some facts straight."

"Yeah, I can get down there a little later. Um, do you think I might need a lawyer?"

"Why? Have you done something wrong?" He half-laughed.

"No, nothing wrong. Yeah, I'll be down there in a bit. Let me just run Morton home."

"Good. I look forward to chatting with you," he said and hung up.

Fifty-seven

I parked out on the street, and we hurried into the house. I let Morton out the back, filled his water dish, then hustled upstairs to put on a cleaner pair of jeans and a button-down shirt. I let Morton back in the house and headed out the front door. A woman walking her dog had stopped alongside my fuzzy car and was taking a picture of it when I stepped out onto the front porch. She quickly yanked on the leash and hurried down the street. I watched her walk down to the corner and turn out of sight. I hopped in the driver's seat and headed down to the police station.

The gravel parking lot across from the station was supposed to have been paved three years ago. The city council, in its wisdom, kept delaying funding and hiring council staff instead. I drove around two big potholes, one that looked large enough to literally swallow the VW Golf. I parked next to a shiny black Humvee, that at first, I thought might be a police vehicle, but the gold spinner rims on the tires and the purple thong hanging from the rearview mirror made me think otherwise.

I locked the Golf and headed into the station. I asked for Aaron at the front desk and was told to take a seat. My escort would be down shortly. Apparently, that meant thirty minutes because that's when he finally showed up. I'd met him before but forgot his name. He was dressed in jeans with a casual long sleeve shirt rolled up above his elbows. His gun and badge were attached to the side of his belt.

I was out of my plastic chair and heading toward him before he called my name.

"Dev Haskell?"

"Yeah, that's me," I said and held out my hand.

"Daren Wengler," he replied, and we shook hands. As we headed toward the elevator, he said, "I understand you had a late-night visitor the other evening."

"Yeah. Fortunately, no real damage other than some holes in the wall I still need to fill, and I've switched back to being a light sleeper."

"Yeah, well, a late night visitor like that can have that effect on you. Glad to hear everything worked out all right. You were down there along the river with the L.T. the following morning?"

"Yeah. I actually ID'd the guy. I don't know who shot him, but whoever it was, I feel like I owe them dinner."

We stepped onto the elevator and rode up without saying another word. When we stepped off, I followed Wengler down to the homicide door. He input a code on the pad, there was a buzz and the door unlocked. We headed into the office. It was filled with too many desks for the room and lots of people on the phone. Wengler headed towards Aaron's office, and I wondered if he might be joining us.

Instead, he took a turn and headed for a desk just as Aaron stepped out of the break room. He saw me, took a sip from his paper coffee cup, and made a disgusted face. "Dev, you want a coffee before we sit down?"

"Based on the face you just made, I think not."

"Can't say as I blame you. How you doing?" he asked and led me down the hall, away from his office, and toward the interview rooms.

"Hey, Aaron. Where in the hell are we going? You said I wouldn't need an attorney."

"I don't think you will, Dev. But I want to get this on tape. Trust me, okay?"

"If I think this is going the wrong way, I'm going to shut up until I get my lawyer down here," I said, remembering my lawyer was Louie, who was probably still nursing one whale of a serious hangover. Aaron held the door open to the interview room and said, "After you."

I gave him a look and stepped in. I sat down at the metal-topped table. My chair was bolted to the floor. There were two files on the desk, no label on either file. A computer sat on the edge of the table. Aaron turned it on and sat down opposite me. He typed in a password and then a moment later gave his name, the date, and the time. After that, he said, "I'm here with Mr. Devlin Haskell. Mr. Haskell, are you here of your own free will?"

"Yes," I said. Not sure I should have even answered that question.

"We're just here for a casual conversation. You have not been charged with anything. I do not plan to charge you with anything. Things are going okay?" he asked.

I decided to play along. "Actually, Aaron, your call was timely. I'm still looking at these missing artists, and I keep coming back to the same far-fetched thought."

"Which is?"

"Which is all four of the guys, start with Chandler Hancock, but then Myles Rossler, Oscar Callum, and Malcolm Webster had some interaction with Kristi McKenzie. I know, I know," I said, holding up a hand and cutting Aaron off before he could say whatever it was he was about to say. "But they all interacted with her in one way or another. She posed for a couple of them, slept with at least one of them, Hancock. Maybe had a brief relationship with two others. I don't know."

Aaron reached into the top file and pulled out a plastic evidence bag. It looked like there was a 4x5 photograph in it. "I want you to try and identify the person in this photograph," he said and slid the evidence bag across the metal-topped table.

I picked up the plastic bag and looked at the image. "Are you kidding me? Where in the hell did you get this?" She had blonde hair, was gorgeous and completely naked.

"Who is it, Dev?"

"It's Kristi McKenzie. This is a photo of the painting that's hanging in Chandler Hancock's office. Actually, in the closet of his office. But how did you get this?"

"You remember your friend, Gerry Berk?"

"I remember him, and he sure as hell wasn't a friend."

"When his body was searched, that photo was in his pocket."

Fifty-eight

Aaron went on to tell me that, along with the photo of the painting, there was also a hand-written note with Kristi's address in Berk's pocket.

"Meaning what, exactly? Was he planning to break into her condo, too?"

"I guess we'll never really know for sure. We have a strong suspicion the handwriting is female and not Berk's. But the bigger question is, where did he get the photo of that painting?"

"Well, I can tell you this much. That condo of Kristi's is covered with framed photos of her in all sorts of beauty pageants. From the time she was a kid. There's even a picture of her as homecoming queen at my high school. She's wearing a cape and a little crown. I'm not kidding. If there's one, there's easily a dozen and a half framed pictures. They're all from beauty pageants. She's wearing formal gowns, dresses, and in at least one she's wearing a swimsuit."

"But this painting, I mean, the thing is virtually hidden in the closet of Chandler Hancock's office. How the hell did Berk get a photo of that painting?" I turned the image over, and at a forty-five-degree angle, the words 'Kodak Moment' ran across the back in light grey type.

"That copy on the back is fairly standard with drug-store versions," Aaron said. "You can send them a digital file, and they make copies for about ten cents apiece. Just for starters, both Walgreens and CVS have that kind of equipment. You can get discount coupons online for the photos. So the fact that he had the image doesn't necessarily mean he was in her unit. Someone could have sent the digital file in, had the image or a number of images printed, and given one to him."

"But what for? And who would know him? He's been locked up for the last ten years."

"And out for the past eleven months before he was murdered."

"Wait a minute. You're investigating who murdered Gerry Berk? The bastard tried to kill me, for God's sake."

"Yeah, and if you didn't know Berk was the guy who broke into your house and attempted to shoot you, we would still be investigating the murder to find out who did it and arrest them."

"Well, yeah, but, I mean, Gerry Berk?"

"Last time we checked, he was still a human being and entitled to protection under the law."

"I get that, maybe, but Gerry Berk?"

"You want to go one step crazier?" Aaron asked.

"I'm not sure. Why, what do you have?"

"Suppose, just for a second, Kristi Mckenzie gave him that photo."

"Kristi Mc— Aaron, where do you come up with this shit? Kristi doesn't know who in the hell, Gerry—" I started thinking.

"What is it, Dev? Spit it out?"

"Okay. I told Kristi about the confrontation I had with Berk a few days ago at noon in the City Salsa House. How he came in after me, and George Estrada and some muscle guy from the kitchen told him to get the hell out. She came to visit me in the hospital. But just for a minute," I added, not wanting to get into her overnight stay.

"And she has a connection to all the missing artists, doesn't she?"

"Yeah. I was going to say tenuous at best, but now I'm not so sure. She posed for that painting by Myles Rossler." I pointed to the evidence bag. "She posed for a statute by Oscar Callum, and she and Chandler got a painting from Malcolm Webster. Now all four artists are missing. All four seem to have disappeared without a trace."

"Would it surprise you to know that she purchased gas up in Warba, Minnesota, just about the time Oscar Callum went missing?" Aaron asked.

"At this point, no. But let me go you one better. How about this? Gerry Berk was shot virtually within sight of her building."

Aaron made a face and shook his head. "Dev, that's sounds a little far-fetched. I mean he had this photo but—"

"And she has a .45 in her unit. A loaded .45. In fact, it's stored in a little drawer just below where that naked painting hangs. I saw the thing. And I don't know if you guys picked up on it, but there was a recently made trail through the grass and weeds cutting across from my car to the dog park at the Upper Landing. Aaron, this is suddenly all coming together. Her husband has been missing for seven months, and she doesn't contact you guys? Finally, gets in touch with me? Come on."

Aaron pursed his lips and drummed his fingers on the metal tabletop, deep in thought.

"I talked to Malcolm Webster's wife earlier today. She said Kristi McKenzie was a very unhappy woman. Never satisfied. If she saw something at your house that she liked, she really wanted it. I think winning all those beauty competitions maybe didn't have the best effect on her life."

"When did you find all this out?"

"Just recently, Webster's wife gave me a bit of the lowdown on Kristi, and Diane over at Find Art could probably corroborate it. Diane's been pushing me to get the word out on these missing artists. Probably figures someone, somewhere, knows something. It's just unfortunate that someone turns out to be Kristi, and maybe she doesn't want anyone to put it all together. Suddenly, it's all making sense, and it was right in front of me the whole damn time."

"And you actually saw the .45 in her place?"

"Yeah, as a matter of fact, brass shells, a full clip, I even checked. And you never found a weapon at the scene of Berk's murder, did you?"

Aaron shook his head. "No, just two shells."

"Brass shells. Well, there you go. It would seem to me that's at least worth a little chat with her."

Fifty-nine

It was just after ten the following morning. I was in a side room, sipping a cup of lousy coffee with Detective Wengler while we watched Kristi being interviewed through the two-way mirror. Aaron and Detective Norris Manning were sitting across the table from Kristi McKenzie and her attorney, some guy named Reginald Beaufort. He seemed very impressed with himself and insisted on being called Reginald. Not Reggie, or Reg, or even Beau, but Reginald.

"Miss McKenzie, recent issues have come to light, and we'd like to gain a little better clarification concerning the disappearance of your husband, Chandler Hancock," Aaron said.

Kristi nodded, and Reginald leaned over and whispered in her ear. When he finished, he looked at Aaron and said, "You may proceed, Lieutenant," clearly trying to take charge of the moment.

Aaron smiled a friendly smile, but I knew him well enough to know he meant it as anything but friendly. "Could you tell us when Chandler disappeared and under what circumstances?"

Kristi looked over at Reginald, and he gave her a nod. "Well, it was about seven-and-a-half months back.

I can't give you an exact date, but I could probably get it off my calendar at home. See, when Chandler worked, when he painted, he would work all day. Oftentimes that might be twelve, fourteen, maybe even sixteen hours in any day. I'd wake up in the morning, and he might have already been working for a couple of hours. He might break for lunch or dinner, but it was not unusual if he didn't. That was just how he was. Same thing at night. I might go to bed, and he was still working, or he may have already been asleep for a couple of hours."

"And where did he paint?"

"We have a three-bedroom unit. One bedroom is just that, our bedroom. Another serves as his office, and the third is his studio. That's where he worked, creating the paintings."

"What sort of work did he do? Portraits, landscapes, contemporary art?" Manning asked.

"Largely landscapes. Once in a great while, a portrait, but not too often. He didn't really enjoy having someone in the studio with him, and he hated the odd commission he might get to do a portrait in someone's home."

"You recall when he may have done his most recent portrait?"

"No, not really, but I could look it up in his files. It had to be four or five years ago, at least. I can't remember the gentleman's name, but he managed a hedge fund of some sort. Chandler created the portrait over the course of a week at the man's home, some mansion out on Lake Minnetonka. When he finished, he vowed he would never do another portrait."

"Did he ever paint landscapes actually on site?" Manning asked.

"Yes, he would do an initial work on site. He had a procedure he would follow. First, he would photograph a number of areas, different angles, you know the routine. He would load those digitally and view them that evening, return the next day and quickly work up four or five rough sketches, as he called them, all in oils. They were things of beauty on their own, and then he would work off one of those, along with the digital image, and create a masterpiece in the studio."

"And then he would sell the masterpiece?"

"Not exactly. Depending on the time of year, there were a number of shows where he might have an item or two or even three on display. Then he had three or four galleries around the country where they would have an annual showing of his work. Those shows usually lasted two to three months."

"Where were these galleries?" Aaron asked.

"New York, San Francisco, New Orleans, sometimes Florida, and then a gallery here in town called Find Art."

"Did he show anywhere else?"

"Occasionally, but in the cities I just mentioned, those were more or less exclusive. They're all highly regarded galleries, and they had an exclusive on his work for that region, provided he was happy with the results of their efforts."

"And was he happy?"

"Yes, quite."

"You hired a private investigator following the disappearance of your husband, did you not?" Manning asked.

Kristi glanced over at Reginald, who nodded.

"Yes, I did. A private investigator by the name of Devlin Haskell."

Wengler was standing next to me. He shook his head and said, "Man, lucky you, that would be one hell of a gorgeous client."

"How did you come to choose Mr. Haskell?" Manning asked, and I noticed his face beginning to grow a little redder at the mention of my name.

"We'd known each other in high school. I was the homecoming queen senior year."

"You were dating one another back then?"

"Maybe once or twice."

"Nothing more serious than that?" Manning said.

"No, in fact, shortly after high school, I met Chandler. We dated off and on, broke up a few times, and eventually moved in together."

She neglected to mention she was two-timing me for three or four months before she dumped me.

"And you've had no interaction with Haskell up until you hired him to look for your husband."

"Yes, that's correct."

"Probably a wise move," Manning said.

"I thought he'd been killed in Iraq."

"If only," Manning mumbled.

"Miss McKenzie," Aaron said, moving on. "We know you were involved in quite a few beauty pageants. You were a princess in the St. Paul Winter Carnival, Queen of the Mississippi Headwaters, Miss Upper Midwest, Princess of the Prairie. Did I leave anything out?"

"Miss Ramsey County," she said, "along with a number of others. But yes, I won all of those pageants."

"Amazing. Congratulations."

"Thank you," Kristi said and flashed her sparkling white teeth.

"You also modeled, or maybe posed, is the term for a statute and portrait, didn't you?"

Kristi suddenly looked unsure of herself. "I may have. I really don't recall."

"Did you pose for a statute done by the sculptor Oscar Callum?"

"Um, yes, I guess I did."

"And did you pose for a portrait done by the famous artist, Myles Rossler?"

"How do you know that?"

"If you would just answer the question, please."

She shot a worried glance at Reginald, who said, "Gentlemen, if we might have a minute or two of privacy, please."

Aaron and Manning stood without another word and walked out of the room. Reginald shot an evil look at the two way mirror we were standing behind but didn't say anything. He stood and leaned against the table with his back to us and signaled Kristi to move over, so she was in front of him, and we couldn't see her. Once she moved over, he leaned down, and they began to talk in hushed tones. Three separate times he had to caution her to keep her voice down.

Just as he settled into his chair and Kristi moved her chair back, Aaron opened the door and said, "Okay to come back in?"

"Yes, please do so. We'd like to bring this to a conclusion," Reginald said.

Aaron and Manning settled into their chairs, and Aaron said, "Miss McKenzie, I believe I asked if you had posed for a portrait by Myles Rossler?"

"Yes, I did," Kristi said in barely a whisper.

Aaron opened a file and pulled out the photo of Kristi naked on the red velvet couch. Her eyes grew wide as Aaron said, "Miss McKenzie, can you identify this image for us?"

Kristi literally shrieked and shouted, "Oh my God. Where did you get that? Just how in the hell did you get that?"

"Gentlemen, if would excuse my client for a moment. Kristi, you have—"

"Shut up, Reginald. Just shut the hell up. You told me they didn't know anything about this and—" She suddenly stopped, seemed to calm down, and said in a tense sounding voice, "That is a painting of me that

Myles Rossler did maybe two years ago. He painted me in his studio, which was behind his house. That painting has been kept in an extremely private collection. How did you get that photo?"

"It's part of another investigation that we—"

"Gentleman, this has been quite upsetting for my client. I'm going to bring this to a conclusion here and now. Should you have any further questions for my client, I insist you direct those to me, and I will see that she responds as quickly as possible. Thank you. It's been, enlightening. Now if you would excuse us, we'll be leave—"

"Actually, Mr. Beaufort," Manning said as he opened a file and pulled out a couple of sheets of paper. "We have a warrant we would like to serve, here and now. Providing us with access to the premises of unit 312 in the Upper Landing complex."

"You, you can't do that. What the hell do you think—Reggie, honey, do something, please. Tell them no way in hell am I going to let them in."

Reginald had a disgusted look on his face and held his hand up to silence her as he quickly paged through the warrant. "I'm afraid this document gives them complete authority to enter and search the premises. We can be there, but we can't interfere."

"Be there? I don't want to be there. I don't want them coming in my place. Do something. That's what you're supposed to do. It's what you promised me you would do last night."

"I'm afraid everything appears to be in order here, Kristi. I suggest you don't say another word, and we follow them to your home."

"But I don't want them to come in and—"

"Here," Beaufort said, handing the warrant documents to Kristi. "You can read this on the way. Gentlemen, I suspect you are aware of the fact that it's a security entrance on Mill Street. We will meet you there. Thank you for your time. Come along, Kristi, and not another word," he said then grabbed her by the arm and headed for the door.

Sixty

Aaron and Manning followed them out the door, and a minute later, Aaron joined Wengler and me in the room where we'd been watching. "We'll be heading over there in just a moment. Manning is already on the way," he said. Wengler nodded and headed out of the small room.

"Dev, I've no idea how long this is going to take. I'll call you if and when we have something. Any thoughts on what you saw this morning?"

"Only that she didn't seem too happy with the idea of a search going on. When you go into Chandler's office, there's a closet in the corner. The painting is hanging on the right-hand side of the closet. Kind of in the middle of a bunch of shelves and above about two hundred pairs of shoes all lined up on racks. Just below the painting is a little drawer. That's where I found the .45."

"Okay. Anything else?"

"Yeah. Just for some giggles, check out her bedroom. She sleeps in a bunk bed. If you spend the night, she asks you if you want top or bottom, and you're thinking this is gonna be some great sex. She's nuts. Hey, you think she and Beaufort have something going on?"

"Not really any of my business," Aaron said. "I guess you might as well take off. If you don't hear from me tonight, give me a call tomorrow morning after eleven. I'm stuck in meetings for most of the morning."

"Okay. Thanks for letting me in on this. No offense, but there's a big part of me that hopes you don't find anything. Although, the odds seem kind of stacked against her."

"We'll see what we end up with. I'd better get over there. Thanks again for your time."

"Always happy to help," I said and forced a smile. Aaron rode down in the elevator with me. We waved goodbye, and I headed out the front entrance and across the street to my fuzzy VW Golf while Aaron went in the opposite direction. I was just backing out of my parking place when an unmarked car drove past. Aaron was in the passenger seat talking on his cellphone, and Wengler was behind the wheel.

I went home, picked up Morton, and we headed down to the office. I sat down behind my desk and made my long overdue phone call to George Estrada.

"Hi Dev," was how he answered. "Glad you called. I was beginning to get worried."

"Crazy last few days, George." I went on to tell him about Gerry Berk's assault and my hospital stay. I left out the part about Kristi showing up in hospital scrubs and spending the night. I gave him a brief summation of Berk getting what few brains he had blown out of his thick skull.

"Sounds like you're lucky to be alive. No loss to society having that character put on ice. We had a couple of incidents with him around here. Asking customers for spare change. Talk about a fast way to shut down a restaurant business. One woman, nice-looking gal, swung by a couple of times, and I saw her giving him money, and not just a couple of bucks, but a handful of twenties. Makes you just want to scream. If you're going to give money, give it to food shelves or a homeless shelter for God's sake. Giving it to a character like that fella just endangers us all for the next three or four days while he's on a bender or worse. I can only hope he was doing yard work or something for her."

I didn't want to ask what the woman looked like. I was afraid he'd say blonde and gorgeous, namely Kristi. I made a mental note to mention it to Aaron. If they needed some way to link Kristi to Gerry Berk, it sounded like George's testimony could help.

"You come up with any way to monitor that cash register?"

"No, I looked at it every which way, including me being the only one to have access, and we, my aunt and I, both decided that's probably not how we're losing money."

"Then what's happening? You told me you were making the night deposits, right?"

"Yeah, and still doing that. No, we're thinking your idea of someone ripping us off in the kitchen is probably more the case."

"The kitchen? What are you thinking? Someone is selling meals out the back door?"

"Not exactly. But it wouldn't surprise me if someone was going through our supplies, maybe the odd liquor bottle from behind the bar, but more likely supplies, butter, flour, chicken, steaks, that sort of thing. A number of people have access to our coolers and pantry. They have to if we're going to expect them to prepare meals."

"Okay, so you want to have someone undercover in the kitchen?"

"I don't think that would work, Dev. Just for starters, everyone there busts their ass, and someone drifting around back there would only be in the way and immediately stick out like the proverbial sore thumb. Plus, if it was you, a number of staff would immediately recognize you."

"You sound like you might have an idea."

"As a matter of fact, I do. It's working undercover, literally."

"Literally?"

"Yeah, in the freezer. You'd have to be there for an extended period of time. I'm thinking maybe four hours or so. It would probably be a good idea to bring some blankets. You think you might be up for that?"

"Yeah, I guess I could. When do you want me to start?"

"How about tonight?"

Sixty-one

When we got home, I let Morton out into the backyard. I turned the table lamp on in the bedroom for him, hoping he chose to sleep in his bed rather than on the couch in the front room. Then I went down to the basement, hauled out a sleeping bag I'd purchased seven or eight years ago and used only once on an ill-conceived camping trip with a woman.

We had driven north for four hours to a campground she really liked up on the Lake Superior hiking trail. To make a long story short, I ended up with a dreadful case of poison ivy. She spent the night in another tent with a guy she met and ended up marrying. When the morning came, she told me she was going to stay a few more nights. They both wished me a speedy recovery and a safe drive home. I think they've got two little girls now. I was invited to the wedding but didn't go.

Anyway, the sleeping bag was supposed to be good to forty-five below, and George had said the freezer temperature was something like minus five on the Fahrenheit scale, so I should be okay.

I drove over to the City Salsa House at eight-thirty that evening. George met me at the back door and hustled me into his office. Along with my sleeping bag, I brought a pair of gloves, a stocking cap, and a quilted jacket, strange attire for a humid summer evening.

George gave me a pair of white pants and a coat that everyone in the kitchen wore in the hopes that I would blend in for the minute or two it would take to walk me through the kitchen.

"We stop serving tonight at ten, so everyone is going to be cranking out the food and keeping an eye on the clock. Once the kitchen is closed, they have to clean up their work stations, that takes maybe a half-hour to forty-five minutes, and then they punch out. Right about nine, they'll be hauling meat items out and placing them in the refrigerators to thaw overnight. The morning crew handles food prep, and that begins at ten in the morning."

"So, where exactly will I be?"

"There's an area in the rear of the freezer. A cabinet, actually. It's been empty for a number of months, ever since we added new shelving. Anyway, I set a chair in there. You can settle in, get comfortable, and wait to see if anyone walks out with a pile of steaks or something. Hauling all the meat out to thaw overnight will have already taken place, so anyone taking out a pile of steaks is probably up to no good."

I held up my grocery bag with the sleeping bag, gloves, stocking cap, and winter jacket.

"Good, I'm going to go start to total some accounts. I'll lock the door on the way out so no one will be coming in here, just cool your heels for a bit. If you have to use the bathroom, there's one right in there," he said and pointed to a door behind his desk.

"Okay, I'll just sit in here and wait for you."

"We close tonight at one-thirty. It'll take another thirty or forty minutes to get the bar cleaned up. If you go out the same back door we came in, it'll lock automatically. And then let's talk tomorrow morning. Okay?"

"Got it. Go do what you have to do and don't worry about me. I'll be fine."

"Once again, I appreciate you helping me out, Dev. Hopefully, you can nail whoever has been doing this."

"Let's see what happens."

Sixty-two

George didn't return to his office for another hour. He carried a plastic trash bag full of cash. "How's it going, Dev? You still up for it tonight?"

"Ready whenever you are," I said.

"Soon as I total this cash up and get it in the safe, I'll take you back there," he said as he settled in behind his desk. He dumped the cash out of the plastic bag and into a pile in the middle of his desk.

"Anything I can do to help?"

"Yeah, that would be great. I'm just sorting the bills into stacks, fives, tens, twenties. You want to help, I'd love it. It'll cut my time in half."

I settled into a chair across from his desk, grabbed a handful of bills, and started sorting. Initially, George was moving about twice as fast as I was, but I gradually began to catch up. After fifteen minutes, George clicked on his adding machine and began to total up the cash at breakneck speed. When he was finished, he wrapped rubber bands around the bundles of currency. He slipped a piece of paper with the amount written on it and stuffed the bills into a canvas bank bag with a leather top and a lock at the end of the zipper. He folded and placed the adding machine tape into the cash bag, zipped the bag closed, and locked it. He spun the dial on what looked like a hundred-year-old safe sitting in the corner, pulled open the door, and set the bag inside. Once he closed the door, he stood, checked his watch, and said, "Let's get you settled in."

I followed George through a twisting hall, past stacks of chairs, a table covered with candles, and into a back corner of the kitchen. No one bothered to look at us. Three guys were busy scraping off large, stovetop grills and applying cooking oil to the surface. Two guys were running trays holding forty or fifty glasses through a dishwashing cycle. Someone else was setting plastic trays full of dirty dishes, glasses, and silverware on a counter. We walked around a corner, and George pulled open a thick wooden door about seven feet high and five feet wide. The lights automatically came on inside the freezer. To say it was cold was an understatement.

"Why don't you slip into your jacket and gloves while I unlock the cabinet," George said.

I quickly slipped on my quilted jacket and gloves then pulled the stocking cap onto my head.

George slipped a key into the cabinet and unlocked the door. "I put this chair in here earlier, so at least you can sit while you're in there," he said.

I stepped over and glanced inside the cabinet. The chair just barely fit in there, and it didn't exactly look like there was much room beyond that. "Looks like it's going to be tight quarters," I said.

"Yeah, I wish we had something better, but that's about it. You sure you're okay doing this? No problem if you want to bow out."

"Yeah, I think it's probably the best way. I could wait in the lot and watch for someone carrying stuff, but what if they go out another door?"

"We've got three exits, so right there, your odds are down to only thirty-three percent."

"So let's do it," I said. I pulled out my sleeping bag and stepped inside then hopped over to the cabinet and backed onto the chair.

"Sweet," George said. "Now, there's this slit in the door, right here," he said, pointing to an opening maybe a half-inch by four inches. "About ten seconds after I close the door, the lights will go off, and you'll be in the dark. But they come on automatically as soon as the door is opened and remain on until the door is closed and the exterior handle is put in place. Figure the last of the staff should be out of here no later than two-fifteen this morning. That's about four hours from now. Okay?"

"I'm on it, George. I'll call you tomorrow morning whether or not anything happens."

"Thanks again for doing this, Dev. Now, any problem, if you're too cold, whatever, you just walk out of here. I don't care if someone sees you. Your health and safety come first."

"Thanks. I'll be fine."

"Well, enjoy," he said and walked out. He closed the door, and ten seconds later, I was in the dark. Over the course of the next hour or so, three people walked into the freezer. One took what looked like a couple of pounds of butter. Another grabbed something off the shelf, and a woman came in and grabbed a bag of ice. Otherwise, it was deathly still and dark.

There was just barely enough room for me in the cabinet. My feet and knees were wedged up against the door and try as I may, I couldn't push the chair back any further. I slowly but surely hiked the sleeping bag up an inch at a time and was able to wrap it around my shoulders.

I had probably been sitting in there for at least two hours. Despite the quilted jacket and the sleeping bag supposedly good down to minus forty-five, I was cold. I chalked it up to a lack of movement and the cramped quarters. The door suddenly opened, and the light flashed on. This was the first person in the freezer in over an hour, and I thought it might be a sign of the end of the night. I just needed whoever it was to walk out with about a dozen steaks, and I'd be home free.

Instead, the guy opened the door all the way then disappeared for a few seconds. The air near the door showed traces of fog as the cold air from the freezer began to collide with the warm kitchen air. Suddenly, the guy appeared again. This time, he was pushing a two-wheel dolly with a wooden pallet and a stack of shrink-wrapped boxes. He groaned as he rolled it in and headed in my direction. He drew closer and closer, groaned a few more times, then began to lower the dolly and the shrink-wrapped pallet. As it started to level with the floor, the pallet scraped against the door, and he actually rose up, suggesting whatever was on the pallet was a lot heavier than he was, and he wasn't a small guy.

As the pallet scraped against the door, the door pushed in maybe half an inch and pressed against my knees as the guy half-groaned. "Shit, that stuff is heavy." Before I realized what was happening, he hurried out of the freezer, and the lights went off.

I pushed on the door to open it, but it didn't move. I tried to push with my arms and legs, but my knees were pressed up against the door and then held in place by the sleeping bag. I couldn't move my legs to either side. I couldn't pull them on top of the chair. I was essentially wedged in place.

I pulled off the glove on my right hand and took the cellphone out of my pocket. Unfortunately, I was going to have to call George. I turned on the phone. The screen illuminated with a red triangle sign that had a white exclamation point in the middle of the triangle. Below that were the words 'NO SERVICE!' I turned the phone off and tried again, same signal. I changed my calling preferences, nothing. In a word, I was screwed and getting colder by the minute.

I pushed against the door in the hope I could move it. Nothing happened. I pounded on the door. Then I pounded and yelled. Then I just yelled. Still no response. Eventually, I inched the sleeping bag up over my head, pulled the cord tight, and tried to massage my legs to keep a semblance of circulation going. I drifted off to sleep more times than I can remember, only to wake a minute or two later. I was cold, but at least I wasn't freezing. I had no idea what time it was. Other than the 'NO SERVICE!' warning, nothing else was on my cellphone screen, certainly not the time. It could have been midnight or ten in the morning, but I had no way of knowing.

Sixty-three

I was half-frozen, my teeth were chattering, and I was more exhausted than awake after not really sleeping for the past twenty-four hours. I heard a noise and shook my head in an effort to pay attention. The lights flashed on, and a moment later, two guys in jeans and t-shirts stood in front of the shelves holding all the steaks. There were a number of stacks of steaks, all labeled: sirloin, t-bone, ribeye, flank, filet mignon, beef tenderloin. One guy held a grocery bag open while a guy with a goatee began tossing two of each into the bag. When they finished with the steaks, they hurried over and examined the pallet of boxes in front of the cabinet.

"No, we better wait for a day or two until they unwrap this. Then we can grab an entire box, and it'll be weeks before they know it's missing," the goatee guy said.

"Come on. Let's get out of here. I'm freezing my ass off."

I was so cold I actually debated for a half-second about calling out to them. But as they turned to head out, I noticed the guy with the grocery bag had a pistol wedged into the back of his belt. Discretion seemed to be the better idea. I sat in the dark for another year or two before the door opened, the lights flashed on, and thank God, George stepped in.

He took one look at the pallet in front of the cabinet and hurried over. "Dev? You in there?"

"G-G-George," I called. "God, I'm f-f-freezing. Get me out of here."

"Oh, what the hell? Hang on just a minute, buddy. Let me move this thing. Hang in there, pal. I'll get you out of there. Don't worry, just a couple of seconds." He took hold of the two-wheel dolly, pulled it back, and rolled the pallet away from the door.

I pushed the door open and attempted to move my legs. They hurt. Really hurt. I started to stand and fell back into the chair. "Shit. My legs, they've been wedged in there all night. God." I leaned forward and began to massage my legs. As I moved, I heard my back go snap, crackle, and pop. "Oh, sweet Jesus. I'm freezing, man."

"Stay there. Let me get you a coffee. Warm you up," George called over his shoulder as he hurried out of the freezer. He left the door open and disappeared.

A moment later, a guy walked in, holding a piece of paper, probably a list of items. He suddenly focused on me and said, "What the fuck, man?"

George hurried in behind him, carrying a steaming mug of coffee. "It's okay, Tony. I got this."

"Dude looks like he slept in here. He break in or something?"

"No, just testing the temperature."

"Testing the temp—"

"I said I got this, Tony. Give us a couple of minutes here."

"Okay, man. Okay. Dude looks like he's half-frozen. Awful dumb shit if you ask me," he said as he stepped out of the freezer and disappeared.

George stepped in front of the cabinet. "Now, this is hot, so keep your gloves on and don't gulp it down," he said and handed me the steaming mug.

I could actually feel the heat from the mug rising on my face. I blew on the mug a half-dozen times and took a slurpy sounding sip.

"Dev, I'm so sorry. I forgot all about the ice cream delivery last night." He indicated the pallet of shrink-wrapped boxes behind him.

"It's okay, G-G-George. I s-s-saw them. Saw the g-guys." I took another sip of coffee, this time not slurping quite so loud. I was moving my feet up and down and my legs from side to side, hopefully increasing the circulation. I was still shivering, but the coffee was beginning to have an effect. I took a couple more sips. I could feel the coffee go all the way down, and there was a warm glow beginning to spread from my stomach. I rolled my shoulders, and they made an audible sound.

"You saw them?" George said.

"Yeah, they loaded steaks into a bag. Two of each kind. Then looked at that pallet, and one guy said they'd take a box once it was unwrapped. There were two of them."

"Did you recognize them?"

I shook my head, took a couple of swallows of coffee, and said, "No. One of them had a gun tucked in his belt. They were in here maybe two or three hours before you and that Tony guy came in."

"Two or three hours? But no one is here until . . . the cleaning crew. Two guys, beard on one of them?"

I thought for a moment. "Yeah, the guy who took the steaks had a little beard, a goatee. He tossed the steaks in a grocery bag the other guy was holding. Took two of each kind."

George turned and looked at the shelving with the steaks stacked one on top of the other. "I'll be damned," he said. "You think you can stand?"

"I think I better. Thanks, this coffee seems to be doing the trick. I might need some help walking until I get the feeling back in my legs, but let's get out of here."

I stood and pulled the sleeping bag down to my knees. George wedged it down around my ankles. I placed my hands on either side of the cabinet and cautiously took a step. It felt like I was standing on two poles, and I couldn't feel my feet.

"Whoa," I said as I stepped out of the sleeping bag and nearly fell. Fortunately, George grabbed me and helped me to the door. I hobbled out of the freezer, holding onto George. Every step seemed to be slightly better than the one before.

We headed in the direction of George's office. As we crossed the kitchen, George yelled, "Tony, go on back there and get whatever you need."

"You got it, boss," Tony yelled then just stood there with two other guys watching us with their mouths open as I limped out of sight.

I stood in George's office, limping back and forth, drinking another coffee, while George was on his computer. I had finally warmed up to the point where I tossed my jacket and gloves onto a chair. I was unaware I still had my stocking cap on.

"Dev, I'm going to do a quick inventory in the freezer and the refrigerators. Shouldn't take more than twenty minutes. I'll bring you something warm to soak up that coffee."

Sixty-four

While George was gone, I used the bathroom then pulled out my phone. Amazingly, I had a signal, and I phoned Aaron to see what the latest was on Kristi. After two rings, I got dumped into his message center. "Hi, Aaron, it's Dev. Just checking to see what you came up with in your search of Kristi McKenzie's place. Give me a call when you can."

George walked back in just as I was hanging up. In one hand, he was carrying a plate with a stack of blueberry pancakes. A large dollop of melted butter was running down the sides of the stack. He held a container of blueberry syrup in the other hand.

"You feel like grabbing a seat and having some breakfast, Dev?"

"I feel like having some breakfast, but if you don't mind, I think I'll just stand."

"How are the legs doing?"

"Good, getting back to normal. I just don't feel like sitting right now or maybe ever again."

He laughed at that and set the pancakes and syrup down on the corner of his desk. He pulled a black napkin wrapped around silverware from his pocket and set it next to the pancakes. "Help yourself."

I poured the syrup over the pancakes, completely covering the top of the stack, and then watched as it dripped down the sides. I cut a small wedge from the stack of four pancakes, and took a bite.

"They're okay?"

"Mmm. Delicious," I said and took another bite.

"Were you calling for a ride when I came in, Dev? God, I'll give you a lift home or wherever you need to go."

"A ride? No, nothing like that. It's another case I'm working on. Matter of fact, you remember that incident here with Gerry Berk?"

"Yeah, that lowlife who came in here looking for a fight." He chuckled. "Remember? You told him we were going to beat the shit out of him and toss him in the dumpster."

"Yeah. Anyway, the police think they might have a suspect in his murder and possibly the murder of a bunch of artists."

"A bunch of artists, you mean like the guy is some kind of serial killer or something?"

"I never really thought of it like that, but yeah, I guess that would be right. Well, except that it's not a guy."

"A woman?"

"Afraid so."

"Isn't that kind of unusual? I thought most serial killers were guys."

"I think, in the US, the current percentage is about sixteen percent of serial killers are female. The nutcase guys who do it are oftentimes in it for sexual gratification. The women usually aren't interested in the sex. More often than not, they're looking for power and profit."

"Strictly business," George said and laughed.

"Yeah. Turns out this gal the cops are looking at is also suspected of killing her fiancé a few years back for life insurance money. She got one point five million."

"She sounds charming."

"She's the same woman you described giving a bunch of twenties to Gerry Berk out on the street. Hot looking, gorgeous blonde."

George gave a slight frown and shook his head. "She was nice looking all right, but she wasn't blonde."

"Oh, yeah, she was, George. She's won a bunch of beauty pageants over the years. God, she's got all sorts of pictures of her in various dresses and wearing crowns and stuff. Posed for a painting where she's just lounging on the couch, completely naked. One very hot blonde."

"That may be, Dev. But the woman I saw wasn't blonde. She was nice looking, very nice looking as a matter of fact, but she wasn't blonde. She had short black hair, and she was wearing leggings. You know, those stretch-pants that go just below the knee. She had a tattoo on the calf of her leg, some sort of design, but I couldn't tell what it was.

"You sure?"

"Oh yeah, positive. I watched her for a couple of minutes. Wanted to make sure that butthead Berk didn't hurt her. No, she had short black hair and that tattoo."

George fired up his computer and ran a series of staff pictures past me. I eventually identified the two guys who stole the steaks. It turned out they were a cleaning crew, contracted through an outside organization.

"In a warped way, it kind of makes perfect sense," George said. "They're in here every morning around five, vacuum, sweep, do the windows, and restrooms, and they're almost always out of here by seven-thirty. I never even considered them. They'd have no reason to ever be in the freezer."

"Except to steal steaks," I said.

"I'll set up a camera in there, and we'll nail their asses. Please keep this under your hat, Dev. I want to get these guys."

"You might want to talk to an attorney or even the police, be nice if you could nail them not just for what they grab in the pictures you take. It would be nice to nail their asses for the profit loss you've experienced over the last two to three months."

"Good idea. Now listen, you're okay to drive home?"

"Yeah, I'm pretty much thawed out," I said. I ran my fork around the edge of the clean plate, picking up the last of the blueberry syrup." I smiled after I licked the fork clean.

"Why don't you take that syrup dispenser home with you? The occasional spoonful makes a nice little treat."

"You sure?"

"Absolutely. Now you're sure you're okay?"

"Yeah, I'll get out of your hair."

"You be sure to send me a bill, Dev. And I'll pass the word. From here on, anything you order here is on the house. Lifetime guarantee."

"Oh, George. You don't have to—"

"No. Go on, get out of here, and take a long hot shower once you get home."

Sixty-five

I let Morton out into the backyard and then cleaned up his mess. He'd somehow gotten into the wastebasket and scattered everything all over the first floor. He'd attacked a pillow upstairs in the guest room. Fortunately, it had been stuffed with cotton and not feathers. I let him back in, and he devoured his late breakfast. I stretched out on the couch, Morton stretched out on the front room rug, and we immediately fell asleep.

A phone call woke me just a little after three. The number came across as 'UNKNOWN', but being half-asleep I answered anyway.

"Hi, Dev. Diane, how are things going?"

"Good, Diane, pretty good, anyway. How about you?"

"Oh, you know the line, same day different disaster."

I laughed and said, "I don't think I ever heard it exactly that way before, but I intend to use it from now on."

"I'm calling to check in on the case you're working, Chandler Hancock. Any new developments? Or for that matter, were you able to build any interest with the police investigators on the other artists missing?"

Interesting she asked the question, but then, I guess it would be a business concern. I decided not to mention Aaron's interview with Kristi and her lawyer, Reginald, or the search warrant for Kristie's place. "Still working on it, but nothing really as of yet. I mentioned the disappearance of the other three artists to the police, and they promised to look into it. That's about all I know."

"You think they will look into it?"

"I sure as hell hope so. They all seem to be related, but the police said, at the moment they simply don't have enough to go on. I got the feeling someone, somewhere, would be keeping an eye on things, and they'll act before another artist disappears."

"Well, you seem to be thinking much more positively than me. Say, I've cooked up a batch of white chicken chili for this evening. Could I talk you into joining me for dinner? I'm thinking a quiet dinner, just the two of us. I wanted to thank you, in some very special way, for all you've done thus far, trying to get the police involved."

Her inflection of 'in some very special way' wasn't lost on me. After my three failed attempts with Kristi, I could sure use a very special thank you. "Yeah, I'd love to. What can I bring?"

"Just yourself and be ready for a good time."

"How about a bottle or two of wine?"

"That would be perfect. Sauvignon Blanc would be wonderful, and I'll owe you big time."

Again with the double meaning, I hoped. "I'll be there. What time?"

"Maybe any time after five. I need a night of pleasure and relaxation, so I'm closing the gallery early. Let me give you the address. I'm up in St. Michael."

"Sounds great," I said. Big deal, a forty-minute drive to see a good looking woman anxious for wine, looking for pleasure, and eager to return a favor. My luck was finally about to change.

No sooner did I hang up with Diane than my phone rang again. "Haskell Investigations."

"Hi, Dev. Aaron, returning your call." He sounded rushed.

"Thanks for calling me back, Aaron. I wanted to see if you found anything during your search of Kristi McKenzie's place."

"We picked up a couple of items. The original painting for starters."

"Kristi lying naked on the red velvet couch?"

"Yeah."

"Isn't that gorgeous? I mean the way she looks."

Aaron ignored my comment. "We also took the statue off her dresser. The one Oscar Callum made."

"Another naked Kristi, can you imagine staring at her for the hours it took to make that thing?"

Aaron ignored that comment as well and said, "We also took the .45 she had."

"Was it in that little drawer in the office closet right below the painting?"

"Yeah, it was right where you said it would be. In fact, we just got the results back from the lab. Ran it for fingerprints and determined when the last time was it had been fired."

"I'm a little surprised she didn't toss the gun in the river. So did you make an arrest? It was the weapon she used to cap Gerry Berk, right?"

"Not exactly, but we were able to identify the fingerprints on the weapon."

"Huh, what do you know. I thought for sure, once you examined the thing, you'd have her. You said you identified the prints. If they didn't belong to Kristi, whose are they? Have you made an arrest yet?"

"No, haven't picked them up yet, but I'm thinking about it."

"Thinking about it? Why in the hell haven't you made an arrest?"

"We haven't made an arrest, Dev, because the fingerprints we found belong to you. Your fingerprints were all over that .45. By the way, from what we could determine, the weapon has never, ever been fired."

"What?"

"You heard me. It's never been fired."

"Well, did she have an excuse for where she was when Berk was murdered? I suppose she told you she was home in bed."

"Berk was murdered between four and five in the morning. You're half-right. She was in bed. Only in bed in downtown Minneapolis, with Reginald Beaufort in his million-dollar condo. We've already seen the security tape of her car sitting in the underground garage. Her cellphone corroborates her location. Beaufort testified in support of her statement, just before he promised to file a harassment lawsuit against us."

"Harassment? Are you kidding me?"

"I only wish."

"Well, the other reason I called is I was on a stake-out last night at the City Salsa House." I didn't want to mention almost freezing to death. "Anyway, I was talking to George Estrada, and he was telling me about some woman waving a bunch of twenty-dollar bills at Berk and handing him the money."

"Yeah, you mentioned this. Did you suggest to him it may have been Kristi McKenzie?"

"I might have, maybe, can't really recall," I said, trying to dodge the question. "But the way he described her, it didn't sound like Kristi. It's pretty hard to forget the way she looks. He told me the woman was attractive, but she had dark hair. Oh, yeah and a tattoo on her leg, on the calf.

"Might have been nice to know this before we made life miserable for Miss McKenzie."

"Well, I called as soon as he told me, but I got dumped into voicemail."

"You home now?"

"I am, but I'm going to head out in a bit. I'm having dinner with Diane, the owner of Find Art."

"Oh, really? Where are you going? Maybe I'll stop by."

"Nice try, but it's a private little get together. She called me, and she sounded ready and willing."

"What's her number? I'll call her back and set her straight then have a squad stand guard out front in the event you decide to show up."

"Very funny. Fortunately, she lives up in St. Michael, way out of your jurisdiction."

Sixty-six

I walked up the block to the Solo Vino wine store and grabbed two bottles of Sean Minor 2016 Sauvignon Blanc. I brought them home, filled a Styrofoam cooler with ice, and set the bottles in the cooler. I shaved, showered, and grabbed a clean shirt. I was pulling onto Interstate 94 at exactly half-past four. Traffic was heavy, in the early stages of rush hour and growing worse by the mile, but I didn't care. I had the radio on a station I liked, the Styrofoam cooler in the back seat, and a full tank of gas.

It took almost an hour to get up to St. Michael on 494. I had the entire night ahead of me and Diane all to myself. Her directions were right on the mark, and once I pulled off the freeway, it was only a five-minute drive to Thirty-Sixth Street.

All the homes were new, very large, and clearly out of my price range. Diane's place was a gorgeous brick house with trimmed hedges and climbing roses on either side of the attached double garage. A large boat on a trailer was parked in the driveway with a vinyl cover snugly pulled over it and next to that a red pickup truck was backed up against the garage door. I pulled in front of the boat and turned off the car, hoping to hide my fuzzy VW Golf from Diane. I walked up the curving brick path with a neatly trimmed little hedge on either side and rang the doorbell.

She answered the door in skintight, black Capri slacks that went just below the knee, a white silk top, and red stiletto heels. It wasn't lost on me that she was bra-less, and I tried not to stare.

"Well, Dev Haskell. Don't you look delicious! Thank you for coming."

"Brought you some wine, Diane. Sauvignon Blanc, per your request," I said and held out the bottles.

"Oh, thank you. I've been dying for a glass, but I didn't want to start until you arrived. Oh, and they're chilled. You are just the best," she said, taking the wine from me. She leaned in and gave me a kiss on the lips, maybe lingering there just a second or two longer than necessary. She stepped back, flashed her dark brown eyes, and said, "Come on back to the kitchen."

I followed her down the marble hallway, past the living room with a red velvet couch similar to the one I'd seen looking through the window at Myles Rossler's house, and into the kitchen. I caught the outline of a very small thong beneath the skintight slacks as she strutted into the kitchen. She had a tattoo of a butterfly resting on a flower on the back of both her calves. There was a crystal vase with fresh-cut purple coneflowers sitting on the kitchen counter. The kitchen smelled wonderfully spicy, and she set one of the bottles on the counter and then opened a large refrigerator door. For just half a second, my mind jumped back to nearly freezing to death in George's freezer.

Diane was bending over, taking her time looking for something in the refrigerator. She looked at me over her shoulder, and as she bent down and said, "Would you mind opening that bottle, darling? I've got some chilled glasses in here somewhere."

She held the pose, although I could see the chilled wine glasses directly in front of her from where I stood. I stared for another long moment before directing my attention to the wine bottle.

Diane placed the chilled glasses on the kitchen counter and then went back to the refrigerator and pulled out a tray with cheeses and a spicy looking spread. She placed the tray next to a plate of crackers just as I finished pouring the wine. She picked up both wine glasses, handed one to me, raised her glass in a toast, and said, "To an enjoyable and very memorable evening. Let the games begin."

She topped up my glass more than once while we chatted at the kitchen counter. When she wasn't topping up my glass, she smoothed the spicy spread on a cracker and stuffed it in my mouth then had me lick the tips of her fingers. I'd lost count of the times she topped up my glass. All I knew was, we were on our second bottle of wine.

She took me out into her backyard. It was very private, with a line of trees and then the Crow River beyond the trees and a state park on the far side of the river. The homes on either side were situated at an angle that gave her absolute privacy. There was a large, raised bed with a number of different flowers: lilies, daisies, coneflowers, and mums. "I love fresh cut flowers, and with these, I can have fresh flowers virtually all summer long."

"They're lovely but must be a lot of work," I said.

"I like to think of it more as a labor of love, and of course, I get the benefit. The soil is exceptionally rich," she said and half-laughed.

"Are you extending this raised flower bed?" There were a dozen sacks of soil at the end of the bed, along with a shovel and a number of eight-foot lengths of timber.

"Yes, dahlias, they bloom in late fall, and I'm hoping they'll give me another month of color. I want the bed ready before spring, which means I have to have it done this fall. I want to extend the bed another five feet."

"Sounds like work," I said as I emptied my glass.

"Mmm-mmm, like I said, a labor of love. Say, are you in any hurry to eat?"

"No, we're on your schedule, Diane. After the past few days, I'd just like to enjoy myself, and believe me, I am."

"Oh, that's so sweet of you. I have an idea, if you're interested. Let's go inside. I think I could use some more wine, and I know you could."

"I should probably slow down on the wine I've got to drive back to the cities tonight."

"Drive back? I was hoping you might be staying for breakfast," she said and raised her eyebrows.

"Well, as long as I'm not imposing, I mean I wouldn't want—"

"Dev? Hello? I've been counting on it. God, haven't you picked up on any of my not-so-subtle hints? Or are you going to make me ask you outright? Ok, I don't care. I want you."

"I'm picking up on that. More than happy to oblige. I'd love it as a matter of fact."

"Well, good, because I've got a little surprise. Come on. Let's get the glasses refilled. Dinner can wait." She wrapped her arm around my waist and leaned her head against my shoulder as we walked back into the kitchen. To tell the truth, I couldn't believe my luck, and after all the wine, I had to concentrate on my walking. I'd already been over-served.

Diane took the wine glasses and set them on the kitchen counter. She opened the freezer door on the refrigerator and took a handful of ice cubes from the ice maker. She put three cubes in each glass and filled the glasses with wine. She handed both glasses to me and followed up with a lingering kiss. She kicked off her red stiletto heels. "Come on. Follow me. I have something special for both of us."

I followed her down a hallway toward what looked like a cedar door. She walked like a fashion model on a runway, placing one foot directly in front of the other. I glanced in as we passed a room, and there, on the wall, was a painting just like Kristi's. A gorgeous naked woman stretched out on a red velvet couch. Only this was a painting of Diane. Right now, I was too focused on the real thing, her fantastic hips just inches away. I didn't notice she had unbuttoned her blouse until she turned and faced me, revealing two small white triangles of skin where a bikini top had covered her breasts. She took hold of her slacks and slowly pulled them down below her hips.

"I hope you don't mind a sauna, but I thought it might be a most interesting way to begin. Here, let me hold those while you undress," she said, taking the wine glasses from my hand. I undid the cuffs on my shirt, felt my heart beginning to pound as I quickly unbuttoned my shirt, and she said, "Oh baby, I just want to eat you up."

After that comment, the top two buttons flew off my shirt as I tore it open and dropped it on the floor. My belt was unbuckled in record time, and I was kicking my trousers into a corner when she said, "Oh, God, look at you. Oh, I really need this."

The boxers and socks came off in one fell swoop, and she handed the wine glasses to me. She was licking her lips and breathing heavily. As I took the wine glasses from her, she pulled her blouse off her shoulders and said, "Go on. Get in there and get comfortable. I don't want to wait another minute. The handcuffs are for me. I liked to be taken advantage of."

She pulled the door open, and I hurried inside. The light was on, and the heater was going. There were two levels of cedar benches, and I climbed up to the second level, set the wine glasses down next to a pair of pink plastic handcuffs, and stretched out on the top bench. I glanced down, and the ice in the glasses was already beginning to melt. Not that I cared. If getting kinky in the sauna was Diane's thing, I was ready for it.

Sixty-seven

It had been more than a little while. The heater seemed to be growing even hotter. It kept making noise, clanging like an old gas furnace. I heard what maybe sounded like the shower running and figured she probably just wanted to be extra fresh.

It was hot and getting hotter. The ice cubes in the wine had melted sometime ago. I got down from the top level and sat on the lower bench. It was a shade cooler but only for a second or two before the heat seemed to envelop me. There was a wooden water bucket at the opposite end of the bench, but it was empty. I looked around for a temperature control, but there wasn't one. I waited a minute or two longer and then, dripping sweat, decided maybe we could start things off by just taking a shower together instead.

I pushed on the door to open it. Apparently, it was stuck. Probably swollen from the heat. I pushed harder, still nothing. I really pushed, and the damn thing felt as hot as a frying pan. Still, it didn't move. I attempted to shoulder it a couple of times, but I might as well have been going up against a concrete wall.

"Hey, Diane. Diane? The door seems to be stuck. Diane?" I shouted again, this time slapping the palm of my hand against the cedar planks on the door. "Diane? Hey, Diane?" I yelled. Now I was pounding my fist against the door. "Diane. Open the door. Diane? Hey, Diane. This isn't funny. Come on. Open the door, honey."

No response. No sound from the other side.

It had been too long. Maybe she fell and hit her head. What if she was lying on the bathroom floor and needed emergency treatment? What if she couldn't get to me and I melted or whatever the hell happened if you were in here too long?

The heater kept cranking away. I checked the thing out, but there wasn't an off button anywhere. The wiring on the back of the thing ran through a metal conduit and out through the wall. I was beginning to feel dizzy, and it wasn't from the wine. I tried to grab the conduit, but it was scalding hot, and I couldn't hold on. I looked at the benches. The planks were an inch thick and appeared to be solidly attached. There was a large knothole in the middle of one of them, and I attempted to lift the plank, but it didn't move. I got down on all fours and crawled beneath the bench then raised up and tried to force the plank up. At first, it didn't move. On the fourth try, it moved ever so slightly, I think.

I took a deep breath, repositioned, and raised my back up against the plank. I heard a slight crack. I dropped to the floor, closed my eyes, and let the dizziness pass. I raised up again and pushed against the plank. This time, the sound of the crack was louder. I did it a third time, and the plank snapped and rose a good inch, tearing my shoulder open against the jagged edge in the process.

I dropped to the floor and laid there for a minute or two. I felt like I was in an oven. I stood and pried up the broken end of the plank, all the while, growing dizzier by the moment. Half the plank was now standing almost straight up at a ninety-degree angle to the bench. The nails were bent and barely attached to the frame. I twisted the plank from side to side, and suddenly, it came loose from the frame.

I gasped for air and sucked in a painful lung-full of hot air. I stepped over to the stove, and using the plank, I lifted the metal cage covering the rocks off the heater. I knocked the rocks off the heater with the end of the plank and then the tray that held the rocks. Below the tray was a plastic box with the logo SAWO and the words 'Power Control.' I smashed the box a number of times with the plank until it shattered and exposed all sorts of wiring. I drove the end of the plank into the wir-ing, getting dizzier and dizzier with each blow. Sparks were flying, and smoke was rising, but I kept on smash-ing the plank into the wiring, gradually tearing the con-nections lose. Suddenly, I felt as if I was falling off a cliff. It was a long, long way down.

Sixty-eight

aron's distant voice seemed to echo in a cave. "Hey, I found him! I found him. In here, fellas. Jesus Christ. What the hell? Was she trying to cook the poor bastard?"

"Pull him out into the hall. Watch it, he's wounded in that shoulder."

"Did she shoot him?"

"I don't think so."

"We got this, sir. Let us do our job. Frankie, start him on an RL IV. Let's get him on the gurney and get him out of here."

It's not that I didn't want to open my eyes, but I couldn't. Somewhere in the back of my mind, I thought it was getting nice and cool.

"They said another twenty or thirty minutes, and it would have been too late. God, all those brass deadbolt locks on the door, talk about nuts."

I opened my eyes and focused on the end of the bed. Aaron and Louie were chatting. I tried to say something, but it sounded like a grunt. Louie looked up at me. "Well, what do you know. He has risen."

"Dev, you gotta knock this shit off," Aaron said. "You want to get together, you don't have to make a scene. We can just meet for dinner somewhere."

I looked around the room. It appeared familiar. Everything was painted white with a window that looked out at a red brick wall. The window was modern and slid from left to right rather than pulled up like the ones in my house.

"How… How did I… What? What happened?"

"You're in United Hospital again," Aaron said.

"Your hot, sexy date decided it might be fun to bake you," Louie added.

"Diane?"

"Yeah, she's a piece of work. While you've been living the life of Riley in here for the past two days, St. Michael police located your artist pals," Aaron said.

"My artist pals?"

"Yeah. All of them. Webster, Callum, and Rossler. She had them buried in a raised flower bed in her backyard."

"Yeah, she told me she wanted to add dahlias to that raised flower bed." Louie and Aaron shot each other a glance. "Nothing on Chandler Hancock?"

"Oh yeah. She was keeping him in a padlocked freezer down in the basement. Looks like she was probably going to add him, along with you, to the flower bed. Of course, I'm forgetting Gerry Berk, but he's down in the city morgue."

"Gerry Berk?"

"Remember the woman giving him twenty dollar bills? Short dark hair, attractive, tattoo on the calf of her leg. Berk was supposed to take you out, but when that didn't work, she met him down along the river. Shot him near the Upper Landing, hoping to point the finger at Kristi McKenzie, and initially, it worked. They found the .45 she used to kill Berk and a half-dozen photos of that Kristi painting at the Find Art Gallery."

"When you told me about George at the City Salsa House and the woman giving Berk the money, it just wasn't adding up, so I called him. His description sounded like your friend Diane. Turns out, 48 hours after Kristi McKenzie purchased gas up in Warba, guess who got a speeding ticket in Itasca County? I'll save you the trouble, Diane Turner."

"You're kidding me?"

"Oh, it gets even crazier. Diane Turner was originally from St. Michael. Guess who else was?"

"I don't know, Gerry Berk?"

"Not even close. Joseph Lauer, Kristi's fiancé. He was Diane Turner's high school sweetheart. By the way, Diane has size five feet, and along with the killing the artists, she admitted pushing drunken Joseph Lauer in front of that car. Said she didn't mean to, but he was going on about how wonderful Kristi was, and apparently, Diane just snapped."

"So, what does all this mean?"

"What does it mean? Well, for starters, we've been able to clear four missing persons and one suspected murder off the books."

"But what the hell? Why? I mean, Diane was running a successful business. She has, or at least had, a great reputation, not only locally but nationally. Why would she do this? Any of it?"

"The short answer is money. All four of those artists would be excellent investments, once word got out they were missing and ultimately declared dead. Diane had close to two dozen paintings and sculptures by them. At today's rates, they'd collectively go for maybe a million bucks. But once they were declared dead, if she hung onto the work, they could fetch two, three, maybe even four times that amount. And all she had to do was sit on the art. I think that was where you came in. Kristi McKenzie, strange way to do it, but she actually wanted to find her husband. Diane at Find Art just decided you might be the perfect person to speed things along, well, until you maybe got too close to the truth, whether you knew it or not."

"This is too weird."

"You're telling me. Hey look, I better get going," Aaron said. "I have to let Morton out. Not to worry, I've got your keys. They were in your pants lying on the hallway floor at Diane's house. Talk about dodging a bullet, Dev." Aaron shook his head as he walked over and patted me on the shoulder. It hurt, and I flinched. "Oh yeah, sorry, I forgot you got some stitches in there. See you later."

Aaron headed out of the room, and Louie just sat there and shook his head. "I don't know, man, never a dull moment, that's for damn sure. Just glad you're okay. Now hurry up and get out of here and back to the office. I need some decent coffee. Catch you at the office."

My stomach growled as I lay in bed. There was a plastic bottle of water on the table hanging over my bed. I twisted the cap off and took a couple of swallows. It really felt good going down.

The door opened about an inch, and someone peeked in. I automatically felt for my gun, but I didn't have it. Kristi stepped into the room and closed the door. She wasn't dressed in hospital scrubs this time, but that was okay. I just wanted to rest.

"Did that police lieutenant tell you what happened, Dev?"

"Yeah, he gave me an update. I'm sorry to hear about Chandler, Kristi. My condolences. I didn't think—"

"Stop right there. No, you didn't think. In fact, you fingered me for his murder as well as killing everyone else in this, this beyond bizarre, unbelievable, dreadful, shitty situation." She was suddenly sobbing. "How could you think it was me? How could you even think that?"

"I'm sorry, Kristi. At the time I—"

"You know what, Dev? At the time, you had your head up your ass. In fact, you always seem to have your head up your ass. Do me a favor, will you? Do not ever, ever call me again. If I ever see you again, I will— Well, just don't ever contact me again. Please. And, I'm blocking you on Facebook," she shouted as she hurried out of the room and slammed the door behind her.

A moment later, the nurse who had wheeled me out to Aaron's car the last time I was here walked into the room. "How are you feeling, Mr. Haskell?"

"Oh, just peachy."

"Good. Can I get you anything?"

"No, I'm fine. Any chance of getting out of here tomorrow?"

"Oh, yeah. I'm pretty sure you will. We'd like nothing better. We, umm, we're going to station someone at your door tonight. You know, in the event some late-night visitor has some kinky idea. Right now, sleep is more important."

"Gee, thanks."

"It's my pleasure. I'm off in an hour," she said, checking her watch. "So I'll see you next time. Until then, enjoy yourself!"

The End

Thank you for taking the time to read **Art Attack**. If you enjoyed the read please consider leaving a review. Just click on the appropriate link, it really, really helps. Thanks in advance . . .

Don't miss the following sample of **Mystery Man,** the next tale in the Dev Haskell mystery series.

Sneak Peek

Mystery Man

Second Edition

MIKE FARICY

Prologue

rtie Walker finished his tonic water with a twist and pushed the empty glass across the bar. He was facing the stage but not really watching, more intent on checking out the few remaining clientele before heading for the men's room. They'd announced last call over the sound system about ten minutes ago. Just two other guys were seated around the bar, three more sat in front of the stage. The crowd had been thin, even for a Tuesday night.

The last dancer was shaking everything she had up on stage in an effort to get a halfway decent tip, but it wasn't going to happen tonight. She had to pay a hundred and twenty bucks just to dance and then give thirty percent of her tips to the manager. There was no way she was going to make any money dancing in a place owned by Tubby Gustafson. The last song finally ended, and she swung around the brass pole two more times. She quickly picked up the tips lying on the edge of the stage, seven dollars, and a piece of paper with a phone number. She tossed the phone number on the floor and headed back to the dressing room.

Artie headed into the restroom, waited until he was alone, and then hurried over to the maintenance closet next to the back stall. He quickly picked the lock and stepped into the closet. He pulled the mask on the top of his head, put the stethoscope around his neck, slipped on his latex gloves, and quickly screwed a sixty-nine cent hook and eye latch into the wooden closet door. He pulled the Snickers candy bar from his pocket, opened the wrapper, and took a bite. So far, so good.

The bartender locked the front entrance. He poured a bourbon and a glass of red wine for the two dancers. They sat at the bar and sipped while he picked up glasses and napkins from the empty tables and set them on the bar. He loaded the dishwasher behind the bar, turned it on, and then turned off the outside neon lights. He poured half a glass of sparkling water and joined the two dancers. They chatted for twenty minutes before he shut everything down, and they all headed out to their cars. Artie Walker waited another half-hour in the closet before he quietly unlocked the door and peeked out.

It was dark, which was a good thing because, if the lights were off, it suggested the place was empty. He placed a hand against the wall and slowly made his way to the door in the dark. He listened at the door for a number of minutes and didn't hear anything. He pulled the clown mask down over his face, opened the men's room door, and headed past the dressing room to the back office.

The office door was marked private, and the lock on the door was a Mul-T-Lock, a state of the art lock that was pick and drill resistant. Fortunately, Artie had a special tool sent all the way from Australia, and he was in the office in thirty seconds and standing in front of the door to the vault.

The vault was what had given him the idea. A walk-in vault in a strip club? That seemed like a lot of overkill. The vault was at least a hundred years old, and maybe the owner, Tubby Gustafson, even got it for free, but the installation had to have cost a small fortune. Artie pulled the combination from his pocket, placed his stethoscope against the steel door, and slowly began to turn the dial. It took no more than ninety seconds before he pulled the door open.

There were two heavy black canvas cargo bags, leather, and heavy, that were sitting next to one another on a shelf. Two cash register drawers from behind the bar were next to them. Artie grabbed the cargo bags. He tossed them out of the vault and into the office. He closed the vault door behind him, spun the dial, and hurried out of the office with the bags slung over his shoulders. He relocked the office door and hurried out past the bar toward the front entrance.

He was almost to the door when he saw the flashing red and blue lights cross the intersection and race across the parking lot headed toward the entrance. That was more than enough warning. He spun around and ran toward the back door.

He flew through the small kitchen. One of the cargo bags bumped into a plastic tray full of glasses, sending everything crashing to the floor. He made it to the rear door, peeked out, and ran across the alley into a backyard just as more flashing lights entered the far end of the alley and sped toward the rear door of the club.

Artie ducked down behind a hedge and heard chatter that he couldn't understand on a radio as two cops jumped out of the car and entered through the rear door. They stepped inside, and a moment later, the lights flashed on. He pulled the clown mask off and waited another two minutes, which under the circumstances, seemed like two hours. He crouched and made his way across the backyard, past a swing set and a sandbox. He hurried up the street toward his car. Fortunately, at this hour, no one drove past.

One

As I opened the office door, Louie said, "You certainly seem to be in a good mood. I heard you whistling all the way up the stairs. Things must have gone well on last night's date,"

"Let's just say, not as bad as it could have been."

"Huh? Not as bad? What does that mean?" Louie asked. He tossed a file on his picnic table desk and leaned back in his chair. Morton settled onto his bed in front of the file cabinet and placed his paws over his head. He'd heard this story before.

"It just means that Sharon didn't say don't ever call me again. She didn't go into the ladies' room and climb out the window. She didn't tell the bartender to call the cops on me."

"This is what makes a good date in your mind?"

"Louie, it was our second date. She's going by the playbook. I met her at that wedding two weeks ago and got her phone number. We met for lunch the following Wednesday. I took her to the restaurant last night and offered to provide dessert at my place. She declined; she's supposed to decline. It's in the women's playbook. She has to prove she's not a slut. Okay, now she's done that. The three-date rule, mission accomplished."

"What?"

"Yeah, she's proven she has morals or at least can pretend she has them. Our next date is tonight, and I'm pulling out all the stops. I've got a dinner reservation at Antonio's for tonight at eight."

"Whoa, big spender."

"This is how it works. After last night when she got the 'I'm not a slut' bit out of the way, now we can have a great time. She can spend the night. She'll no doubt be wearing something super sexy. I've got clean sheets on the bed and clean towels in the bathroom. She can be as wild as she wants to be because she's already demonstrated she's not easy. It's the third date, Louie. This is the way things work."

"Gee, who knew? Well, keep me posted."

"Yeah sure, reporting in to you will be the first thing I think of. Just remember, I might be a little late coming in tomorrow morning. In fact, I might not be in until noon, you never know."

Louie had an afternoon full of court dates, and I had a stack of job applications I had to wade through for an insurance client. I was online all afternoon, checking property tax records, looking for arrest histories, and speeding tickets on close to fifty job applications. Mercifully, everyone checked out just fine. We were home a little after five, and I took Morton for a walk. I set a bottle of pink Prosecco in the fridge. Sharon loved the stuff. I showered, shaved, put on a reasonably clean shirt, and a dark sweater to hide the shirt wrinkles. I was seated at Antonio's at 7:45, fifteen minutes early.

Sharon arrived stylishly late at 8:10 and looked like a million bucks. She wore a tight, black cocktail dress with lace sleeves and a scoop neck. Nothing was left to the imagination, and a number of heads turned as she waved and then strutted to our table. Her dark hair was swept back over her shoulders, and she looked like she was going to bounce out of her top at any moment. I loved it.

"Hi, Dev, sorry I'm late. My car's in the shop, so I had to Uber over here," she said, then leaned down and kissed my cheek. "Mmm-mmm," she moaned softly and lingered a second or two before she sat down.

Uber over? Yeah, right, how perfect. She probably had a friend drop her off. Now it would just be natural that I'd offer to give her a ride home. Then once we're in the car, I'll offer a glass of pink Prosecco at my place, and that will start the clock ticking to try out my clean sheets.

"Well, you're certainly worth the wait. You look great," I said.

"Thanks, I was running short on time after dropping off the car, so I just threw on any old thing. Hope you don't mind."

"Mind? You kidding? You look fabulous."

"Oh, thanks, you're so sweet," she said, shrugged, smiled, and gave my hand a squeeze.

Yeah, the third date was it. I could tell. We had dinner. I ordered pasta, and Sharon had lasagna. We ordered a bottle of wine with dinner, took our time, no rush. I kept her glass filled and listened to everything she said. She only answered two text messages during dinner, so that was a plus. I paid the bill, and we headed out to the parking lot. Once again, Sharon turned all sorts of heads as we walked out, holding hands, and she rested her head against my shoulder.

The entrance to Antonio's has a twenty-foot red canvas awning over the top. It was a lovely early fall evening, a warm temperature, but not hot. We walked out the door and stopped to let a car pass before stepping into the parking lot.

My first thought was, who knew there would be two red 2011 Chevy HHR's in the parking lot? Then I glanced at the license plate as it sped past and out onto the street. I recognized the number on the plate. It was mine.

"Hey, asshole," I yelled.

"Excuse me?" Sharon said and pulled her arm away from mine.

"That car that just shot past, that was mine."

"Yours?"

"Yeah. Someone just stole it. What the hell? I can't believe it. They just stole my car from right in front of me." I pulled my phone out and dialed 911.

"911 Emergency services."

"Yeah, I'm standing out front of Antonio's restaurant, and some bastard just drove off in my car."

"Did you know the individual?"

"Know him? You gotta be kidding. Hell no, I didn't know him. What the… Look, my car was just stolen, right in front of me. He's headed east on Fifth Street."

"Do you know the license number?"

I gave her the license number.

"Color and make of the car?"

"Yeah, it's a red Chevy HHR. The year is twenty-eleven."

Sharon had her phone out and was texting someone. I was on the phone with 911 for another four or five minutes. A shiny black Toyota suddenly pulled into the lot. Sharon waved her hand, and the car came to a stop.

"Sorry about your car, Dev. I'm going to grab this Uber and head home."

"The cops said they'd be here in thirty or forty minutes. I was thinking we could maybe grab another glass of wine. Check out the dessert menu if you wanted to—"

"Thanks, but I've got a crazy day tomorrow. I should probably just head home."

"Well, um, do you want me to stop by once I file my report with the police? I could bring the bottle of pink Prosecco." It wasn't what I'd planned, but a night at Sharon's or even just an hour or two was better than the dry spell I'd been going through.

"Oh, that's sweet of you," she said, sounding like she didn't mean a word. She followed up with a fake smile. "Maybe we both need a little break."

A little break? So far, I paid for a night of drinks and dinner on the last two nights. I'd certainly put in the time, not to mention the money.

She opened the back door on the Uber and slipped in, then looked at me and locked the door. No kiss, no hand squeeze, not so much as a wave. I read her lips as she spoke to the Uber driver. '*Just go, please, and hurry.*'

TWO

I watched the Toyota turn the corner and disappear from sight. Great, just great. What could be worse? A black SUV in a distant corner of the parking lot turned on its headlights and pulled out of the parking space. It pulled up alongside me as I stood beneath the canopy waiting for Sharon to come to her senses and return. The passenger window on the SUV lowered, and unfortunately, a familiar voice said, "Get in, Haskell."

Fat Freddy Zimmerman. Righthand thug to the city's crime lord, Tubby Gustafson.

"Perfect timing, Freddy. Like things aren't bad enough. Hey, it's turned into a pretty lousy night, and right now I don't really need to—"

"I'm asking nicely, Haskell. Get your worthless ass in here while you can still do it under your own power." With that, the backdoor opened, and a very large individual stepped out, smiled, and extended his hand toward the inside of the car.

I'd had just about enough. "Hey, Freddy, sorry, but I'm going to take a pass. It's been a lousy night. Someone just ripped off my car. It was my third date with a woman, the night everything was supposed to happen, and she ended up going home in an Uber. For the record, just in case you're not picking up on it, I don't feel like talking to Tubby tonight. How about we set an appointment for some time tomorrow and I can just—"

"Get his worthless ass in here," Freddy said and raised the window.

The thug started toward me, minus the smile. "Hey, Freddy, were you even listening. I said—" The thug placed a hand the size of a ten-pound ham on my shoulder and started to force me toward the open door.

I slapped his arm away, made a fist with my right hand, and put everything I had into a punch headed straight for his solar plexus. He caught my fist in his massive hand and began to squeeze, all the while smiling. I started to groan as he slowly increased the pressure, and then just when I thought he was going to break all four of my fingers, he wiped the smile from his face and gave me a head butt. I saw stars just before everything went black.

"We're almost there. Wake that idiot up," a distant voice seemed to echo somewhere in my thick skull. I felt some not so gentle slaps across my face.

"All right, all right, knock it off. I'm awake. I was just resting my eyes," I said. I could barely recognize my own voice.

My statement brought a chorus of laughter from all four thugs in the car. I opened my eyes and focused in on the guy who had head-butted me. He didn't smile, and

I noticed a red welt on his forehead after coming in contact with me. Let that be a lesson to him, although it didn't seem to bother him all that much.

"Nice of you to join us again, Haskell," Fat Freddy said without turning around. "You'll be in front of Mr. Gustafson in just a minute, so pull yourself together."

I couldn't breathe through my nose. I glanced down at my sweater. Fortunately, it was black, so the blood from the head butt I'd received more or less disappeared. The thug with the forehead welt held out some sort of a baby butt-wipe in my direction.

"I'm fine."

"You might want to clean the blood off your face and chin," he said.

I dabbed and wiped and asked for another butt-wipe and then another one after that.

Fat Freddy laughed and said, "I knew you were always a shit head, Haskell." He followed up with another laugh as we turned into a crowded parking lot and headed for the building at the far end. The neon sign across the top of the building flashed the name of the place twice, Bare Facts. After that, the sign went dark for a moment before the letters flashed on one at a time until the entire sign was lit up. Then the sign flashed two more times before returning to one letter at a time. I recognized the place and had even visited a few dozen times, at least until I learned Tubby Gustafson owned the place, after which I pretty much stayed away.

The driver pulled the SUV to a stop opposite the front door. Actually, a set of double doors with neon lights designed to look like a pair of female legs in cowboy boots, one on either side of the doors. A childish idea that was probably great for business based on the three guys standing just outside the entrance having their picture taken.

"Let's go," Fat Freddy said as he rolled out of the front passenger seat. The large thug next to me opened the door and stepped out. He gave me a quick nod of his head, indicating I had better get out and fast. I thought it best to comply. Another thug joined us.

Fat Freddy said, "All right, Haskell, I don't want you talking with anyone along the way. You just keep your fat head down, keep that big mouth shut, and follow me. When we get to the office, I know you'll act the perfect gentleman. All right, let's go."

As we stepped in through the neon legs, the SUV pulled away and headed into the crowded parking lot. Inside, the place was jammed. Guys stood two-deep at the bar, all the tables around the stage were filled, and guys were standing against the walls on either side of the stage. The crowd was attired in everything from three-piece suits to shorts and work boots. Three women were currently on stage. One spun around on a brass pole while the other two danced along the front of the stage. Four more women, clad in see-through negligees, were working the crowd offering lap dances.

"Keep moving," one of the thugs behind me shouted over the music. He pushed me forward just to make his point. Everyone was focused on the three women working the stage, and no one noticed us as we headed down the hall past the dressing room and toward an office door marked private. Fat Freddy knocked on the door, smiled, and held it open for us.

"Behave," he said, issuing a warning as I stepped past him.

Three

Another muscular thug with a neatly trimmed beard and an open collar white shirt beneath his dark suit stood in a corner. He had his hands politely clasped in front of him, and he nodded at Fat Freddy as he stepped into the office. Fat Freddy nodded back. The thug looked at me, snapped his fingers, pointed to a chair in front of the desk, and I sat down.

Tubby Gustafson was seated behind the desk and didn't bother to look up. He was busy pushing keys on an adding machine. His fingers were moving in a blur, and there must have been at least five feet of partially rolled adding machine tape draped across the desk. Behind Tubby was a large steel door leading into a vault. The door was painted black and looked about a hundred years old with elaborate leafy gold trim around the edge of the door and the combination dial. The door was only partially open and was made up of a number of inch-thick steel plates.

Tubby's fingers flew across the adding machine keys for another minute or two before he hit a button, causing the machine to crank for a bit before it fell silent. He pressed a key, advancing the paper tape a couple of inches, then tore off the tape and glanced at whatever number was at the bottom.

"Damnit to hell," he half-shouted and tossed the tape onto the desk. "I'll kill whoever did— Well, if it isn't Private Investigator, Dev Haskell. How nice to see you. Perfect timing."

"Always nice to see you Tub… err, Mr. Gustafson."

"Tell me, Haskell. How is that business of yours working out?"

"My business? It's keeping me busy. I've got a few major clients now that provide regular work."

"Really?" Tubby raised his eyebrows. "Regular clients. You don't say. Are you making any money?"

"Oh, you know how it is, sir. I manage to keep the wolf away from the door, and then just about the time things seem to be going well, something unexpected happens."

"Unexpected?"

"Yes, sir. As a matter of fact, just tonight I came out of a restaurant with a friend, and my car was stolen right in front of my eyes."

Tubby smiled. "A friend, interesting. A business friend?"

"Umm, not exactly," I said.

"Well, I know how things go, Haskell. You get a hundred dollars in the bank, and suddenly, you need a hundred and ten to repair the furnace or pay the water bill."

"Yes, sir, something like that."

"Haskell, I'm going to give you the opportunity to experience a decent client. Without a doubt, the best client you will ever work for. What do you say?"

"Well, sir, umm, yeah, that sounds nice. What company would this be?"

"Not a company, Haskell. An individual. A wonderful individual. Namely, me," Tubby said and then extended his hands, palms up as if he was welcoming me into a church or something.

"You, sir?"

"Correct, and let me be the first to say congratulations. Lucky you."

"What exactly is it that you would like me to investigate?"

"Just one little thing," Tubby said, sounding like he was dangling the only option for freedom in front of a desperate prisoner.

"One little thing?"

Tubby nodded as he pushed his chair back and stood. "Come over here, Haskell," he said, urging me forward and wiggling his index finger.

I slowly stood and walked around the desk as Tubby pushed the vault door open. I looked inside the vault. The walls, floor, and ceiling were all steel. The vault was maybe ten feet long, six feet wide, and one side had a series of shelves. The shelves were all empty.

"Did you want me to paint this or move the shelves somewhere?"

Tubby shook his head then said over his shoulder, "You were right, Frederick. Why do I even bother? Haskell, the opportunity I'm presenting to you is to locate the items that are missing from this vault. To be specific, two black cargo bags that disappeared barely twenty-four hours ago."

"Someone took them out of this vault?"

Tubby smiled and said, "Correct. You're beginning to catch on."

"Who has access to the vault? Do you lock it?"

"It's always locked. It was opened last night at seven minutes after two in the morning, and the cash drawers from the registers behind the bar were placed in the vault. Like they are every evening after close. At twelve minutes after three, an individual opened the vault and left with both cargo bags. Show him," Tubby said and snapped his fingers.

The thug with the neatly trimmed beard and white shirt ran his fingers across the computer keyboard on the desk. An image appeared of an individual in a clown mask, wearing blue latex gloves and dressed all in black. He had a stethoscope plugged into his ears and was slowly working the combination dial on the door to the vault.

"Any idea who this is?" I asked.

"That's for you to find out," Tubby said.

"Who knows about this vault? Obviously, it's not original to the building. Did you have it put in?"

"Just for starters, certainly anyone who has ever ventured into this office knows about the vault. I had it installed three years ago for the express purpose of preventing just such an incident. Damnit to hell. Whoever did this is going to pay, big time!" Tubby's temper was suddenly ramping up. "I want you to find out who in the hell did this and find out fast."

The individual on the computer screen opened the vault and disappeared inside. A moment later, he stepped out of the vault with two large, black cargo bags slung over his shoulders. He seemed to look up at the security camera. The clown mask suggested he was laughing, and then he raised his middle finger and waved it at the camera before he disappeared. Tubby's face went crimson.

"Have you contacted the police?" I asked.

"The police? Really, Haskell? Please, use your head and don't make me think you're as stupid as everyone keeps telling me."

"I'll try to see what I can find out. I'm going to need a list of your employees. Anyone you can think of who has been in this office. I'll need the name of whatever company installed the vault and the names of anyone with access to the vault. Oh, and there's one other little problem, sir."

"And what in God's name is that?"

"My car was stolen this evening at—"

"At Antonio's. I'm aware of that, and for your information, we've already recovered it, and it's waiting for you out in the parking lot. I only hope you will return the favor and be as efficient when dealing with my particular problem."

"Recovered it? But how did you even know? I—"

Tubby held up his hand and said, "Silencio. If you would please simply focus on the task at hand."

Four

I left Bare Facts armed with about twenty pages worth of names and addresses of employees, former employees, dancers, the company that installed the vault, a number of accountants and attorneys who worked for Tubby, vendors, and various individuals who, for one reason or another, had seen the inside of Tubby's office. Not to mention the image of the guy wearing the clown mask and giving Tubby the finger, talk about living dangerously.

One thing became crystal clear, this was mission impossible. And then there was the question of who stole my car. Obviously, Tubby arranged the whole episode. Thanks to him, my third date with Sharon had been ruined.

When I walked out of Bare Facts, my red car was parked directly in front of the place. Two thugs smiled, and one of them opened the driver's door for me. Once I was inside, the thug who had opened the door took a pocket square from his suit coat and rubbed it across the door handle, pretending to make it clean. It wasn't lost on me that what he was really doing was removing any fingerprints.

Still, it didn't make sense. Tubby could have grabbed me anywhere at any time. Ever the eternal optimist, I drove past Sharon's condo, thinking if there was still a light on, it might make sense to call her and offer to come up and give her a back rub or something. Alas, the lights were off, and the place was dark. It was now approaching midnight after all.

I drove home, parked my car in the garage, then went inside and let Morton out into the backyard. I got the coffee ready for the morning, let Morton back in, and we went to bed. Nothing against Morton, but he wasn't who I'd hoped would wake up next to me in the morning. I tortured myself thinking about Tubby as my new client for the next twenty minutes until I drifted off to sleep.

I was up two hours before Morton made his way downstairs. I let him out the back door and returned to the laundry list of names and addresses Tubby had printed off for me. Twenty pages worth, and I knew there had to be more. I went through the list, checking the names of potentials. Certainly, Tubby's band of desperados, starting with Fat Freddy Zimmerman, were all potential culprits. Of course, there was also the company Tubby got the vault from and the crew that installed it. I was overwhelmed, to say the least.

Morton and I were in the office a half-hour before Louie arrived. I was on my computer looking up folks on Tubby's list, and it wasn't going well.

"Dev?" Louie said. He stood in the doorway with his hand still on the doorknob. "Oh my God, what happened to your nose?"

"Nothing good." I went on to tell him about my car being stolen, Sharon taking an Uber home, the thug's head butt, and Fat Freddy Zimmerman taking me to see Tubby at Bare Facts.

"So, you're going to take on the investigation?"

"Louie, this is Tubby Gustafson we're talking about. You don't tell him no."

"What did the police say?"

"The police? He's not going to report this to the police, and I sure as hell won't. God only knows where this stuff came from, but two canvas duffle bags filled with cash or drugs or diamonds or something. It's gotta be worth a million, plus."

"And what are you going to do if you find it? Who knows how many people you'll be up against?"

"If I'm so lucky to find out who is involved, I'm giving their names to Tubby and running for cover. Let him deal with it. I just want out of this whole thing as soon as possible."

"Yeah, I get that. But do you think Tubby will go for it?"

"I think he'd like nothing better."

"Any chance of linking up with Sharon again?"

"Mmm, might be a good idea to give her a couple of days to calm down, and besides, I don't want her anywhere near Tubby Gustafson and his group of bottom feeders. I can't think of a faster way to end my chances with her. If she ran off because my car was stolen, can you imagine what she'd do if she knew Tubby Gustafson was now my biggest client? In fact, my only client. I just want to get some answers on this deal and get the hell away from it as fast as I can."

To be continued...

Thank you for taking the time to check out **Mystery Man.** Better grab a copy to learn how absolutely crazy things get.

Books by Mike Faricy
Crime Fiction Firsts

A boxset of the first four books in four crime fiction series:

Russian Roulette; Dev Haskell series
Welcome; Jack Dillon Dublin Tales series
Corridor Man; Corridor Man series
Reduced Ransom! Hot Shot series

The following titles comprise the Dev Haskell series:

Russian Roulette: Case 1
Mr. Swirlee: Case 2
Bite Me: Case 3
Bombshell: Case 4
Tutti Frutti: Case 5
Last Shot: Case 6
Ting-A-Ling: Case 7
Crickett: Case 8
Bulldog: Case 9
Double Trouble: Case 10
Yellow Ribbon: Case 11
Dog Gone: Case 12
Scam Man: Case 13
Foiled: Case 14
What Happens in Vegas… Case 15
Art Hound: Case 16
The Office: Case 17

Star Struck: Case 18
International Incident: Case 19
Guest From Hell: Case 20
Art Attack: Case 21
Mystery Man: Case 22
Bow-Wow Rescue: Case 23
Cold Case: Case 24
Cash Up Front: Case 25
Dream House: Case 26
Alley Katz: Case 27
The Big Gamble: Case 28
Bad to the Bone: Case 29
Silencio!: Case 30
Surprise, Surprise: Case 31
Hit & Run: Case 32
Suspect Santa: Case 33
P.I. Apprentice: Case 34
Rebel Without a Clue: Case 35

The following titles are Dev Haskell novellas:
Dollhouse
The Dance
Pixie
Fore!
Twinkle Toes
(*a Dev Haskell short story*)

The following are Dev Haskell Boxsets:
Dev Haskell Boxset 1-3
Dev Haskell Boxset 4-6
Dev Haskell Boxset 7-9
Dev Haskell Boxset 10-12
Dev Haskell Boxset 13-15
Dev Haskell Boxset 16-18
Dev Haskell Boxset 19-21
Dev Haskell Boxset 22-24
Dev Haskell Boxset 25-27
Dev Haskell Boxset 28-30
Dev Haskell Boxset 1-7
Dev Haskell Boxset 8-14
Dev Haskell Boxset 15-19
Dev Haskell Boxset 20-24
Dev Haskell Boxset 25-29

The following titles comprise the Jack Dillon Dublin Tales series:
Welcome
Jack Dillon Dublin Tale 1
Sweet Dreams
Jack Dillon Dublin Tale 2
Mirror Mirror
Jack Dillon Dublin Tale 3
Silver Bullet
Jack Dillon Dublin Tale 4
Fair City Blues
Jack Dillon Dublin Tale 5

Spade Work
Jack Dillon Dublin Tale 6
Madeline Missing
Jack Dillon Dublin Tale 7
Mistaken Identity
Jack Dillon Dublin Tale 8
Picture Perfect
Jack Dillon Dublin Tale 9
Dublin Moon
Jack Dillon Dublin Tale 10
Mystery Woman
Jack Dillon Dublin Tale 11
Second Chance
Jack Dillon Dublin Tale 12
Payback Brother
Jack Dillon Dublin Tale 13
The Heist
Jack Dillon Dublin Tale 14
Jewels To Kill For
Jack Dillon Dublin Tale 15
Retirement Scheme
Jack Dillon Dublin Tale 16
The Collector
Jack Dillon Dublin Tale 17

Jack Dillon Dublin Tales Boxsets:
Jack Dillon Dublin Tales 1-3
Jack Dillon Dublin Tales 4-6
Jack Dillon Dublin Tales 1-5

Jack Dillon Dublin Tales 1-7
Jack Dillon Dublin Tales 6-10

The following titles comprise the Hotshot series;
Reduced Ransom! Second Edition
Finders Keepers! Second Edition
Bankers Hours Second Edition
Chow Down Second Edition
Moonlight Dance Academy Second Edition
Irish Dukes (Fight Card Series)
written under the pseudonym Jack Tunney

The following titles comprise the Corridor Man series:
Corridor Man
Corridor Man 2: Opportunity knocks
Corridor Man 3: The Dungeon
Corridor Man 4: Dead End
Corridor Man 5: Finger
Corridor Man 6: Exit Strategy
Corridor Man 7: Trunk Music
Corridor Man 8: Birthday Boy
Corridor Man 9: Boss Man
Corridor Man 10: Bye Bye Bobby

Corridor Man novellas:
Corridor Man: Valentine
Corridor Man: Auditor
Corridor Man: Howling

Corridor Man: Spa Day

The following are Corridor Man Boxsets:
Corridor Man Boxset 1-3
Corridor Man Boxset 1-5
Corridor Man Boxset 6-9

All books are available on Amazon.com

Thank you!

Contact the author:
- Email: mikefaricyauthor@gmail.com
- Twitter: @Mikefaricybooks
- Facebook: Mike Faricy Author
- Website: http://www.mikefaricybooks.com

Published by

MJF Publishing